George Bor
Yuri Vinokuroff

Kill to Live

The adventure begins!

Yuri Vinokuroff

Book Two

PUBLISHED BY MAGIC DOME BOOKS

This book is entirely a work of fiction.
Any correlation with real people or events
is coincidental.

ALL BOOKS BY THE AUTHORS:

War Eternal
a LitRPG series by Yuri Vinokuroff

I Will Be Emperor
a space adventure progression fantasy series
by Yuri Vinokuroff

Kill to Live
a LitRPG progression fantasy adventure series
by George Bor and Yuri Vinokuroff

The Hunter's Code
by Oleg Sapphire and Yuri Vinokuroff

The Order of Architects
a portal progression series
by Oleg Sapphire and Yuri Vinokuroff

TABLE OF CONTENTS:

Chapter 1

Planet Heart of the World

(all names have been translated into the human language selecting the best analogy in the human language)

THE CHIEF STRATEGIST WAS CALCULATING the probability of success for a second attack on the Galaxy's seventh stellar arm. The first offensive had not been successful. The defenders had pushed back waves of Lirdags and their minions, but still had lost more territory than they could afford.

From birth, the Chief Strategist's brain was connected to the giant bio-computer that was the heart of their civilization. This contact allowed the Strategist to make calculations at a speed unavailable to any living creature in the Universe. He was just finishing the current session of calculations when he felt a soft but insistent vibration. A kind of alarm demanded to interrupt the connection, so as not to overload his mind.

Having finished analyzing the regrouping of the Twelfth Fleet, the Chief Strategist returned to reality and was surprised to see, in addition to his usual servants, a representative of the Intelligence Lair in the room. This was the Chief Scout himself, which meant the matter at hand was serious.

After exchanging the traditional greeting, the Chief Strategist looked at the Chief Scout with greatest attention.

"What prompted the noble Chief Scout of the Intelligence Lair to honor a humble strategist with his presence?" The Chief Strategist asked.

"Probable activation of an A-class threat, esteemed strategist," the Chief Intelligence Scout replied in the same polite and unemotional manner.

"Did I hear you right?" The Chief Strategist was older than anyone in his noble lineage. He didn't suffer from hearing loss, but an A-class threat was highly unlikely. The current operation, which had been going on for two centuries, was being waged by the Lirdags against a fading civilization. This current conflict qualified as a C-class threat.

"You heard me right, dear Chief Strategist. Our long-range reconnaissance systems have detected vibrations corresponding to the manifestation of the human Ideal in our reality."

"Is that so?" The Chief Strategist said. He was curios and alarmed at the same time.

Memories surged through his mind like an electric current. This threat was assigned the highest class by his kind, and was the reason he rose so high among the ranking of the race. The previous Chief Strategist was destroyed by these very Ideals of Humanity, in the only defeat in the history of their race.

It's a good thing the predecessor died in a space station explosion. With such shame, he would have faced a long and painful death among his kin. The Lirdags still bore the stamp of shame — back then, they had to flee to the farthest reaches of their domain. The blow of the Ideals was so crushing that their race took many generations to recover. But they learned from their mistakes and came back to this world only to find that their ultimate terror had vanished without a trace.

Lirdagi forces had grown immeasurably larger. Their onslaught was fast and decisive. But, for some unknown to the Chief Strategist reason, the most powerful weapon of Humanity never showed up on the battlefield, even as they stormed its main planet. This threat was taken out of the complex equation by the humans themselves, as such, raising the efficacy of the Chief Strategist's calculations many times over.

Yes, Humanity fought back with the help of its Seniors to the last. But without the variable of the perfect tool in the face of Ideals, the conquest went much faster.

Book Two

After the conquest, the Lirdags dug through the minds of Humanity's Seniors and found the places where the Ideals were preserved. The Chief Strategist personally visited one of these sites. Under his leadership, the Lirdagi elite troops performed a controlled awakening of a human Ideal, which was their greatest mistake.

That day forever left a mark in his mind. A completely naked human female emerged from the capsule in which she was found. She had virtually no internal energy reserves and they thought it was easy prey. They were wrong.

The monster had torn apart half of the Strategist's guard with her bare hands, and he himself had to flee to the orbit in a ship. From there, the Lirdagi fleet used destructors to tear the planet to shreds, and then patrolled the Universe for a long time, trying to find any burst of energy indicating that an Ideal was still alive. The paralyzing song of the Ideals sometimes still played in the depths of the Chief Strategist's consciousness when he slept.

The Chief Strategist had always prided himself on the absence of any feelings that might hinder him in the fulfillment of his duty. His cold mind was born free of fear and doubt. But back then, on that distant planet, he truly felt primal terror for the first time. So he gave the order. From that day on, all further Ideals conservation locations were destroyed along with the planets.

However, not all of the Ideals were located, and some of the vile so-called "free men" suddenly showed courage and determination in taking them to unknown destinations. Some Ideals were found, but the Chief Strategist knew for sure that the main weapon of Humanity was still present in this Universe.

Together with the Intelligence Lair, they developed an alarm system that would alert them if a human Ideal attempted to tap into their system. In the hundreds of years that followed after the final enslavement of Humanity, there were several such alerts. They all proved to be false. Nevertheless, remembering the power of the best warriors of the species, each signal was immediately assigned an A-class threat level. Right away the Chief Strategist recalled that the last such signal had been about two hundred years ago.

All this flew through his mind in a moment. Without waiting for instructions, the scout put the point of the desired planet on the holographic map. This planet was far in the back of the Lirdagi Association of Eternal Life. No representatives of the superior race were stationed there, only human scum put in the service of the Great Life.

"Has the Regent been informed?" The Chief Strategist asked more for the sake of order. He knew very well that the scout had to do that before coming to him.

"Of course. That's not all. We received another signal. One node is destroyed and before it went out, it infected three neighboring nodes with a virus. We've had no record of such a breakdown since the first war against Humanity."

"Was there really an Ideal hidden from our eyes on that forgotten planet?" Frowned the Chief Strategist. "It has been under our control for nearly eight hundred years, and all of it had been scanned, hadn't it?"

"Absolutely," the scout nodded. "But we both know how well people can shelter what's important to them."

"Yes," the Chief Strategist said. "We do. We can't ignore those signals. Neither can we send a fleet out there without solid evidence. Mother wouldn't approve of us wasting resources."

The Chief Strategist's mind involuntarily reached out to his race's bio-computer. This calmed him and allowed for a quick analysis of the situation. The current scenario was still within the range of possible errors, but such a double coincidence required immediate action.

His calculations took less than two seconds. "Deploy the Seeker. Let him investigate the zone of alarm."

"Got it, Chief Strategist," said the Chief Scout, bowing slightly before leaving the room.

Servants disconnected the Chief Strategist's feeding tubes from his large body, and he rose from his working bed. His corpulent body had long since lost the ability to move on its own, relying instead on a gravitational platform.

Floating on it, he approached the enormous porthole and looked down from the top floor of the Seer's Tower, as his residence was called among the commonfolk. Below, in the vast azure ocean, his kin lived on many small islands, enjoying their life. Most of them considered him a sort of god and had no idea what was really going on inside his tower. Only a few elites were aware that their Association of Eternal Life was waging war in the Universe for the benefit of the entire race. Not that many Lirdags remembered the existence of Humanity. The Chief Strategist hoped it would remain that way, and that his many children would continue to enjoy the delights of life while he and the rest of the elite ensured their well-being.

*   *   *

After equipping the squad with samples of old Confederate weapons, scavenging from the rank-and-file bandits had become meaningless. Spending time and effort on looting to end up with a dozen ruined leather armors and a few low-quality swords was futile — these had no value for us. But I remembered that we were not alone. The new settlement of Wolf's former prisoners was currently bare and defenseless. The people there could make use of any rusty knife, not to mention a dozen spears and some combat bows.

"We need to check out the construction site," I said, sending a command to the CES to map out a route. The increased power of the Brist module restored only a small part of the abilities I had in my previous life, but it already made things much easier.

There was no longer a need to constantly ask

my subordinates for directions, and I finally stopped feeling blind in my own home. I could focus on more important tasks than finding my way to the base.

The squad was still under the impression of the recent battle. Throughout the interrogation, I heard the voices of the fighters left to guard the perimeter. They hadn't thought to turn off their headphones, and the exchange of opinions whispered over the airwaves.

My unit gradually gathered around. The CES provided the shortest route to the cluster of people, and we set off. We ran in silence because I gave out all the instructions and a detailed analysis of the operation at the base. There were many aspects of the situation that concerned me, but some details needed careful consideration before presenting them to the personnel.

Overall, everyone was more than satisfied with the operation. The guys had never experienced such overwhelming superiority over the enemy. A mere handful of fighters had destroyed a unit five times their size, without losses or injuries, and in less than a minute.

I would need to talk to them about that. At the very least, we needed to discuss the aspects of psychological resilience against their own ambitions. The Confederacy's armor and weapons gave the wild foresters an unprecedented sense of invulnerability. But I knew all too well that such delusions could end very quickly and, at times, fatally.

We only had the equipment of the Juniors available. It used to be the simplest and most widely used throughout the entire human habitat range. Similar sets were stored in all police departments and civil defense points.

Now, during the period of decline of this planet, such equipment seemed like the pinnacle of progress. Any sword or RE-gun of the Seniors would leave my guys no chance. They wouldn't be able to do anything, just like the naked raiders couldn't do anything against them.

And I was almost certain that sooner or later, we would encounter those wielding such weapons — the local system was too advanced for that not to happen. It was alien and repulsive, but that didn't mean I would allow myself to ignore the enemy's capabilities.

As repulsive as it was, the Lirdagi system was also efficient. It had been working for a long time and had a large coverage. Based on the basic RE production values, the total power of the alien system on one planet could reach five hundred thousand RE. This is assuming the entire population lived like those villages I had already seen.

With such power, it was theoretically impossible not to have tools to utilize the raze-energy — there were advanced users of the system somewhere on the planet. The real Seniors of the aliens, not this rabble that had received a couple of pieces of ancient metal as a gift from their leader.

Where there are Seniors, there is full equipment and support. The modules of the human system had enormous resources, but they also needed maintenance. This meant that somewhere, probably in the Center, there was a serious material base. And the master of this hub of civilization was already aware that something was amiss in his domain. Measures had surely already been taken.

Ditras had good reason to worry about the number of enemies. By local standards, an army of a couple of thousand men was monstrously large. It was impossible to confront such a number of enemies alone.

However, the warrior did not take into account many other factors. Maintaining a large army has always been very expensive. While the bands of raiders were sitting in their well-established bases, they required only as many resources as they could consume themselves. Things changed drastically when they needed to go somewhere, especially to war.

The army needed something to eat and drink; somewhere to sleep; some way to interact with each other. Our prisoner mentioned that the Regent had ordered a truce between all the factions. This meant that relations between raider leaders were very tense, but now, the units would be getting together at the borders of the forest.

The greatest burden would fall on the territories closest to us. Villages would be robbed of every last drop of RE and perish. Fields would be destroyed, bringing famine as early as next season.

At the moment, the enemy had no

information about our exact location. Moreover, they did not know my identity or the forces at my disposal. The raiders would need more time to investigate and search for the cause of Wolf's camp destruction. They certainly wouldn't find anything on their own, but in three days, the nameless would arrive.

According to the dukuna's stories, these creatures were not just a strange anomaly. The locals couldn't see their names, but they couldn't see mine either. What did that mean? That they had insufficient access level or here was a system error. In my case, the latter was more likely, whereas with the nameless, it was probably the former.

Trees and bushes flashed by. I was so engrossed in analyzing the current situation that I didn't notice the changing landscape. At some point, a tree ahead shuddered and began to fall. Only then did I automatically switch to my surroundings, uploading my conclusions to the CES. In the coming hours, I needed to develop a battle strategy against significantly superior enemy forces, using all available tools for the analysis.

"Halt," I raised my hand, and the squad behind me stopped.

Several men were gathered near the fallen tree. Soon, we heard the sound of axes. Even when we approached within ten yards, the men didn't notice us. Ditras shook his head in disapproval.

"Fielders," he grumbled. Apparently, the foresters never allowed themselves such carelessness.

"Good day, gentlemen," I called out loudly, causing a genuine wave of panic. A couple of men dropped their tools and ran into the forest. Another immediately crawled under the fallen tree, while three others turned to face us with axes in hand.

"Achilles!" One of them exclaimed with relief. "It's Achilles, guys! Boy, did you sneak up on us. We thought you were them raiders!"

"We were stomping around like wild elk," Ditras grumbled again.

"Where are your leaders?" I asked.

"Vens and Nikos are setting up the log frames," the man answered, as if everyone should have known this. "Over there, beyond the hill..."

"Thank you," I nodded and headed in the indicated direction. The CES confirmed that the main concentration of people in the area was in that direction.

"Look at them," one of the workers whispered quietly. "What beasts!"

"Quiet," said another. "Beasts or not, they're on our side. We're their guests, you know."

"And Achilles, what a man. He's practically naked himself, but had outfitted all his men in armor. Why would he do that?"

To the inhabitants of this world, such an approach seemed strange indeed. Every leader, if they participated in battle personally, aimed to protect themselves first and foremost. In this regard, I seemed eccentric, which was not a bad way to disinform the enemy.

My chances of survival were much greater than those of my armor-clad companions. Simple skin enhancement of an Ideal could withstand blows better than most of the Juniors' equipment. Such armor would only restrict my movements without providing any advantage.

Once again, I reminisced about my former Ideal armor. Perhaps it had been waiting for me at the place of my awakening.

Chapter 2

The Enemy of Humanity is strong and treacherous,
It punishes all who resist it.
There is nothing you can do if you fall into the off-
spring of hell,
You can only die with dignity,
Without betraying the Spirit of Humanity,
With Faith in your soul and Hope in your heart.

"Book of Sorrows"
Verse 20

WE CLIMBED THE SLOPE of a gentle hill and saw the construction on the other side. Nikos was spacing out the buildings according to the rules of the foresters — not a single tree was harmed. Even some bushes remained intact. We could see the foundations of a dozen houses. For some reason, the workers were laying only the first rows of logs and then moving on to the next structure.

The head of the settlers and the chief architect were found in the center of the future village. They were discussing something over a diagram drawn on the ground.

"Good day, gentlemen," I said.

"Hello, Achilles," Vens said with visible joy. The young man looked very tired and exhausted, but extremely satisfied. "What brings you to us?"

"Business," I replied. "How is construction going?"

"If there are no incidents, we'll have our first houses completely ready in seven days," Nikos said. "We're laying the foundation now. Vens will take over the construction from there. He found some competent people who know how to work with lumber among his own. I got a message from the dukuna that I need to head south."

"We'll manage," Vens said. "We have enough food supplies for three weeks, even if we don't find anything else. We've already found some berries and plenty of game. We haven't touched the grain yet. I wanted to clear a couple of plots, but the ancestors forbid it."

Vens looked at Nikos, clearly showing whose ancestors were doing the forbidding. Nikos didn't even raise an eyebrow. For him, the tribe's traditions were more important than any benefits of agriculture.

"You need to finish in three days," I said. "Build fewer houses. Send people out to hunt. On the fourth day, minimize movements as much as possible."

"Is there news?" Vens grew somber. For him, recent events were already far behind. He clearly hadn't expected the past to catch up with the refugees so soon.

"You could say that," I said. "I don't have anything specific yet, but you should wait it out anyway. If something changes, I'll send someone from my team or come myself."

"We can fight, Achilles," Vens said. "There are hunters and men familiar with combat among us. How can we help?"

"If it comes to me needing your help, it will be the beginning of the end. No offense," I smiled. "If you can protect the settlement, that will be enough."

"Of course," Vens said. "We have two dozen axes and three bows. Plenty of knives, so we can make spears. Even the women are ready to stand up for their freedom. You don't need to worry about us."

"About the weapons," I said. The refugees' determination was impressive, but reality was merciless. If I made a mistake and a couple hundred raiders came to the village, its population would perish to the last person. "Vens, get a few people who can go into the forest. There're some weapons and armor there. I'm sure you could use it all. Cat, take them, then return to the camp."

"No problem," Cat said.

"We'll be grateful for any help," Vens said. "We

don't have a lot of real weapons."

"Let's hope you won't need it, after all," I smiled. "Have a good day!"

I had learned everything I needed to know, and it was time to leave. The settlers were adapting and trying to build their lives. There were no conflicts with the locals. All that needed to be done was to give the former prisoners enough time for rehabilitation and recovery, which was my task. In the years since the war, nothing had changed. Protecting the civilian population was still one of the main priorities of the Ideals.

"Have a good day, Achilles," Vens said. "And good luck. For all our sakes."

He called over a couple of men passing by. Cat waited for the group to take to the forest, and we headed back to the base.

The scanning systems were silent, which was somewhat reassuring. At the very least, I was now sure of the security of the foresters' territorial borders. Uninvited guests would receive quite a welcome, but I had far fewer resources than I would have liked. The exact figures could be calculated in the lab, but I knew that the perimeter wouldn't hold for long. I needed a backup plan.

The modules required energy to perform. The Savannah had used part of the transformer's reserve to close the tunnel with the enemy squad, and I could repeat a single activation without a problem — this didn't even require my participation. But what would happen when the perimeter was attacked simultaneously from ten directions, or if fifty paths were opened in one day?

I had three days to find a solution. The size of the territory wasn't changing. If the line was breached in one place, there would be nothing to hold back the enemy forces. If such breaches occurred at three different points three miles apart, we wouldn't be able to contain them. We simply wouldn't have time to plug all the holes.

Calculations of all possible scenarios showed us failing. The difference in forces was too great. The CES accurately confirmed my own worst predictions. By the time we arrived at the base, I was in a rather bad mood, which is perfect for finding solutions in hopeless situations.

"You have one hour to rest," I said. "Recharge the batteries and check the armor reserves. Fill everything to the maximum. We're switching to energy-saving mode from now on. We need to conserve our strength. Ditras, tell Cat when he returns. Dismissed."

The fighters didn't go underground, but I went straight to the lab's workroom. Herman was still in the same place, as if he moved at all while I was gone.

"Congratulations, Achilles!" Herman said. He didn't take his eyes off the terminal screen, on which images of some diagrams were quickly changing. "It's an amazing victory. The system reported the annihilation of two enemy squads."

"Thanks," I smiled. The kid was quickly picking up the lingo and was already using terminology that the locals didn't understand at all. How long had it been? A little over a day? "Have you eaten anything?"

"I'm not hungry," Herman said.

"When did you last rest?"

"I'm sleeping right now," the boy answered cheerfully. "The system showed me the brain function diagram of the Seniors, the real Seniors, and the sequence for deactivating the rain spheres. I'm a Senior, right, Achilles? Is that why you took me with you? And you're a Senior, too?"

"You'll become one if you get enough rest," I said. "As for me, let's just say we're very similar."

"I thought I had to study a lot," Herman said.

"Every being has its endurance limit," I said as I approached the control terminal of the defense system. "For you, because of your gift, that limit is very high. But even you can't go on forever. From now on, you need to sleep at least three hours a day. Otherwise, your learning speed will drop a lot within a week."

Herman looked away from the screen, where an image of some communication node was being dissected.

"Does it matter what time of day I rest?" he asked.

"No."

"I'll rest now, and then get back to it. It'll give me a chance to check the wake-up signal settings."

The boy left, and I immersed myself in studying the module operation reports. The Savannah had spent ten RE to close the tunnel. Under the most favorable conditions, we would accumulate several hundred units of raze-energy while we waited. Part of it needed to be reserved and not touched. Another part would be used for recharging weapons and armor. Some would be spent on replenishing ammunition during the assault. In the end, I was left with about two hundred RE, which was clearly not enough for two dozen tunnels. Even with fifty people in each, that'd be already a thousand.

The squad warriors started coming into the hall one by one. They were charging their batteries, then leaving. Ditras was the last to arrive.

I was buried in the reports, trying to find ways to quickly move between the path exits, but everything proved to be too energy consuming. A tunnel that moved humans used an enormous amount of energy. I couldn't sustain it on my reserve.

"Looking for options?" Ditras asked. He finished charging his equipment and sat down on one of the empty chairs. "Do you think we can handle it?"

"We can," I said. "I'm assessing our resources right now. Ideally, we'd need to triple our energy intake, and then we could relax."

"Maybe we could breed more monsters and let them roam the forest?" Ditras suggested. "You understand we can't be everywhere at once, right? Only the wind can get to the other side of the forest in a few moments."

I froze, then slowly turned to look at him. There was a hidden brilliance in Ditras's words that I hadn't noticed myself. The idea that came to me required careful planning.

"Ditras, where did you get that moss you used on Harvey?"

"That's not something I want to brag about," Ditras said. "Our ancestors forbid us from using such methods, even against our enemies."

"Can you get more or not?" I asked. "We're facing an invasion of raiders that could wipe out any memory of the foresters. I respect traditions and understand your hesitation, but the situation demands that we use any resources available. I'll take full responsibility before the ancestors."

"Yes," Ditras said. "I have one more dose. It's enough to put three people to sleep or get one to talk."

"Let me see," I said.

Ditras reached into a small pocket on his armor, usually used for spare batteries, and pulled out a handful of green fibers. He handled them with bare hands, making me believe that the plant wasn't poisonous when raw.

"This is smoss," Ditras said as he handed me the fibers. "We use it when we need a good night's sleep. Just a couple of strands are enough to ensure no dreams disturb you until morning."

"But you found another use for it," I said, examining the unremarkable stems. There was nothing shameful in this. On the contrary, I would have been surprised if no one had studied the properties of such a plant. As it usually happens, it's impossible to discover all the characteristics of useful plants without casualties.

"Many winters ago," Ditras said, "our ancestors found the first smoss field in the valley. At that time, there was discord in the tribe, and some warriors decided to join one of the raider groups. They stole our relic but couldn't escape the forest."

I nodded silently. The rebels were caught and turned into test subjects. Partly to test the properties of the plant, and partly to set an example. A very effective method.

"Activate property recognition system," I ordered, walking over to one of the lab's devices. The transparent cover of the analyzer slid aside. I placed half of the fibers inside, and the other half I put into a small test tube filled with water. "What valley? I thought it was just the forest around here. Is it near those ruins on the mountain?"

"No," Ditras said, "that's just what we call the place. The forest's defense isn't uniform. There are protected places, where it's impossible to live, but where you can hide for a short time."

He was talking about buffer zones — a strange feature of the Lirdagi protective fields. We had discovered that the aliens didn't have a uniform coverage of the territory, and their barriers always had thinner sections. To conceal this vulnerability, the Lirdags would set up a twin circuit in such places. Sometimes, these cavities stored important control nodes, because it was very difficult to penetrate them.

"One of our guides had miscalculated his strength once," Ditras continued. "He should have died, but he was kicked out of the tunnel he was taking in a safe area. He spent two days recovering and nearly went insane from the continuous whispering of the monsters. When he returned, he collapsed in a delirium. For a day, he talked nonsense about the eastern path and a place where the walls of the tunnel transpose. Then he died."

"We need to go there," I said. "There might be something more interesting than sleep moss."

Analyses complete

The CES displayed the results before me, and I briefly got distracted. Under the influence of the Lirdagi fields and their monsters, the plant had mutated into a strange mix of moss and grass. As a result of this change, a powerful narcotic began to condense in it. A slight overdose could easily kill an ordinary person, even in its raw form. That's what happened to Harvey. If this poison was refined a bit, the results could exceed all my expectations.

Smoss was the best solution to our problem, and I already knew how to use this discovery. Defense and transport tunnels were necessary for moving living forces, but that wasn't their only function. The lizards were very different from humans. Many substances harmless to us could kill them, and vice versa.

When arriving on a new planet, the aliens needed time to adapt. The second generation of Lirdags could easily live in the new conditions, but it took time. Fortified points, like the one described by Ditras, provided that time for the Lirdags. With enough energy input, they could form a complete dome. The barrier was filled with an atmosphere familiar to the lizards, achieved through a system of small penetrations.

It was similar to a regular tunnel but much smaller. Even a tiny object couldn't be sent through it; it simply wouldn't stay within the walls of the path. But gas was an entirely different matter.

"There's definitely nothing there, Achilles," Ditras said. "I've been there a couple of times myself. Just a small field overgrown with smoss. No other grass, no bushes, no trees. If you go there when smoss blooms, you could easily die."

"Thanks for the warning," I said. I didn't want to spend my energy reserves on Detox. "It's already mid-summer. When does this plant bloom?"

"We don't know. We just try not to go there unless we absolutely have to. In one trip, you can pick enough smoss for the whole season. After that, it loses its properties."

"We definitely won't manage in one trip," I said, estimating how much fibers we'd need. "Get George. You went with him, right?"

"I'm on it," Ditras got up from his chair. "Should I get anyone else?"

"No need," I shook my head. "The three of us can handle it. Let the others rest."

I went to the storage and conducted another inventory. This time, I was interested in laboratory equipment. I'd seen a decent stock of containers for collecting bio-material but didn't pay much attention to it the last time I was here. During the cleanup, my subordinates had stashed the boxes in a far corner, but they were careful with them.

I got a hundred standard chemistry flasks and twice as many regular test tubes. That should have been enough. I also grabbed a couple of plastic boxes to pack the cargo for transport. Then I went to the surface, where Ditras and George were already waiting for me.

"Let's go," I said, handing the boxes to them.

The round trip would take several hours. By the time we came back, Herman would undoubtedly wake up and return to his studies. As I continued walking, I formulated a request to the CES. Given the opportunity, it was worth channeling the boy's energy in the right direction.

One thought kept bothering me. The Lirdags were renowned for their bio-technologies. So far, I hadn't seen directly modified humans, only those enhanced by the local system, but I was sure the lizards had done more. Sooner or later, I would encounter these people. Should I consider them to be Lirdags, or humans? How many could there be? What should I do with them?

In the past, I did what I was best at, which was killing enemies. Moral questions were resolved by the Council. That arrangement suited me. But under the current circumstances, it seemed the time had come for me to answer such questions myself. The great Achilles was no longer above politics.

Chapter 3

*There are many ways for our Enemy to infiltrate the
Mind.
If you keep it unprotected,
Repulsive commands, against which you are pow-
erless, will flood your Mind.
Such is the price of Humanity's downfall,
Having surrendered itself to the infernal System.*

*"Book of Sorrows"
Verse X*

WE MOVED FASTER without the carts. The foresters were used to running, and their armor didn't
hinder them at all. It wasn't very heavy and was
tailored to fit perfectly.

The journey to the eastern edge of the foresters' territory took us about three hours. Along the

way, we passed an abandoned village and quickly checked to ensure that the residents hadn't left anyone behind. Soon, we reached the memorable site of our encounter with Fiend and his raiders. The CES indicated that we could reach the buffer zone from this point, but George led us further.

"This path runs close, but sometimes the monsters change their position and wait right at the exit," George explained. "It's better for us to go to the next gate."

The group of raiders destroyed by the Savannah had also taken this path. I cross-checked the data and confirmed there was no mistake. I trusted George with dealing with the tunnel, since transporting a small group of people wasn't difficult for him. He needed only a few minutes to prepare, and we found ourselves on the path.

"You're very 'heavy', Achilles," George said. "I don't know what changed since the first time, but now it feels like I'm leading ten people."

I checked his energy consumption and noticed that the alien system was indeed reacting aggressively to my presence. Last time, I had much less energy in reserve, making it harder to detect. Perhaps it had to do with my connection to the lab equipment.

I commanded the CES to disconnect from the base's security system, and George immediately felt better. This was something to note for later. My connection to the human system was getting stronger, and the enemy might notice it before I was ready. From now on, I decided to work with the modules only in the lab's workroom.

"We're almost there," George reported after a short while. "I'll close the path now, and we'll get out at the center of the valley."

"Wait," I said. "Can you take us a bit further?"

We were only about a hundred yards away from the site where the second raider squad had perished. There was unlikely to be anything left of them, but it was still worth checking.

"No problem," George said. "I can do it now for sure. What did you do? I feel a lot better."

"I disconnected myself from the base," I replied. "The path thought we were carrying it with us."

"Got it," George nodded.

Ahead, we saw the first victim of the tunnel collapse — it was the guide. He had managed to run further than the others, as if he knew salvation was near. But then he died and his body was torn apart. The Chucklers didn't care about the dead, but they could use their bodies to intimidate living enemies.

Further down the tunnel lay the bodies of the raiders. Some were behind the tunnel's walls, but what I saw was enough. Of the ten bandits, only half were armed, but each of them carried a woven crate on his back. All the crates were empty.

"These aren't our guys," Ditras said, stopping briefly by one of the bodies.

"They were after your smoss," I said.

"No one knows about the valley," George objected.

"The group's guide tried to reach the entrance to the valley," I said. "They have almost no weapons, while Harvey's group was armed to the teeth. Every one of these guys has an empty crate for cargo, but you didn't schedule any deals. Where else could they be going?"

"Is that good or bad?" Ditras asked.

"Bad for you," I replied, "because you're unaware that your secret places are known beyond the forest."

"And for you?" George asked.

"For me it's good," I said. "Let's go to the valley. You still have to get us back."

Finding this group was pure coincidence, but it played into my hands. Harvey had tried to be the first to carry out the Regent's order, which was the only reason for him taking the risk and crossing the foresters' border.

This group came to the forest with entirely different intentions. They were hunting for the most valuable cargo. Any liquor was like baby formula compared to smoss extract. People never stopped inventing ways to escape reality and destroy themselves faster.

We returned to the breach point in the path and stepped out into the valley. Ditras was right — aside from the mutated plant, there was nothing in this pocket of space. I was in for a disappointment — we didn't find the main perimeter control node right away. The node wasn't needed for control, but rather for blocking, which was a simple precaution. I could interfere with the aliens' field using the Savannah, and that was enough. I couldn't control Lirdagi equipment anyway, but that didn't mean that no one else could.

"Get as much moss as you can," I said. "I'll take a look around the area."

The guys nodded in unison, set the boxes on the ground, and took out their knives. I walked along the border of the buffer zone and heard the howls of the Chucklers from behind the barrier. I counted ten of them. If not for the barrier, the monsters would have already overwhelmed me with their fields.

In forty minutes, the fighters had filled the boxes to the brim. The weight changed insignificantly, though. It was time to head back.

It was getting dark when we arrived at the base. Though I didn't need any rest, my men did. They wouldn't last long at my pace.

"Go rest," I said as George handed me the second crate of smoss. "Tomorrow, we'll need to patrol the southern side of the territory."

The dukuna and the other villagers probably hadn't reached their destination yet, but we needed to act now. If my plan worked, I'd gain a significant advantage.

The workroom was a complete mess. I stood frozen at the door, crate in hand, unable to decide whether what I saw should make me laugh or get angry. The CES had precisely executed its task and loaded Herman with data. I thought I'd come back to find a decent assistant, but things turned out to be much more interesting.

The boy's impatient and curious nature demanded immediate application of the knowledge he had acquired. He not only managed to absorb the data but also put it to use.

Most of the available space was taken by a multi-stage purification and distillation system. Herman had used half of the flasks available at the lab and somehow found a burner and hoses. He had protective goggles on his head and was now watching the bubbling green liquid at the center of the setup.

"Finally!" The boy screamed, rushing toward me. "I tried to contact you, but couldn't. I thought something broke."

"I disconnected from the base," I replied.

"Why?! What if something would have happened?"

"Ditras's men stayed here, and the CES would have reported on any danger."

"What's the ultimate goal?" Herman asked, switching to a completely different topic with a businesslike tone.

"What are you talking about? What is this?" I asked, sitting down on the only free chair.

"What do you mean?" Herman said. "You changed the training program and ordered the system to give me data on chemistry! I read everything. I even waited for you for a while. Then I tried to contact you. But you didn't respond. So... Oh!"

He darted to the flask with the green liquid and quickly turned off the burner. Then he turned the valve on the hose and transferred the distilled liquid to the next container.

"Then I decided to see what chemistry was for," the boy said. "I found smoss in the analyzer and figured you wanted to do something with it, but I didn't know what. So I had to assemble a dual-purpose distillation system with multiple end-result options. And you didn't respond! Now the middle result is almost ready, and I don't know what to do next!"

"Gas," I replied with a smile. "I need to get the smoss substance into a form that can easily be turned into gas."

"I need three more flasks and a coil," the boy said. "Can you help set it up? I can't reach. And stoppers. Where will we get the stoppers? There's nothing like that in the storage!"

"We'll seal it with film," I said. "There's a slot for packaging materials in the analyzer."

"How do we get the raw material there?" Herman asked. "It'll start evaporating the minute it comes into contact with air!"

"How did you figure that out?" I asked.

"Simple," the boy snorted. "System, display smoss formula three!"

Next to me, the terminal came to life, displaying the molecular structure of the substance. The CES confirmed the young scientist's calculation, and I just shook my head. Herman's gift was beginning to unfold in full force. I had first expected the training to take a couple of months before the first results could be seen, but back then I didn't have any technology at my disposal.

The boy's information absorption rate was at its peak. His age, character traits, physical attributes, and other factors had converged at one point, and now I just needed to direct the prodigy's energy in the right direction.

Over the next six hours, we worked in the lab together. We had to move part of the setup closer to the analyzer because the first sample started to evaporate five seconds earlier than calculated. Then we ran out of flasks and had to use test tubes. By the end of the work, we had an entire crate of such tubes.

The purpose of the large containers was clear to me even before the experiment began, so we placed them separately. We still needed to come up with something for the small ones — they weren't big enough to store a decent volume of the smoss liquid. We needed to either use several containers at once or find another way.

"Done!" Herman said in a tired voice, sealing the last test tube.

"Great work!" I smiled. "Go rest. You'll continue in the morning. Tonight, I'll set up the training program for working with modules and the lab's security system for you."

"Make it two streams, if possible," the boy replied with a long yawn as he walked to his room. "You can set them up right away. I'll filter them myself."

I sat still for a couple of minutes, thinking of everything that had happened that day, then began moving the crates to storage. I would need to tell Ditras and the men not to touch the crates. This is when the CES came alive with a message.

"There's no rest for the wicked," I said, reading the report. Not for me, at least. I had to decide whether to act based on the new information or stick to the original plan.

* * *

Node 234, edge of the forest

"Is that you, old hag?" The head of the raiders and owner of Nodes 234 and 236 frowned as he watched an elderly woman appear at the edge of the forest. She raised both hands in the air, still holding her staff. "Put your hands down, old woman, I'm not about to think you'll whack me with your cane."

"Thank you, noble Spatus," she sighed with relief, leaning on her stick. "You've always been kind to all of us."

"And they always criticize me for it," the raider leader laughed heartily.

He was genuinely proud of being a good person, at least in his own opinion. When the other raider commanders took everything by force, he obtained what he needed through negotiations. Because of this, the few independent human settlements around, which included the foresters, brought their goods to him first.

Spatus always met his quotas for the masters, even in bad times, and his friends-turned-rivals were furious. Some even tried to go to war against him, but "Fat Spat", as his enemies called him, was too clever to lose. He traded surplus goods for high-quality weapons and equipment for his elite.

His neighbors quickly found themselves biting off more than they could chew, especially after Spatus, with the Masters' approval, seized Node 236. In doing so, he rid it of the outright tyrant they had for the leader, who had nearly turned his territory into a lifeless desert. Having the resources of two nodes, Spatus could have expanded further, but he needed the Masters' approval for that. He also was perfectly content with how much he'd already had.

He had everything: things, delicious food, beautiful women. Unlike other raiders, his wives lived with him willingly, bearing him numerous children and being quite satisfied with their lives. Two of his eldest had already come of age and now stood beside Spatus in battles.

He gave the deceptive impression of a fat, clumsy man, which led to more than one opponent to underestimate him. Beneath the layer of fat were strong reinforced bones and powerful muscles that allowed the stout man to move with a speed unattainable for nearly anyone else. Because of this, he was a very serious warrior. Combined with his intelligence, one could say he was extraordinarily serious.

The dukuna approached Spatus, limping, and bowed deeply. "Greetings, Master. We rely on your protection and kindness. We are ready to pledge our loyalty to you and humbly ask to settle on your lands."

"Why would I want that?" Spatus asked. "You are useful to me when you hunt game and bring in skins and meat. If you settle on my land, what will you do? You don't even know which end of the plow to hold."

"We don't, you are right, Master," the dukuna said. "We still ask to stay. We can decide later how we will help and what we will do. Together with you, of course. We did not come empty-handed. We also have information on the strange man from the mountain. I heard the Regent is searching for him."

"Is that so?" Spatus turned serious in a flash.

Of course, he had heard the Regent's call. All the raider leaders in the area had heard it. But as for Spatus's little kingdom, it had not taken direct part in this operation. Back then, the raider had cursed irritably, looking at the promised reward that could have been his. But he couldn't go against the will of the Masters. Now things could turn out differently.

"Speak, old woman! Tell me everything you know! Masters save you if you lie to me."

"Of course, great Spatus," the dukuna bowed again. "I wouldn't even think of it. His name is Achilles, he came with Wolf's prisoners."

"Where are those traitors now?" Spatus asked.

"I don't know, he led them somewhere deep

into the forest. But he left some of his equipment with us. We thought it would be useful to you."

The dukuna waved her hand, and six old men brought three stretchers full of stuff and dumped them onto the grass.

Spatus's face twitched. It wasn't the best equipment, but what could you expect from those idiots Wolf had on his team. The man didn't care a bit about the strength of his own guard. In any case, everything the dukuna brought was worth money, and some of it would be useful for his recruits.

Spatus shook his head in displeasure as he glanced at the human riffraff that were the foresters, who stood at the edge of the forest, afraid to step out. Any good raider could easily kill several of these wretches. Yet somehow, someone had managed to take down not just one or two, but several equipped and armed raiders, and then destroy an entire camp.

Spatus looked at the piles once more, estimating the amount of equipment. It looked like it had been taken off at least two dozen fighters. He'd heard that the Wolf's army had been completely wiped out and Wolf himself killed.

"What else do you know?" Spatus asked.

"I know where he went. A forbidden place where our ancestors don't allow us to go. I know for sure he is there."

"Are you certain, old woman?!" Spatus said menacingly, looming over the trembling dukuna.

"I swear on my life and the lives of all my kin."

"Well, if you swear, then so be it."

Any other raider in Spatus's place would already be gathering his fighters. Any other would be rushing to get ahead of his rivals and earn favor with the Masters. But Fat Spat was in his place, exactly where he belonged.

Spatus turned to his sons, who had been silent until then. "Graham, take this junk and haul it back. Pierce, go to Naum — that bastard owes me for the last shipment. Tell him that if he wants to settle the debt, I'll take half the Masters' reward for catching that man." Spatus had no intention of risking his own people, but he didn't want to miss out either. "Plus the debt for the shipment. That'll be the whole reward! In return, we'll give him the enemy's location and guides to get him there. We'll give him the guides, right?"

"Of course, noble Spatus," the dukuna bowed. "My people are at your full disposal."

At the last moment, Spatus thought he saw a triumphant glare in the old witch's eyes. Then he decided that he'd mistaken, because it simply couldn't be. The human herd knows its place well.

Chapter 4

And though we cannot support you with power, O Children of Humanity,
For we are weak and frail compared to our Enemy,
The power of the right word is great,
For in times of trouble it calms the Soul and guides to the True Path.

"Book of Hope"
Verse I

I RETURNED TO THE WORKROOM and opened the Brist's report again.

Area scanning complete
Phalanx modules detected: 7 units
Distance:
- 20 miles: 1 unit

Direction: Southwest
Condition: Damaged
Status: Fit for use after full service cycle
- 23 miles: 2 modules
Direction: North-Northwest
Condition: Operational
Status: Critically discharged
- 33 miles: 4 modules
Direction: East
Condition: Operational, partial modifications made
Status: Fit for use after removal of modifications

I needed at least four modules of this model, but the more we had, the better. The third option was the most enticing in that sense. We could get the four modules we needed in one go and move on. But there were downsides.

The first was the distance. The modules in the first two options were significantly closer, and a few extra hours on the road could be critical. The second issue was the condition of the modules. In the first two cases, the equipment had clearly not been used, but the third was different. After my visit to Wolf's camp, I was very wary of the local modifications to standard equipment.

Four whole modules. Each could connect up to thirty people to the system. It was hard to imagine what the local craftsmen might have repurposed them for, but they definitely weren't using them for their intended purpose.

The first option wasn't viable, because it had only one module, which was damaged. I had no way to repair it, except perhaps to dismantle it for parts. It wasn't worth the risk for such a dubious benefit.

The second option was better — the modules were close and recharging them wouldn't be a problem, in theory. We'd just connect them to the lab system and they'd be ready to work in a day. In practice, it was much more complicated. The backup power for all the equipment was provided by a built-in raze-energy battery. Until its capacity was filled, the equipment would remain a pile of scrap metal. Filling each module would require at least fifty RE. I wouldn't have time to offset the energy expenditure with a new Hass-Arss pack.

So I actually only had one viable option. The time of the other modules would come later. But I was bothered by the location of the equipment in option 3. The CES showed a schematic map of the area, according to which, the Phalanxes were located in the territory of those same drug manufacturers whose caravan I had so successfully destroyed.

I wasn't interested in the raiders' activities. It was highly likely that their product didn't reach ordinary people and was used by the raiders themselves. Should it be deadly when used for some time, I had no objections to the self-destruction of the bandits. I didn't like the fact that their base was very close to Wolf's camp, because most of the raider groups involved in searching for me would now be gathering there.

I needed a day to complete the operation. We definitely couldn't manage it faster. By then, the arrival of the nameless would be near. Most likely, they'd be showing up at ground zero, aka Wolf's camp, as well.

In the end, my squad and I could find ourselves right next to the enemy's army and in the center of a raider group preparing for a big war. Even with some basic means of communication, the enemy, or even one escaped raider could put an end to my plan. But I couldn't just let four working Phalanxes go.

I needed additional information. A detailed inspection of the area revealed the operation of a blocking field, which made me think there was another relay. The distance between them matched the minimum coverage of one node.

However, the Phalanxes themselves were located away from the main raider camp. I went to one of the terminals and initiateв manual scanning mode, which led me to discovering an interesting detail.

This raider settlement was much larger than Wolf's camp. If the destroyed raider base was essentially a fortress, this one was almost a city. There was a fortress too, but it was much smaller. The rest of the territory was occupied by small houses and strange long buildings that looked like warehouses.

Controlling such a large settlement constantly and effectively would be very difficult.

Logically, there should have been special law enforcement squads, something like the Humanity's police. The main strike force and the leader himself lived in the fortress. That's where the most valuable equipment and provisions were stored.

Considering how important the technology of the past was to the raiders, it was strange that here, it was located in a large building on the outskirts, almost at the settlement's border. Although, there was protection set up. The Brist gave out information about the presence of a dozen guards and a couple of surveillance modules like the Beacon I've seen earlier.

If we acted quickly and discreetly, we could potentially capture the Phalanxes with our own forces. But what would we do with them afterwards? Unlike the Amina, the Phalanxes didn't have their own engine. Each unit weighed a ton, and we wouldn't be able to escape hauling such a load on our own. Carts weren't an option for us, either.

I realized that I had already moved on to planning the operation, the decision was practically made. I needed to wake up my squad, but decided to give the fighters a bit more time to rest. There was an opportunity for me to prepare the operation in peace, so I tasked the Brist with locating all active power sources in the designated area. Then I assigned the CES to develop a forecast and the most effective plan for the operation. There were a few details left to think through, but as always, they took up the most time.

Book Two

In the past, maintaining the system in working condition was not part of the Ideals' functions. With Humanity's vast, practically infinite support, we focused on one thing only: destroying our enemies.

With a mere gesture, we moved massive space armadas across the Universe. Billions of Juniors would board ships or enter portals to appear wherever we, the Ideals, needed them the most.

Not to mention all the specially trained people we had to repair, restore, and deploy the system. There were Juniors, Seniors, scientists, and simple workers, all working towards the common good — the Victory of the Humankind. And together, we won.

Now, I mentally thanked those visionaries who decided that an Ideal was not just a machine for killing Humanity's enemies. We remained part of the human community not only in reports but also internally. Thanks to our uniqueness, we could use our practically limitless capabilities for various purposes. Our consciousness and mind had turned into a very versatile tool.

The same visionaries invented the CES — a highly complex bio-computer, which was far ahead of its time even by the Confederacy's standards. The Ideals were further upgraded by the CES and turned into an overwhelming superior power. We outplayed the Lirdags on their own playing field.

In its modified version, the CES could originally be installed in the consciousness of Seniors and even Juniors. Unfortunately, the war between the two races was fought not only on the physical field. Neither side shied away from any means of jeopardizing the enemy, as the main goal was victory.

Therefore, just like us, the Lirdags, used our captured soldiers to create viruses specifically targeting the CES. They disrupted settings, hampered analysis, and in particularly successful cases, killed the host.

So, in addition to the physical confrontation, there was a battle between the best minds of both races, constantly inventing new threats and countering enemy know-hows. The network of our fighters continuously expanded, contracted, broke, and reformed. It was truly an everlasting process, in which we, the Ideals, also participated.

At our command, the CES of the subordinate forces would turn on or off, or reboot. It did everything to maintain the combat readiness of the units and equipment entrusted to us.

Even now, I had the ability to upload all the necessary information into Ditras and his men, but I needed our human system. And to bring it online, I needed equipment. That was the current priority.

I got stuck in front of the computer for several hours, planning, forecasting, and assembling nodes like puzzles, trying to achieve maximum efficiency and best outcome with minimal resources.

I was lucky that the local system was mostly built on our human blocks. More precisely, the system used the Lirdagi pseudo-living bio-relays, but the connection to the conquered Humanity, due to physiological differences, was made based on our equipment.

The main control modules and the most complex blocks that were the visible part of the entire system were called Cerebrums. They had been ripped out of the former planetary infrastructure of the human system. These blocks were the cells or nodes that interacted with each other, creating continuous coverage of the system in the interstellar space of the Galaxy.

Now I needed to restore this system because there was no other way. I had an emergency protocol for such a situation, but its implementation would require sacrifices, and not just on my part.

I had to act. I brought up the holographic image of the base again, giving it one last skeptical look. The base's security worried me a bit. After all, it remained a civilian structure. Even considering its specific features — it could probably be called "semi-civilian" — it was far from command bunkers capable of withstanding prolonged orbital bombardment. Fortunately, orbital bombardment wasn't a threat in the near future, but beyond that — who knew.

Our base also made me worry. Initially, I thought it was minimally equipped. I even specifically checked the most likely locations for additional rooms on my first visit. While there was no doubt about the safety of the bunker, only recently did I realize that the layout and power of the equipment used corresponded to a class-six shelter, not class-eight as I initially thought. A request to the security system yielded nothing. Only accessing it with administrator rights revealed the full picture to me.

At the moment, we were only using one level of the base, specifically its lab. It was located above the others because the scientists needed access to the surface to work with the bio-replicator. But the lab's staff was small, so most of the base's capacities were idle. This was inefficient, as the equipment still consumed energy.

The scientists had made the best decision, but the way they implemented it raised some questions. Why hide all evidence of the lower levels so thoroughly? I was interested in the entire structure of the facility. I thought I might need to use all of it some time in the future, but I wasn't in a hurry to break through walls. Perhaps the staff had a serious reason for sealing off most of the base. Surveying it also required time, which I didn't have, so I decided to rely on the system's data.

According to the plan, the base had four underground levels, each approximately 5400 square feet, totaling 20,300 square feet of usable space.

A hundred people could comfortably fit here; even more, if they were crammed. The protective and camouflage fields would hide the activity inside the base for a while, but only until someone took a closer look. A thorough scan of an orbital satellite would show increased energy consumption, especially since the production of raze-energy was constant.

Interestingly, some specific traits of the Lirdagi race worked to my advantage. Almost all of the lizard equipment could be considered semi-living. While human armies were formed "around" us — the Ideals — as the centers of decision-making, the Lirdagi armies were formed around the Queens — like those in a hive — who literally produced these armies. Moreover, their armies were commanded by the Lords — specially bred beings, the so-called Higher Race. The Queens were simply "reactors" for offspring production.

When conquering planets, systems, and sectors, the Lirdagi armies moved on, leaving a small number of troops on the planet as a garrison. With limited reproduction means, they physically couldn't "exponentially" produce the necessary number of new soldiers, let alone spaceships.

Considering that several centuries had passed since this planet was conquered, there likely weren't living ships in the system. There must have been a small number of satellites in orbit, and overall, primary control has been delegated to the subjugated local mankind. This gave me hope that I could manage quickly. I definitely didn't want to hide — passive defense is the path to defeat. I needed to attack, restore the system, and expel the cold-blooded invaders from the planet, or better yet, bury them there.

"Ditras!" I called out, reaching the soldiers' room. He immediately opened his eyes and looked at me with a completely alert gaze, as if he hadn't been sleeping at all. "Wake up the guys. We've got work to do."

Within ten minutes, all my fighters had gathered in the main hall. While I was waiting, I had cleared a part of the room and set up one of the terminals to project images of what I'd be talking about. This was just one of a thousand briefings for me, but the foresters' first. Information in images instantly captured their attention.

"So," I began, "as you all know, we are expecting a visit from a very large number of very unpleasant guests. At the moment, we're not fully prepared, but we are on our way. An hour ago, I received information that there is equipment I need beyond the forest borders. Here."

A map of the forest and the surrounding territory came up on the wall. Then it shifted to the side, and the raider settlement appeared in the center.

"Do you know who lives next to Wolf?" I asked.

"Baka," Ditras replied. "We don't deal with him. He's too arrogant and insolent. Once, he sent his men to negotiate, suggesting he'd graciously take us under his wing. We refused. The next time he tried to attack. He hasn't visited since."

"Those are his men we found on the path today," I said. "This leader knows enough to use your paths at his discretion."

"He doesn't harm us, though," Ditras objected. "If he crossed the border, we would respond."

"I see," I sighed. I didn't mention that the foresters were constantly in danger because of this. It was already suspicious that someone was using the tunnels and the Brist didn't notice. "Let's move on to discussing the operation. Our task is to capture and transport four Phalanx modules to our base. Like this one." I walked over to a nearby unit and patted its casing.

"Each weigh a bit over two hundred pounds," I said. "Which gets me to my question: what means of transportation do we have for delivering such loads?"

"Carts, of course," Bers said. "What else could haul it? If we use a sled, it'll wear us out."

"If I understand the question correctly," George said, "we need something akin to ancient wagons."

"Exactly," I nodded.

"Baka's men didn't come alone the first time," George said, frowning. "Their guide nearly died but managed to drag some contraption over to us. It was like a cart, only flat and without wheels. It stank like a pack of dead opossums."

I stared at George for a second, trying to understand what he meant. It was hard to believe, but in this world, such an option might indeed exist.

"Well," I said, smiling broadly, and gave the Brist new search parameters. "That settles my question. Let's move on to discussing the operation itself. It's time to shake up this damn hornet's nest."

Chapter 5

As long as we remember, the Human Spirit cannot be crushed.
As long as we believe, we cannot be broken or divided.
As long as we have hope, there is still a chance for us and our children for a different future.
When the Protector of Humanity arrives one day, we will be ready.

"Book of Hope"
Verse XVII

THE BORDER OF THE FORESTERS' TERRITORY was long behind us. My fighters were silently running through the dense forest. This time, I chose the route. None of the guys had been to Baka's territory, and I didn't want to waste time finding a path or accidentally bumping into the locals. We were already running out of time.

We made a short stop at the tunnel entrance, as I decided to leave a few surprises for anyone who might follow us. The CES indicated an almost certain probability of pursuit, and I completely agreed.

As soon as the enemy learned about our sabotage, they would definitely try to reclaim their property. Our main task was to delay being found out as long as possible, and to make the chase as regrettable as possible. If anyone had time to regret anything before they died.

The only downside to my plan was the lack of communication between squad members. I had to spend a considerable amount of time distributing targets and splitting tasks.

The briefing dragged on, but now everyone knew their roles. The final adjustments to the plan would have to be made on-site.

Due to the delay, we would arrive at the location later than planned. The guards around the target object would likely change or shift positions. I didn't rule out an increase in the number of guards during the daytime. And then there was the issue of camouflage. All in all, we had a much better chance of remaining unnoticed at night.

For the guys, the difference wasn't significant — camouflage cloaks worked equally well at any time of day. But I would have to come up with something. Either spend RE or use my surroundings if I had a chance.

I had planned the route in advance and uploaded all the details into the CES. We were taking the most remote and desolate parts of enemy territory. The Brist unequivocally indicated that there wasn't any active technology of the past in this area, and ordinary people didn't venture into such depths.

The raiders believed in their complete superiority on their land, which wasn't surprising. The shepherds tended the flock for their Masters, sheared it, and sometimes slaughtered it. In this respect, they were no different from Wolf. I hoped it would remain that way until it was too late.

"Open area ahead," I said quietly, and my words were passed down the line. "Three hundred yards. Speed up."

We didn't know how the operation to capture the modules would go and what resources we'd need, so I had told them to conserve energy in advance. Not wanting to use camouflage, the fighters crouched slightly and doubled their pace. I thought to myself that if we were in the human system, they would move quicker. The Acceleration matrix was available even to Juniors, which my guys could be considered.

The sprint took less than a minute. We crossed the open area and disappeared back into the forest. Only a few miles remained before the raider settlement border.

It was almost dawn, and we needed to be extra cautious for the remainder of the journey. While the raiders themselves were unlikely to wander into the forest near their city, there could easily be ordinary people. Loggers, hunters, gatherers — the people had to utilize all the natural resources around to sustain themselves.

"Hello!" Someone's voice came through the earpiece, and I immediately stopped. "Can anyone hear me? Is this thing working? Someone, please respond?"

"Who is this?" Ditras asked cautiously.

"It's working!" Herman exclaimed joyfully. It was indeed him. "Ditras, where's Achilles? I see he's also online, but he's not responding."

"Here," I said. "Did it work? Is everything as I said?"

"Yes, I figured out the frequencies," the boy replied with pride in his voice. "Just as you said, everything was tied to the Savannah, and it only covers the area within the perimeter. I switched everything to the Brist. And lowered the signal transmission density! Came up with that myself! It might have a delay of up to two seconds now, but the connection will work throughout the coverage area."

"What's he saying?" Anar asked. "I hear the words, but I don't understand anything."

"We're connected now," I explained. "Herman, is this a secure channel? If we enter a scan zone..."

"No one will notice you," the boy said. "I've thought of everything. Due to the signal delay, it's nearly impossible to trace. The individual encrypted packets appear as white noise. And the transmission intervals vary. The only problem is that the communicators are weak. They won't last more than a day in this mode. But there are options. They just need manual adjustments. I've already prepared a plan and will handle everything once you return."

"Good job," I said. "Can you monitor us manually? We're currently three miles from the target. There's a route in the Brist's memory."

"I already found it," Herman said. "What should I look for?"

"The patrol schedule and live forces in the area," I said. "And any living creatures on our route."

"Give me a minute."

"Yep," I said. "Let's rest while we can."

Now I had a dispatcher at the base — little Herman, who was already making my life much easier. And he was still learning.

The fighters immediately sat down on the ground. They understood that this might be the last opportunity to rest for the day and tried to make the most of it. There were about thirty yards to the edge of the grove where we had stopped. I approached the first row of trees and stood in the shadows.

The terrain ahead went up slightly. In the distance, the outlines of the raider settlement were visible. There were several small villages nearby. A bluish smoke hovered over each of them. A full cloud of smog hung over the city itself. It looked like three was a factory at work there, though that was unlikely.

"Five hundred yards ahead," Herman's voice came through. "A cart with three people. They're heading toward the city. There are workers in the field one thousand yards away. Six of them. It's better to go through the groves on the right. Two miles out — a couple of hunters in the forest. Villages — three miles out. There are more people there. You'll have to try hard to go around them. There's a passage slightly to the left of the main route."

"Let's move," I said, returning to the squad. The others had heard Herman's comments and didn't ask any questions.

Forty minutes later, we reached the edge of the city and lay down in dense bushes. There was no wall around the main settlement. Immediately beyond the first buildings was a field overgrown with thick grass, which wasn't very convenient for us. The camouflage cloaks would spark and use up some energy interacting with the surroundings. We had to crawl to the nearest buildings the old-fashioned way. Fortunately, Herman informed us that the first line of warehouses was empty and there were no people there.

"Spread out," I said. "We proceed according to the initial plan. Now that we have communication, it makes the task significantly easier. The numbers remain the same. Bers, Cat — you control the area and maintain the route of retreat. The rest, come with me."

Herman checked the area around the warehouse we needed twice and reported that there was a change in guards. The patrol routes remained the same. The night shift had gone back to the city. Since the number of enemies hadn't changed, I ordered us to stick to the original plan.

"Achilles," the boy hesitantly said. "There's something strange about this building. The modules are operating normally, but I don't see what's connected to them. I mean..."

"There are no standard connections," I said. "I also thought it was odd, but the raiders had made their own modifications to the equipment. We'll figure it out on-site."

"The Phalanxes are at maximum throughput," the boy said. "There might be people inside that we can't see."

"Thanks," I replied. The fighters took their positions. "Ready in five minutes."

Bers and Cat climbed onto the roofs of the warehouses and prepared to shoot. Their task was to eliminate enemies on the nearest towers, of which there were three. Four pairs of guards patrolled the area. The entrance to the building was guarded by a Beacon. Another one was set to monitor the gates.

The area around the building was enclosed by a simple fence made of rope netting, with makeshift barbed wire scattered across the surface. In essence, such a fence could only help against wild animals or stray wanderers. It couldn't stop a determined enemy. We froze in the shadow of the nearest building. The gate to the area was on the other side. The third tower was at the edge of Cat's shooting range, who was confident in his abilities.

"Begin!" I said when I saw the guards appear. "Three, two, one!"

I sprang into action. Out of the corner of my eye, I saw several emitter flashes. Two more flashes appeared above. The first pair of guards died instantly.

"One down," Bers reported.

"Two down," Cat said.

One of the second pair of guards was already lying on the ground with a hole in his chest, while the other was just turning towards me. His mouth was slightly open as if he was trying to finish a sentence. His eyes began to widen.

Trust in a combat group is one of the most important qualities for a successful operation. I trusted my people, so I kept running towards the barrier. A shot flashed past my shoulder. I swung my sword and cut through the netting. The HFS felt no resistance. I didn't even need to turn on its power supply.

One more strike, and a triangular piece of the netting fell to the ground. I ran further, my fighters followed. The ground around the warehouse was packed down to the density of stone, which helped our camouflage. The snipers controlled the far corner of the building, where the third pair of guards was about to appear. We were running in the opposite direction.

"Who the hell are you?!" Someone shouted, and I saw the last pair of guards ahead. I ducked. Emitters fired on my right and left. On the other side of the building, my fighters were also shooting, but I couldn't see the result.

"Clear," Bers reported.

I stopped for a moment and heard nothing. No one paid attention to the guard's shout, which should have raised alarm under any circumstances. But that would have been if these soldiers had taken their duties seriously. The local guards apparently considered their work at the warehouse a sort of vacation.

"Move the bodies to the walls," I ordered. "Herman, the patrol on the adjacent street?"

"Ten minutes," the boy said. "They've gone inside some building."

It wasn't worth touching the Beacons yet. The warehouse was made of rough planks, and the CES had marked the weakest points. I approached the necessary spot, and activated the high frequency sword field. The sharp stench of smoldering wood filled the air. Three strikes, and I carefully placed the cut-out section of the wall down and stepped inside.

I waited and listened. A couple of minutes later, Ditras and the others joined me in a small room of the warehouse. The walls were made of poorly fitted planks, and the entire structure was full of gaps. The air reeked of decay and filth.

"Bodies?" I barely moved my lips.

"By the exit," Ditras said. "So the men could see them."

Based on the Brist's data, the main security detachment of ten people was supposed to be inside. They weren't heavily armed, but they had access to the alarm system and needed to be neutralized quietly. We could find and capture the control room, first. Then we wouldn't need to be discreet and could just eliminate everyone.

"Split up," I said after considering the options. "We need to find the head of security. He's somewhere in this part of the building. Don't engage until all targets are identified."

The warehouse was divided into two unequal parts. The biggest one was near the main gate, where the Phalanxes were. The second part consisted of a corridor and a dozen identical rooms, one of which we were currently in.

I slightly opened the only door, and three of my invisible fighters scattered in different directions. I decided to wait. My subordinates had a better chance of remaining unnoticed and completing the task. So far, everything was going smoothly, and there was a chance we could avoid using our own energy.

"I've got four," Ditras reported. He had gone to the right alone. "They're having fun."

"We've got five," George reported a few seconds later. "Awaiting orders."

"Moving on," Anar added. "Two more rooms."

I found it strange how quickly the fighters adapted to the new communication devices. If Herman possessed a rare gift, the others were ordinary Juniors, who had been running through the forests with bows in hand just days ago. Now I was hearing the familiar roll call of a coordinated assault group over the airwaves.

I was still amazed at how correctly they reacted to my orders and how adequately the foresters executed them. It had been a long time since I had "lowered" myself to commanding such small groups. I was used to dealing with numbers that had many zeros. Yes, at a certain point, human armies had become mere numbers to me.

At the beginning, I was concerned about how men, who had lived through roughly equivalent of the Humanity's "medieval" period, would react. And I was pleasantly surprised. Despite its strange and truncated form, the foreign system had inadvertently ensured the adaptation of the guys to new living and combat conditions.

In essence, they possessed all the necessary skills from birth. This knowledge just didn't belong to them personally but was waiting for the right time in the network archives.

"Found one," Anar reported. "At a desk in the last room. Seems unconscious."

"Let's go," I ordered.

In the distance, three doors slammed simultaneously. There were a couple of screams, then silence. The emitters left the enemies no chance. In the enclosed space, my subordinates had an undeniable advantage.

I stepped into the corridor and headed towards Ditras. The warrior had dropped his camouflage and was waiting for me by the door. In the small room, I saw four dead raiders. Two had managed to grab their weapons. Ditras shot another in his sleep. The fourth died on the floor, pants off, alongside a woman he and his friends were "having fun" with.

"What about her?" I nodded at the unconscious woman with a trickle of drool coming out of her mouth.

"Seems drugged, but alive," Ditras said.

The room George was in looked similar. The raiders had been drinking there: there were empty clay jugs and food leftovers on the floor. In the corner stood a half-empty crate filled with small bottles, each one sealed tight with a cork.

I took one and opened it. A pungent smell of alcohol and smoss hit my nose. After several hours of processing this stuff in the lab, I couldn't mistake it for anything else. The raiders had taken the simplest route and started adding the drug to some kind of brew. The local chemists hadn't come up with anything more complex.

I noticed that there were no empty containers in the room. Despite the overall mess and the impression of a whorehouse, there wasn't a single bottle used for drugs on the floor. This meant that even when drunk, the local guards hadn't touched the reserves of the more debilitating drug.

"Let's go to Anar," I said. "Ditras, find a way into the main area, but be careful. There might still be some raiders left in the warehouse."

My subordinate nodded silently and left. George and I continued down the corridor. There was only one open door at the end. Anar was waiting for us inside.

"A patrol is heading your way," Herman reported. "They'll be at the main gate in about seven minutes if they don't get delayed again."

We needed to hurry. "What do you have?" I asked.

"One raider," Anar replied. "He didn't even move when I opened the door."

The last raider was lying face down on the table. There was a smoldering hole in the back of his head from an emitter shot. This bandit was dressed a bit better than the others but looked significantly worse. His skin had a greenish tint, visible even in the dim light that came from the tiny window. The corpse's hand clutched a nearly empty bottle with some drops of the drug left in it. Apparently, this guard had gone further in his entertainment than the others.

The room's setup was more like a command post. At the very least, it was significantly cleaner here. I found the alarm control panel on the far wall. It was just two primitive button terminals with wires disappearing into the floor.

A drug-addicted head of security? I knew that the concept of "discipline" was foreign to the raiders, but this went against all common sense. These raiders got way too relaxed.

I calmly pressed the buttons labeled "Disable" on both terminals. Again, no surprises — a standard human control panel. Universal, like all the other standardized equipment, with partial modifications to meet the specific needs of the site.

Now we didn't have to fear the sudden

appearance of the main enemy forces.

"Cat, Bers," I said, "we're going with the first plan. The alarm is disabled."

"Got it," Bers responded for both. He was the older brother and often took responsibility for both of them.

"Dear ancestors..." Ditras's shocked voice suddenly came through the earpiece. George and Anar immediately looked at me.

"Ditras?" I said. "What's going on? Did you find a way into the main area?"

"I did," Ditras said. There was some scuffling and background noise over the air, then Ditras spoke again. "But I wish I hadn't. You'd better see for yourself, Achilles. Sixth door on the left. I'm waiting."

I quickly left the room I was in and headed to where Ditras was. Behind the sixth door was a short corridor, at the end of which stood the pale Ditras. Behind a flimsy partition, there was a sense of vague movement. I heard rustling sounds and strange sobs.

"There..." Ditras began, but I didn't wait to hear and flung open the only door.

"Damn it!"

Chapter 6

And the dark clouds will scatter in the Sky,
And the spawn of evil will flee in panic,
And with cleansing blade and light,
The Great Warriors of Humanity will pass through,
leaving not a single Enemy of Humankind alive.

"Book of Hope"
Verse XXI

THERE WAS A SILENT CROWD of people behind the door, several dozens of them. Their greenish skin was covered in ghastly sores — they were rotting alive. The smell in the security corridors seemed like the fresh air of a mountain meadow compared to the stench of the main room. The faces of the warehouse inhabitants looked like grotesque masks, marked with greedy impatience and fear.

Book Two

Most people, if you could call them that, could barely stand. The crowd moved in a strange, unnatural way, as if something was pulling them back. Their heads were slightly tilted back, which only exacerbated the horrific scene. Long ago, in what felt like another life, I had watched movies about zombies, or the walking dead. The people before me looked exactly like those creatures.

"Give it!" Croaked the woman closest to me. I could only identify her gender by the sagging breast protruding from her torn shirt. In every other aspect, she was indistinguishable from her neighbor. "Give it!!!"

These words seemed to break a dam of sounds, and the silence was replaced by moans and cries. Someone tried to push forward, but they were immediately shoved back. People reached out to us with hands mutilated by festering wounds, repeating the same words.

"Give it! Give it! Give it! Give it!!!"

"What do they want?" George muttered in confusion, raising his emitter and aiming it at the crowd. "Achilles?"

The weapon had no effect on the people. Either they didn't know what it was, or they didn't care. The latter seemed more likely.

Once, I had visited the slums of Zail-Tau — a criminal underworld where human scum from across the galaxy gathered. There were places like that in the Confederacy, too. It was easier for the government to contain all the undesirable elements in a few places rather than chase them among the normal population. Prostitution, robbery, and drugs — the three pillars on which Zail-Tau society rested. The slums were the epicenter of these vices. But even there, I had never seen anything like this.

"Drugs," I said grimly. "They need the drugs the raiders are giving them."

"Why?!" Anar asked. "That's insane!"

"Not at all," I shook my head. "It's actually a very effective business model for the local leader. Look at the floor."

I had already carefully examined the room. Behind the crowd was an empty section of the warehouse where the Phalanxes stood. From each module, dozens of "leashes" extended in different directions. Thin cables were attached to each inhabitant of the warehouse, turning them into appendages of the Lirdagi system.

I saw hideous patches of pulsating bio-mechanisms on the backs of people who were lying on the bare floor. These were the connection points to the network.

"Scan," I commanded, and the CES revealed an astonishing sight.

The people rotting alive emitted a monstrous amount of RE. It was as if I were looking at a squad of Seniors. The energy production levels of many exceeded fifteen units. But the consequences of such acceleration were evident in the ulcers on their bodies and the madness in their minds.

I clenched my jaw and walked straight through the crowd. Only the Phalanxes interested me in this place. And Baka — I really wanted to meet the local raider leader.

"Give it!" The croaking cries echoed behind me. "Give it! Please, give it! He's going to eat me alive! Don't you see?!"

The last words caught my attention. I stopped and looked at a young man barely standing on his feet. His RE output level had dropped to ten. The bio-mechanical growth on his back pulsed more vigorously than those of the others.

For a second, I silently studied the growth's activity, then struck along the man's back with my sword. The young man let out a wild scream and fell to the floor. The growth landed next to him with a slap, and the crowd recoiled several feet. It was quiet for a few seconds.

"Give it!" Someone cried again. "Give it!!!"

"Kill them all," I said to my soldiers. The young man's spine was nothing but a memory. The living connection had devoured part of his body. The people could no longer exist separated from the Lirdagi bio-mechanism.

"Achilles..." Ditras said. "These are people..."

"Not anymore," I replied. "And not for quite some time. Execute the order."

"Batteries..." George began, but I just shook my head.

We'd need the charge later. Starting work on the Phalanxes before completely disconnecting everyone wasn't an option. If we did that, the living growths could react aggressively to the interfer-ence.

Though it was unpleasant, I have had experience doing this, unfortunately. The nervous systems of the warehouse inhabitants were under the control of parasites. If they sensed a threat, the crowd of emaciated people would turn into rage-driven animals. The last remnants of their sanity would vanish. This had happened many times when we tried to rescue prisoners on Lirdagi planets. After dozens of failed attempts and massive casualties among the Juniors, a clear decision was made — if you see a person with a living connection, kill them.

I shook my head, getting rid of the illusion. My guys were performing so well that I kept forgetting they weren't professional Confederate warriors. A week ago, they were still hunting game in the forest, unaware that there were creatures in the world far scarier than those in the woods.

"Everyone out," I said.

"But Achilles," Ditras frowned.

"Get out! And close the door behind you."

The guys exchanged puzzled glances and quickly headed for the exit. Anar was the last to leave, and as he closed the door, I saw a glimmer of gratitude in his eyes.

It seemed that a long sleep hadn't done me any good, and I had become more human. I smiled — my psych supervisor Colonel of the Medical Service Oxana Eli would be proud of me. The Confederacy had created an entire scientific department, the task of which was to ensure that we, the Ideals, didn't lose our human roots. Humanity has always been afraid — and I can't blame them for it — that at some point, we would embrace our true nature and proclaim ourselves gods. After all, we were practically gods.

Before, I wouldn't have even thought about it and would have simply given the order. An order that would have seemed very cruel to the men I now led. But I was sure I was right to take on the task myself. It's better to face questions from subordinates later than to see one of the half-crazed lunatics bite into their throats.

I shook my head and looked at my sword. It was time to get to work.

One hundred and eighteen. That's how many half-humans I killed over the next couple of minutes. I stopped when I found the barely living body of the last prisoner in the far corner.

"Come in!" I shouted, and one by one, my slightly embarrassed fighters came inside. They clearly felt out of place and were unusually silent.

"Don't touch this one," I nodded at the half-corpse and gestured around the room filled with dead bodies. "It's better to see it once. I'll say it again — these are no longer people. Mercy. That's what we just showed them!"

I approached the Phalanxes, which were all linked into one network, so it was enough to connect to just one module. I touched the control panel of the lead module and deactivated the entire system. This should have sent a signal to the raiders' base power supply system, but the CES didn't detect the necessary channels for that. The connection was crude and primitive.

As soon as I disconnected the Phalanxes, a tremor went through the room. The growths on the bodies of the deceased people started to twitch and deform. They demanded a response from their hosts, but none of them, except for one, could react.

From the corner of the warehouse came a guttural roar. In the dim light, the twisted body of the last survivor stirred, and a moment later, he jumped straight into the air toward George. It was an impossible jump for any living being. If he were human, his tendons would have torn from the strain. But this creature was no longer a he, but an it, with a cocktail of combat stimulants surging through it. It didn't feel pain from tearing muscles, or the weight from the pulsating mass of flesh on its back. Only rage and the desire to kill.

George jerked back. The mad creature's twisted fingers scraped across the chest plate of his armor, leaving deep scratches. If it had been George's throat instead of metal, he would have been dead.

Ditras reacted first. A beam of energy struck the side of the modified monster, throwing it to the side. The creature immediately sprang up from the ground and launched a new attack.

"What the hell is that?" Anar shouted.

"Shoot it in the head or the limbs," I said. "It's the only way to stop it."

There were a few more shots and the room finally went silent. Only the heavy breathing of the fighters and the quiet rustle of the ventilation systems in the modules could be heard. The disconnection of the network parts was almost complete. It was time to start loading.

Ditras approached me. "Achilles," he said. "I'm sorry, I didn't know. It's just…"

"It's just that all these creatures looked like people," I finished for him, raising my voice so everyone could hear. "You're not the first to think so. Long ago, I was in your place. Back then, I couldn't give the order and tried to save the victims. My people died as the result of my hesitation."

"Better to see it once," Ditras whispered, shaking his head in shock. "Who could be capable of doing something like this?"

"Prepare for loading," I said, leaving his question unanswered and walking toward the gates. It was clear who was responsible for the existence of this place.

"A patrol will be with you in a couple of minutes," Herman reported.

"Wait for my command," I said and slipped outside.

Last night, the Brist had discovered the equipment we needed. The use of internal combustion engines was considered an ancient relic throughout the entire galaxy. I hadn't even thought to look for transport with such characteristics.

The local society ignored all accepted norms, and there were several ghastly-looking platforms not far from the main gates of the base. They resembled fossilized relics of past eras with rusty fans on their tails, but the Brist couldn't be wrong. The transport was operational, and I intended to use it. I just needed to figure out how.

But first, I had to deal with the guards. From what I knew, such equipment was quite fragile and could be easily damaged during a firefight.

There was a small pergola with crates under it near the main gates. I quickly cut a section of the fence and took cover in its shadow. Soon, I heard the approaching voices of the guards.

"Six people," Herman reported. "No heavy weapons or armor."

"Got it," I said.

"Did you hear what Raul's planning?" One raider said in a raspy voice. "He said the boss has gone too far and he's going to punish him."

"How interesting?" Another raider said. "Raul doesn't have the guts. Baka is in good standing with the Regent. You should talk less shit, Krest."

"You're asking for it, Jasek," Krest said. "I'm no bitch to gossip. I got it from trusted sources. Mountain himself told me."

"And what did he say?" Jasek asked. The mention of this Mountain seemed enough to eliminate any further questions.

"He told me that Raul promised to cut off Baka's balls and shove them down his throat the next time they meet. He also said he'll carve his name on Baka's forehead, so he's reminded every time he looks in the mirror that Raul is no one to mess with."

"Liar!" The other guards said in unison.

"Ask Mountain," Krest said. "But I have a feeling it's no lie. Otherwise, why would Baka be gathering so many people?"

"That's because of the Regent," Jasek said. "What does Raul have to do with it? I have a buddy in the citadel who told me there's some unrest. That's why they're gathering everyone for a meeting and heading to Wolf's territory today. Something happened there, but I don't know what. Just passing on what I heard. Apparently, Raul will be there too, and the other gangs."

"Why is it so quiet in the incubator?" One of the raiders said suddenly. "And the watchtowers are empty. Hey, assholes! Anyone here?!"

"Fire," I said quietly.

Two synchronized shots rang out, and panic erupted behind the fence. The guards were clearly not expecting an attack and didn't try to run right away. Their time was irretrievably lost.

"Shoot the runners," I said, rising from my cover.

There were four raiders — two with swords, two with spears. Everyone was screaming, lost in what was happening. I took off, darting through the pre-cut hole in the fence. The nearest enemy managed to swing his spear, and I chopped his right arm off. Then with a backward motion, I took off part of his face.

Energy: 209/1000

Attention: Absorption of raze-energy is limited without full deployment of the System

8,906% of the enemy's raze-energy absorbed

I pushed the corpse toward the second guard and saw a sword glint to my right. Parrying the attack, I use my sword to finish him off.

Energy: 216/1000

Attention: Absorption of raze-energy is limited without full deployment of the System

7,103% of the enemy's raze-energy absorbed

"Run to the citadel!" Yelled Krest, who was covered in the blood of my first victim. "I'll…"

Energy: 225/1000

Attention: Absorption of raze-energy is limited without full deployment of the System

9,908% of the enemy's raze-energy absorbed

The sentence was cut off by a prolonged wheeze. My sword pierced Krest's throat. I didn't want to wait for them to finish their conversation. The last guard dropped his spear and bolted, running in a straight line, the way only people unfamiliar with long-range weapons would run. A charred hole appeared in his back, and I headed back to the warehouse.

"Get rid of the bodies," I said. "Anar, George — drag the first module to the exit."

Several precious minutes had to be spent fiddling with the unfamiliar engine of the archaic vehicles with controls in the form of levers. The contraption hovered above the ground thanks to a thick, inflatable rubber skirt. It was something like an ancient prototype of a glider.

The smell of fuel filled the air. Either there were holes in the energy conduits, or it was the normal state of this piece of scrap metal, but I had no other choice. This was the best transport option available.

On the second attempt, I managed to move the vehicle in the right direction, causing part of the fence to collapse. Dust billowed out from under the skirt. This contraption roared like an infantry platoon in a tavern. If our entire brawl with the guards had been rather quiet, now the whole city probably heard us.

I drove the vehicle through the open warehouse gates and headed straight for the Phalanxes. My fighters lifted the first module off the ground and hoisted it onto the empty rear platform. The machine sagged noticeably but quickly leveled out.

"Get another one," I ordered, jumping to the ground. "George, you'll drive this thing. This lever controls forward movement. This one is to stop." I figured he would handle the controls better than the others.

"Got it," George replied.

"Cat, Bers, prepare for retreat," I ordered, running to the second Phalanx and activating it. "When we pass by, you should already be on the ground."

Loading the other modules took a few more minutes. The guys quickly hoisted the equipment onto the platforms and climbed up themselves.

George grabbed the control lever uncertainly. I waited until their transport left the warehouse and then moved my machine to follow.

"They heard you," Herman reported. "Two nearest patrols are heading to the warehouse. Five and seven men."

I immediately stopped the vehicle. Its momentum was monstrous. The edge of the skirt tore down the pergola, but the contraption finally came to a halt. I needed to take care of the remaining vehicles.

I ran along the sides and slashed the skirts on two remaining transports, then climbed onto each one and made deep cuts in a cluster of hoses. Various fluids sprayed into the air. The damage might not be fatal, but the raiders wouldn't be able to get these machines back in working order quickly.

A minute later, I was already speeding out through the gates. The first group of raiders appeared from behind a nearby warehouse. I couldn't hear anything from the engine roars, but they were clearly unhappy. George's transport raced along the designated retreat path. I slowed down again and picked up the other fighters.

"Let's go!" I said. "We'll have another chance to meet the local leader."

Though our new transport was very noisy, it was also quite fast. Much faster than any cart. Not exactly a glider, but thirty miles per hour was a fantastic speed for the local conditions, especially with a load.

"Achilles," Herman's voice came through the earpiece about ten minutes into the journey. "Three vehicles are moving after you. Five men on each."

"Thank you," I replied.

"And one more thing," the boy added. "I'm seeing a large squad on the other side of town. Forty people. There's armor and several emitters. The Brist says it's the settlement leader's forces. They're heading to Wolf's camp."

"Thanks," I said and called Cat over. "Take the controls. This is for steering. This is the brake. To go forward, press here. Turn here. Try it."

"Why?" Cat asked.

"Achilles?" Ditras called out, looking our way from the first vehicle.

"You're going on alone," I said. "Don't stop anywhere. Your main task is to get the equipment to the base."

I jumped off the moving vehicle, rolling over to absorb the impact.

"Where are you going?" Cat's voice rang out in my earpiece.

"I'm going for a walk," I replied. "Don't wait for me. I'll get to the base on my own."

Then I turned and started jogging toward the nearest grove. This was my chance to get up close and personal with Baka.

Chapter 7

If we remember the Greatness of Humanity,
We will know what made us strong in times past,
And this will give us incredible strength,
Especially if we remember where to seek our Ideals.

"Book of Hope"
Verse VI

THE PURSUERS WERE IMPOSSIBLE to miss. I heard the first sounds of their vehicles at the edge of the forest. By that time, my fighters had already disappeared in the distance. The smell of lousy fuel and smoke lingered in the air.

Three fueled carts raced after Ditras and the guys. The raiders couldn't rely on sound to track their prey because the engines of their own vehicles drowned out any noise around. But there was a distinctive trail in the high grass, which was a sure way to lead the raiders to my men.

Herman was right. There were five raiders on each vehicle, including the driver. All were armed with bows. Judging by their enthusiasm, they knew nothing about what had happened at the warehouse, which meant I didn't have to worry about the safety of the cargo. My guys had enough battery charges for another fight.

I thought the pursuers might catch up with them before they reached the path, because the raiders were moving faster than Ditras's group. They were lighter and more familiar with how the fueled carts operated. But I didn't intervene, I had a different task.

"Attention everyone!" I said as I headed into the forest. "If the raiders get too persistent, let them get closer and shoot them down. We can't have any of Baka's men returning to the city. Herman, you're in charge of monitoring the distance."

"Maybe I should come with you, Achilles?" Ditras offered once again.

"You're in command, Ditras," I replied. "Don't worry about me."

"As you say."

"Herman, I need a visual on the route or at least a direction. You can upload it through the Brist. I have access to it. Limit the communication channel, so I only hear you. Connect the others only if necessary."

"I can't keep up!" The boy yelled, and I realized I was already loading him with tasks as if he were a trained operator, even though he had only skimmed the basics of his training. If everybody could learn so quickly, there wouldn't be a single training school for Seniors in the Confederacy.

"Work at your own pace," I said. "It's not urgent. Just give me a direction for now."

"Four miles west," the boy said. "They're heading toward Wolf's camp almost in a straight line. There's a decent road there. Speed is three miles per hour. It'll take them about four hours to reach their destination. The Brist sees two carts. Similar to yours or slightly larger."

"Got it," I said, breaking into a run. "Give me a list of their equipment and troop composition."

"Two minutes," Herman said. "Disconnecting the main squad. Got it! Now I have two channels! Too bad I only have one mouth and can't talk to everyone at the same time."

"You don't need to," I said, smiling. "Don't clutter the channel with unnecessary information. Learn to transmit data efficiently. We can chat back at the base."

The boy didn't respond. Soon, a list of the raiders' probable equipment appeared before me, and I concluded that Herman had heeded my advice. I uploaded the received data into the CES. It was just a mock preparation. The main decisions would have to be made on the spot.

The limited RE once again restricted me in what I could do. I was getting tired of having to constantly maneuver and conserve energy. This was not my typical way of waging war. In this world, I often felt the urge to activate external fields and unleash my full power. Chasing every armed thug around was becoming quite annoying and rather exhausting.

There had been a small chance to replenish the reserves during the warehouse sweep, but it hadn't panned out. I had realized this after the attempt to separate the parasite from the first prisoner. The connection model was unfamiliar to me, but it was just as effective as all the others.

The Lirdags knew how to extract and conserve valuable resources. The parasites drained their hosts with remarkable efficiency. Every scrap of RE was immediately siphoned into the alien system. These creatures even managed to send one last surge to their masters at the moment of the host's death, while they contained no energy themselves.

This was the only type of lizard bio-technology that yielded nothing upon destruction. The parasites lived solely at the expense of their hosts' bodies. Simply put, they ate the humans alive until the latter died. If the energy output wasn't sufficient enough, the parasites devoured the flesh of the host more aggressively to compensate.

One hundred and nineteen victims — a bad day by any measure. The fact that I couldn't do anything to help those people didn't change things. Saving everyone was impossible, and that wasn't the true goal of the Ideals. We were meant to eliminate the threat to our entire species, and we had successfully done that. But then something went wrong.

"Ready!" Herman's voice came through the earpiece again. "The squad is almost at their destination. The pursuers are closing the distance. Ditras ordered an ambush to avoid leaving any traces."

"A reasonable decision," I said. "Prepare a couple of aerial channels just in case. If anyone tries to follow the guys on the path, direct them to the gas tanks. We might as well test those out."

"It won't be necessary," Herman reported a few seconds later. "We shot down the enemy transports on approach, Achilles. The Brist doesn't see any survivors."

"Give me a map of the area," I requested. "I need a suitable place to wait for the raider squad."

"Will this work?" Herman responded almost immediately.

I saw a map, with a road connecting two raider territories in a nearly straight line. There was just one spot where it made a slight loop around a high hill, which was on my side. On the other side, the road hugged a small stream. This created a narrow corridor about two hundred yards long.

"This will do," I said, slightly adjusting my direction.

Despite having transportation, the raider squad was moving quite slowly. Probably, there wasn't enough space for all the fighters on the cart. The CES had already provided rough calculations and tactical plans, but it needed to physically see the terrain. I did too.

I ran the rest of the way without stopping. This mode of travel was still unfamiliar, but it required no additional effort on my part. My body had recovered enough not to expend resources on such simple actions. In essence, I didn't have any equipment, because the high frequency sword didn't really count.

I arrived at the location an hour before the enemy, which was more than enough time for proper preparation. I walked around the forest, inspected the future battlefield from all sides, and chose my position. I had a little over two hundred units of energy in reserve, and expected to come out of the upcoming skirmish on top. All that was left was to wisely play the advantage I had.

Node 214 (Responsible — Baka)

Borders with Node 213 (Formerly responsible — Wolf)

"Hurry up, you idiots!" Baka shouted from his seat. "If that bastard Raul arrives before me, I'll skin you all alive!"

Baka kicked the raider who was driving the cart. The big guy hunched his shoulders and tried to pretend nothing had happened. The scrawny leg of the raider leader couldn't cause him serious harm. But that didn't make Baka's wrath any less dangerous.

Baka was so thin he was almost transparent. Neither abundant food nor a sedentary lifestyle could change that. Sparse strands of dark hair awkwardly covered his extensive bald spot. There used to be jokers who dared to make fun of it, but the last one had long disappeared — he was sent to the incubator a couple of years ago in a state of extreme overdose.

Baka was in a foul mood, and everyone around knew that. The usually noisy group of his raiders was now extremely silent and focused on not making any mistakes.

"Why so quiet, you bastards?" Baka snapped. "Did you shit your pants? Sing something! We're not going to a funeral!"

A dozen foot soldiers marched ahead of the group. Behind them moved the transport with the elite. Baka protected these fighters and didn't send them out unless absolutely necessary. The fifteen brutes were equipped with ancient armor that had been purchased for a fortune in the Center. If not for Baka's favor with the Regent, he wouldn't have been able to get this equipment.

Then came Baka himself. His cart was fitted with a luxurious chair, which was a source of special pride for the raider leader. Apart from this chair, there was nothing else on the transport. Even the driver sat on the bare floor. Usually, a couple of drugged-up girls sat next to Baka, but this time he decided to leave them in the camp.

Another fifteen fighters were eating dust at the tail end of the group. These were the future zombies, who were recruited from ordinary residents and hooked on drugs. In case of danger, this cannon fodder turned into a pack of animals that mowed down everything in their path. Such liberties could only be afforded by the Regent's favorites, and Baka never failed to remind everyone of that.

Even before leading his gang, Baka had realized one simple thing — his brains were a far more important tool than any muscles. Finding thugs to swing swords for him was easy, but there wasn't another genius like himself even in the Center.

He never suffered from modesty and was fully sure of his righteousness. After all, he was the one who came up with the recipe for the drug made of the forest savages' herbs. He was the one who got the former leader of his node addicted to the poison and ingratiated himself with him. And when Cyclops finally turned into a vegetable, Baka seized power.

Using drugs to help fuel the Regent's equipment was also his idea, which caused real excitement in the Center. Or rather, he was informed that the Regent was pleased to learn about the resourcefulness of the leader of his herd. But that didn't matter. The main thing was that he got noticed.

Baka had planned to expand his territory at the expense of his neighbors, but it wasn't as easy as he had thought. Raul turned out to be an arrogant bastard who outright refused to try the drugs even in the company of his noble neighbor. And Wolf was a complete psycho, with whom Baka was afraid to deal at all.

Everything had been relatively calm in his lands until that idiotic order came from the

Regent. Why the hell did they have to leave and go to Wolf? Weren't there enough other fools who would rush at the Center's command to do whatever was necessary?

There was another reason Baka was so upset, though. He was reluctant to admit it to himself, but it was too difficult to overcome his own fears. Something had changed in the last few days. First, there were rumors about Wolf's death and the destruction of his camp. Then came the order for a general meeting of all neighboring gangs. It was a good thing that temporary truce had been declared. At least that idiot Raul won't dare attack him in the meantime.

Baka had been preparing to confront his neighbor for trespassing and had even laid the groundwork for it, but Raul somehow got wind of it. Someone had blabbed about the burnt village on the border between the two gangs, and the culprit hadn't yet been found. But he would be — found and sent to the incubator.

"Halt!" Came a shout from the front of the group. The leading ten stopped, and Baka leaned over to see what was happening.

"Why the hell did you stop?" He barked.

"There's an elk, boss," one of the fighters said.

"You're the elk, idiot!" Baka snapped. "Have you never seen an elk before?"

"It's headless," the fighter said.

"Juka, don't piss me off!" Baka said. "If I have to get off this cart, you'll be the headless one! Now move!"

Suddenly, a strange crunching sound came from the right, followed by a loud hissing noise. The front cart began to tip over, the group's elite fighters falling to the ground. Baka turned toward the unusual sounds and saw the head of his best fighter, Maity, separating from his body. The body remained standing as the head flew a couple of yards and fell to the ground. Baka found himself staring into the surprised lifeless eyes of his best killer.

"Attack!" Baka screamed, not taking his eyes off Maity's head.

His scream was echoed by someone else, but the voices were more frightened than threatening. The bushes to the right of the road rustled as if someone was crashing through them straight toward Baka's cart.

"Fire, fire, fire! What are you waiting for, idiots?" Baka yelled, backing away.

A few shots were fired haphazardly into the bushes. It surely wasn't a coordinated attack, for which his army trained for days and wasted a lot of precious energy. They would pay for this screwup as soon as they got back to the city. Baka turned toward his elite squad and tensed up.

Of the fifteen fighters, fewer than half were still standing. Many hadn't even activated their armor — something that should have been done immediately. A human figure moved with unreal speed among his soldiers. A chill of impending death ran down Baka's back. The only thing he could make out was the glowing sword in the hands of the killer slaughtering his men, and even that only because it got momentarily stuck in the skull of one of them.

"He's alone! Do something, you idiots!" Baka shouted, kicking his driver hard. "Start it up! We're getting out of here!"

The man reached for the levers but slumped to the side, choking on his own blood — a knife handle protruded from his throat. It was a knife every raider in his gang carried, somewhat of a brand. It bore the engraved symbol of smoss.

Baka struggled to tear his gaze away from the spurting blood of his driver and looked toward the battle. The crazed intruder stood amid a pile of bodies, staring indifferently at Baka. Then, he disappeared, just vanished into thin air.

"Damn it," Baka said, taking the control panel for the zombie horde from his chest. "Let's dance, bastard."

The single button pressed into the metal plate with a distinctive click. There was no turning back. The capsules embedded in the collars of the death squad received the signal and injected their contents into the fighters' bloodstream. Baka dashed to his chair and activated the built-in protection. The horde didn't care who they tore apart. They lived for only a few minutes, but it was always enough to eliminate the problem. The shield would last ten minutes. He would be the only survivor. That was the plan.

Several suicide zombies rushed past Baka. Their faces were twisted with rage, veins bulging all over their bodies. This was his last weapon, typically used for intimidation. Perhaps some of his fighters would die, but it was their own fault — they should have done their job better.

Baka managed to focus on what was going on and realized he had been worrying needlessly about the lives of his men, because all of them were already dead. In the middle of the road stood a half-naked man, covered in blood from head to toe. He looked indifferently at the approaching zombies. There was no fear, not even the slightest doubt in his gaze. Only a cold calculation of the necessary moves. It was the same look Baka had when calculating the profit from goods sold to the Center.

A second passed, then another. An ordinary person simply could not move at such speed. No one could kill three zombies at once. But terrified Baka saw this man doing just that with his own eyes.

The first wave of zombies died in mid-air — they just fell apart. A trail of blood and a ghostly trace from the glowing sword hung in the air.

"Three," Baka counted his dying fighters in horror. "Seven. Come one, somebody!"

He was now shouting at the top of his lungs, but no one heard him. His main defense had turned into a deadly trap, and Baka knew it. When the last of the zombies died, the stranger slowly moved toward his cart.

As he approached, the stranger carefully examined the protective dome and only then turned his ruthless gaze to Baka.

"Are you Baka?" The man asked, his voice frightfully calm.

"You don't stand a chance!" Baka shouted. "You have no idea what's coming for you! You'll never break through my defense! My men will be here soon!"

"Your men are dead," the stranger smirked slightly and ran his sword across the energy dome. Blue sparks flew in all directions. "Your defense will last another minute and a half. Are you Baka?"

"Yes, you damn psycho!" Baka shouted. "I'm Baka! I'm the master of this territory, and I can give you anything you want! Let's make a deal! What do you want?!"

"Raul sends his regards," the stranger smiled. The protective field over Baka went out, and the raider saw a knife in the stranger's left hand. It had the symbol of smoss etched on the blade.

Chapter 8

Tall buildings that touched the sky we had,
Spaceships delivered the Children of Man to any
point in the Galaxy.
Nothing remains for us now.
Only the bitterness of defeat and the animalistic de-
sire to survive, no matter what.

"Book of Sorrows"
Verse VIII

IT TURNED OUT THAT the raiders' vehicles moved quite well on water. I stayed at the battle site for almost two hours, which was very risky, but I needed to stick to the plan to reach my goals. Dealing with the bodies of the bandits was unpleasant, but if everything worked out, I would end up on top.

I briefly stopped the captured cart in the middle of the river and kicked the collected junk overboard. Clothes, shoes, most of the armor — it was all hopelessly ruined, and there was no sense in dragging this trash along. I kept only the weapons and equipment of Baka's best warriors.

Among the armor, I found several pieces that suited my fighters. A dozen emitters were nearly out of commission, but I took them, too. I had to admit that Wolf took much better care of his men's gear. I got the impression that Baka had managed to acquire artifacts from an ancient era, but he hadn't bothered to learn how to use them.

I glanced briefly at a separate crate and smiled with satisfaction. Two dozen standard batteries — my main prize. The risk of this venture was definitely worth it. Now my fighters wouldn't have to restrict themselves as much.

Neither would I. But, as before, only for a limited time. Out of the options the CES offered, I chose one of the most energy efficient ones. I had to do some prep work, but throughout the entire fight, I used only four Acceleration matrices and my high frequency sword, which now needed to be recharged. So I had significantly replenished my own reserve.

I now had almost six hundred RE at my disposal, all thanks to the last group of bandits. Baka had kept them in reserve, and I didn't immediately understand why. Then I saw that they were suicide soldiers, but not ordinary ones — they were pumped full of the same stimulant used to boost

RE production in the warehouse prisoners. Only, these poor souls didn't have parasites on them.

Baka turned out to be very talkative and noisy. I got enough information to consider another visit to his town. This might become my priority after addressing the main issues.

The last pile of shredded breastplates was thrown into the water, and I returned to the control levers. I couldn't fully restore the transport, and I didn't take Baka's cart, as it would have presented a different picture than I wanted.

I had to use whatever was at hand to patch up the air skirt, which had been slashed at the start of the battle. Among the raiders' gear, I found a primitive torch that one of the fighters had used instead of a sword. I took a piece of material from the sole of the second machine and welded it in place as a patch, hoping it would hold until I reached the base.

The squad had long crossed the forest's border. George over-exerted himself and dragged everyone through at once. I'd hoped he'd have enough time to recover before the next mission.

"Herman," I said. "When the squad arrives at the base, relay my orders to them. The modules need to be delivered to the workroom. Prepare a place for them. Can you handle connecting the Phalanxes to the lab system?"

"The same way as the others?" The boy clarified.

"Yes."

"No problem, Achilles!" Herman said. The boy

still enjoyed new tasks. I hoped this period would last as long as possible. "I can also make new monsters if you want. I'll ask Ditras to feed the bio-replicator."

"No need," I said, looking for a convenient spot to get ashore. "We'll deal with that when I return. The guys need to rest."

"Got it," the boy didn't argue, though I could sense his impatience and eagerness to conduct an independent experiment. "When should we expect you?"

I estimated the distance and replied: "In about three hours, if I have enough fuel and nothing happens on the way."

"Would you like me to map out a safe route?" He offered, and I just shook my head with a smile. Herman adapted surprisingly quickly, even for a gifted Senior.

"Go ahead," I said. A strip of sandy shore appeared ahead, and I steered the transport towards it. Two miles down the river was enough to guarantee losing any potential pursuers. The oil slicks on the water would quickly be carried away by the current, and there was no vegetation in the middle of the river. It was unlikely that any search party would go far enough to find me.

A familiar map appeared before my eyes. Herman had taken the specifics of the vehicle into account and charted a route through empty fields. He even marked potential observers along the entire path. There were only five such points, and they could easily be avoided.

I was contemplating future plans. The situation was developing rapidly, and I hoped to finish all preparations before the main events began. There were still too many gaps in my plan, but now I had more opportunities to cover them. It was time to expand the Junior squad — I had the resources, I just needed to find the right people. This was something that could be discussed with Ditras.

I didn't want to recruit anyone from Wolf's former captives. Ideally, new recruits should come from the foresters, who had already proven themselves in battle. Although, there was another issue with that. My thoughts smoothly transitioned to the dukuna. I needed to wait for the results of her negotiations.

"Herman, can you find the dukuna and other villagers?"

"How?" The boy asked, puzzled. "They don't look any different from ordinary people. I mean, maybe they do, but I don't know what parameters to load into the Brist."

"For now, just check the southern direction," I replied after a moment of thought. "If there are no large raider groups or other threats there, we'll expand the search parameters. Ideally, the dukuna should have led her people to the nearest settlements. If she managed to negotiate with Spatus."

"I'm on it," the boy said and disconnected for a while.

During that time, I managed to cover a quarter of the route to the nearest tunnel and bypass two observation points. The map was guiding me to one of the paths at the junction of Baka's and Wolf's territories. In any other situation, this area would have been the most dangerous, with its border patrols, watchtowers, and fences.

However, I had already realized that the local gangs were far from proficient at defending their territory. Their main concern was gathering resources for the Regent, and most issues were resolved through personal negotiations. With some luck, it would be possible to almost completely clear the lands adjacent to the forest. The only problem was that I didn't have enough people to control them at the moment.

"The dukuna is four miles from Spatus's main settlement," Herman reported. "I found a way to search for the guides. There are more of them near Miss Tina."

"Well done. What about enemy forces?"

"Hard to say," Herman replied. "There's no one near our border, but I see a strange group moving east. There are only three people and four guides. I can't tell if they're ours or not."

"Understood," I said. "That's all for now."

I reached the forest border without any incidents, thanks to the well-prepared route and the speed advantage of the captured transport. I had to spend some time clearing the path, but with the support of the Brist and Savannah, it turned out to be much easier.

By the time I got to the base, the Phalanxes were already in place, and Herman was excitedly running around two wagons that my fighters had brought. His face and hands were covered in grease.

"What are you doing?" I asked.

"Upgrading the captured transport," the boy quickly replied. "I'm trying to figure out what to do with the engines. We don't have that kind of fuel, and I don't know what it's made out of. We could analyze it and try to synthesize something similar, but I'm not sure if the machines will work after that."

"When did you manage to learn the principles of such technology?" I asked, jumping to the ground.

"I didn't," the boy said, crawling under one of the transports. "I only got to the part of the principles of raze-energy and moving mechanisms. But that doesn't work here."

I squatted down beside him and asked: "Why?"

"Because we don't have spare batteries," came the muffled voice of the little scientist from behind the rubber barrier. "These contraptions are great, but it's not worth taking batteries from Ditras and the others."

"I think that's a solvable problem," I smiled and stepped over to my wagon.

"What do you mean?" Herman asked as he emerged from under the cart. "Or do you just happen to have a box of spare functional raze-batteries lying around?"

"As a matter of fact, I do," I replied, pulling

out my precious loot from the side of the transport and placing it in front of the boy.

Herman's eyes lit up with a thirst for action. He looked skeptically at the pile of batteries, then at me, then back at the batteries, and finally, with a feigned neutral tone, he said: "I need a couple of hours and six, no, nine batteries. If you don't mind that I use some of the transformer's power to charge them."

"I don't mind," I said. The task was indeed important. Three working transports could get us to any part of the forest in less than an hour. Such an advantage was worth any expense.

Without another word, the boy grabbed part of my haul and dashed off to the base's entrance shaft. I just shook my head and started unloading the rest. I immediately set aside the armor pieces and emitters I had earmarked for my squad, leaving the rest on the transport.

George was there when I went down underground. The guide was eagerly gnawing on a field ration as if it were the best delicacy in the world.

"Feeling better?" I asked.

"Yep," George replied with his mouth full. The dry lump of ration got stuck in his throat, so he washed it down with water from his flask. "Great stuff! Feels like I've eaten half a moose!"

"We need to run over to the settlers and take them some weapons," I said. "They're on the third wagon. Can you handle it?"

"No problem!" George replied and headed for the ladder to the surface. "How was your trip?"

"Successful," I smiled.

Herman had filled all the free slots in the transformer with power cells and was intently monitoring the charging indicators with one eye. The other eye was fixed on the terminal screen, where various connection diagrams and standard battery configurations were flashing by. Ditras and the guys were looking at him, laughing.

I checked the energy reserve in the lab's system and nodded in satisfaction. Everything was going well. Herman had connected the Phalanxes by the book, and all that remained was to start the replication process and feed the living alien aggregate.

For the next couple of hours, I was busy increasing the Hass-Arss population in my territory. If any of my former comrades had told me that I would be breeding Lirdagi creatures and worrying about their health, I would have punched them in the face. But life had turned out to be stranger than any fairy tale. Although, my fairy tale was quite lousy so far.

I didn't have enough meat, so the guys were sent to the ruins on the mountain. Fortunately, the delivery of bio-material had become significantly easier. Herman went with the squad to check the functionality of the test sample on the move. I had no objections. Thanks to the boy, we managed to tackle a huge number of tasks and significantly simplify everyone's life. He deserved to have some fun.

I didn't want to just stand around while

waiting for the feed delivery, so I grabbed a couple of ration bars from the warehouse, poured myself some water, and sat down at the terminal. I needed to devise a perimeter security system. If my enemies weren't complete idiots, they'd conduct thorough reconnaissance before invading. What they'd see depended entirely on me.

"Display the perimeter energy flow system," I ordered, and a full schematic of the Lirdagi protective dome unfolded before me.

Every defense had weak points. Sometimes it was easier to completely destroy a barrier than to spend time carefully breaching it. I faced a rather complex task of turning the well-oiled lizard system into an impenetrable obstacle course that no one would want to mess with.

I decided to start by installing redundant channels and disturbance points within the tunnels. I couldn't directly control this structure, but that wasn't necessary yet. Energy clusters were sent to designated sections of the perimeter and adhered firmly to the main nodes. The Savannah was operating at the limits of its capabilities. I methodically worked through each tunnel, requiring the CES to visualize all the changes I made. I moved on to the next path only when the final result satisfied me completely.

The second step was placing and activating the small breaches. I deliberately positioned them in the most conspicuous spots and placed the central node near the base to ensure we had the quickest access to the entire system. I'd also send all our supplies of poisonous gas there today. The Savannah had managed to create a fully functional pocket for our weapon of mass destruction. All that was left for me to do was link each of the dozens of breaches to a specific canister.

The result of my efforts was a very ugly and chaotic structure, tied into a tight knot. If any one element was disturbed, the entire construct would inevitably collapse, burying the careless intruder.

Of course, with enough experience and determination, this knot could be untangled, but I was betting that the enemy wouldn't waste time on this. It didn't fit the psychological profile I had created of the local society's rulers. For them, demonstrating their superiority was crucial, and to do that, they needed to act quickly and decisively, not sit around for hours untangling the knots of someone else's defense.

The task now lay with the Hass-Arss. So far, I had created a second pack and allocated it territory that wasn't far away from the first pack. I'd create a third once the caravan returned with supplies. I left two clear paths in the hunting grounds, which were necessary for several reasons. We needed a normal exit from the forest ourselves, but that wasn't the most important thing.

It was more crucial to create the illusion for the enemy of a single convenient route. If the dukuna's negotiations went smoothly, this path into the forest would soon become known to the enemy. I adjusted the geometry of the hunting grounds slightly to ensure we had freedom of movement. For now, that was enough.

Since I didn't yet have information on the results of the foresters' negotiations with the raiders, I had set the Brist to track the group of people and guides that Herman had found. If we dismissed certain inconsistencies, this group could be exactly what I was waiting for. I linked the module's reports to the CES, and all there was to do was wait for the results.

"We're back!" Herman said cheerfully as he burst into the workroom.

"How did the tests go?" I asked.

"Better than I expected! The speed is up by a quarter. There's almost no noise, just from the fans. The range is about one hundred and twenty miles. Energy consumption is a bit higher than forecasted, but still within acceptable limits."

"Congratulations!" I smiled.

"Have you finished with the monsters?" The boy asked. "If not, can I take care of the rest? Please!"

I didn't mind, and went to feed the bio-replicator. "Go ahead."

The guys were just finishing unloading. I was pleased to note that all the fighters had swapped their combat armor for sets of the Alive armor — none had forgotten my instructions. I just had to put on gloves to avoid getting smeared with poisonous blood.

"Don't go anywhere," I said as I descended into the tunnel. "We need to talk."

On the way, I checked the location of the

group of people I was interested in and estimated the time we had. I distributed the meat and returned to the fighters who had settled a bit further from the entrance.

"I understand that you're all very tired, but the situation demands decisive actions from us," I said. "You have two hours to rest. Use them wisely. Then, we have another mission."

"What's this one going to be?" Ditras asked, not a hint of complaint in his voice.

At that moment, the replication of the first hound was completed, and the creature burst to the surface. The fighters tensed slightly but didn't reach for their weapons. Such things were gradually becoming routine for them.

"A little demonstration," I smiled. "We'll leave the armor and emitters at the base. I hope you haven't forgotten how to use bows and arrows?"

Chapter 9

And sooner or later, the Children of Man will rise, engulfed in Hope,
Against the evil creatures, they will stand resolutely in battle,
Reviving their essence, armed with the Strength of the Spirit.
They will remember the past and rise, breaking the yoke of the Enemy of Humanity.

"Book of Hope"
Verse V

"WE'RE BETTER WITH THE BOWS than with any ancient gadgets," Bers responded with a smirk. "If it's a hunt, I'll give you a run for your money with your fire thrower, Achilles."

The other fighters smiled. Despite their

fatigue and the many events of the past few days, the squad's morale was high. Perhaps it was because we had managed to complete several missions that the foresters deemed suicidal and impossible. Not without reason, I must admit.

"Then you'll get to show off your skills," I said. "Our enemies plan to infiltrate the forest. They'll be led by guides from your village. We need to meet them and show that they have no business here."

"That's just our usual work, Achilles," Ditras said. "Only I always took more people with me. How many raiders will there be?"

He was certain we'd be dealing with raiders. There were no other adversaries in the vicinity.

"Not sure yet," I admitted. "I estimate no more than thirty."

"It'll be tough to hold them off with just five bows," Ditras reasoned calmly. "There will be five to seven archers. We need to scout the area in advance. Scaring them off isn't hard, but if a serious fight breaks out, we may be in trouble."

"I'll help," I said. This dispelled any questions and doubts among the squad members. The fighters exchanged glances and visibly relaxed. "For now, you can rest."

They slowly dispersed, and I headed to the warehouse. I needed to finish preparing the perimeter. Another Hass-Arss burst from the burrow in the ground, racing past Cat, who instinctively jumped aside.

"Damn it!" The warrior muttered angrily, spitting in the direction of the fleeing hound. We still had two more monsters and a leader to complete the third pack.

I found Herman in the workroom. He was working tirelessly, effectively performing the duties of an entire team of scientists. He had managed to gather three screens from different terminals around one table and was surrounded by holographic projections. He had even started an audio lecture on bio-mechanics to fully occupy himself.

"Can you handle the replication of the leader?" I asked.

"If we don't change anything, I can manage," the boy replied, distracted.

"What do you want to change?" I asked.

"I'm not sure yet," he said. "I'm exploring options. The replicator has a very wide range of settings, but they're kind of confusing. For example, if you alter the hormonal system of the template, you can change the final specimen's skin color to yellow. Imagine a yellow pack leader! But then other chains are disrupted, and the success rate of the experiment drops. I'm trying to find an option that doesn't disrupt anything."

"Then it's better to try on a regular hound," I advised. "Leaders have a lot of additional capabilities built in. If something goes wrong, the whole pack could suffer."

"You said that just in time," Herman muttered. He quickly glanced at me and then started changing the replicator settings.

Theoretically, the boy couldn't do much

damage. Any changes could be rolled back. The CES reported the replication progress to me in the background, and I could intervene at any moment. The worst-case scenario would be if a hound went out of control in the middle of the base and tried to attack one of our people.

But for that to happen, a lot of factors would have to align — from a failure in the defense system to the presence of an unarmed person in the monster's path. Herman had considered those possibilities. I was pleased to note that he was prioritizing safety and control settings. I felt I could leave this experiment entirely in the hands of the young Senior.

I moved most of the canisters of liquefied gas from the warehouse to the surface and loaded them onto one of the transports. At first glance, Herman's modifications were imperceptible. The engine and control mechanisms remained the same. It was only when I activated the equipment that I felt the real difference.

A powerful turbine came to life under the cart's bottom platform. The transport rocked and lifted into the air making very little sound. A large fan began spinning at the rear. Lubricate it a bit better, and only the whisper of air would be heard. I even stepped away about ten yards and was surprised to realize that I could hardly hear any noise. Herman did an excellent job!

It was just a few miles to the barrier section. Now this distance seemed minuscule. After all, proper means of transportation significantly changed one's perspective on how near or far something was.

The pocket created by the Savannah was not part of the barrier in the strict sense. A dozen points of tension, placed in the right order, slightly distorted the overall field. After installing and connecting all the canisters, I would remove the plugs, and the cavity would disappear. The procedure would have to be repeated to get back in.

It was long and tedious, but this option had one undeniable advantage — no scan, even with administrator rights, could detect the location of my traps. The enemy would have to track each breach to understand where it led. And I had tried to turn the ventilation system into a maximally tangled knot. I even added twenty percent of decoys that led back into the forest.

Attention!

Control group changes detected!

I carefully set the second crate on the ground and switched to the CES report. The group of guides had reached their destination. It turned out to be a small settlement seven miles from the foresters' territory. According to the dukuna, a different leader operated there. Spatus's lands ended quite a way from this settlement. The CES suggested the possibility of an alliance. That suited me just fine, even if it added one more link to the chain.

For about five minutes, I watched as our future guests prepared. Determining the composition of the group within the village was quite challenging. I had to wait until the entire group set off. I had previously placed simple markers on the guides' companions and was somewhat surprised to see that they didn't leave with the scouts.

Composition of the likely enemy squad: 25 units

Composition of the support squad: 4 units

Probability of having conditional allies among the support group: 97%

Arrival time at tunnel H4U6: 2 hours 23 minutes

Tunnel crossing time: 48 minutes

Threat potential: low

There were no serious opponents among the scouts, which seemed strange, but suited me perfectly. Our raid on Baka's territory was still not discovered, but everyone in the area already knew about the death of Wolf and the destruction of his camp. The dukuna had brought Spatus generous gifts, so the enemy must have assumed we had serious weapons. Sending a bunch of ragtag scouts into the forest under these circumstances was very reckless.

I returned to my task and began placing the canisters on the ground. At the same time, I worked remotely with the Savannah, guiding a separate breach to the neck of each vessel. I needed to replace the film stoppers with energy seals, which required a certain level of caution.

The process took almost thirty minutes. Then I stepped out of the pocket and sequentially removed all the fastenings. The tiny platform, filled with open canisters of powerful poisonous gas, shimmered and disappeared. Now it could only be discovered if one knew the exact location of the entrance. I deliberately erased all traces of interference in the protective circuit. Now I could head back.

It was still too early to wake up the fighters. With some time left before the operation, I decided to check on Herman's experiment. The CES informed me that the third pack was fully assembled and had begun energy feedback.

"Congratulations on the successful completion of your experiment," I said, entering the room.

"That's no fun," Herman grumbled. "I can't even surprise you! You always know everything!"

"I know that you succeeded," I smiled. "I didn't delve into the details."

"Really?"

"Absolutely," I nodded, and that was my mistake.

The young scientist immediately took a deep breath and unleashed a torrent of data and statistical analyses on me, so overwhelming that I felt a sharp lack of oxygen. I was drowning in a sea of terms and theories that Herman was spouting like a machine gun.

"Stop!" I said at one point. "What do you mean you need to involve some of the settlers for the second phase?"

"Well, that's what I'm trying to explain!" The boy exclaimed. "Aren't you listening to me? I just need a few volunteers with a neutral interaction index relative to the global absorption matrices and open access to their innate energy systems. Or at least partially open. Is that so difficult?"

"Now listen to me, Herman," I said sternly. "Experimenting on humans is a very slippery slope. It can lead you somewhere far from where you originally intended to go."

"What does experimenting on humans have to do with this?" The boy looked at me in surprise. "I'm researching changes in the Hass-Arss. I need volunteers to test a theory. It's completely safe! They won't be in any danger. They just need to stand near the hounds' territory. If nothing happens, they'll go home. That's all."

"What changes did you make to the replicator molds?" I asked suspiciously. "Show me the schematics."

Herman hesitated a bit but followed my order. Two blueprints appeared on the screen. The first was the original, and the second was the one the boy had assembled. There weren't many changes, but they affected key areas: the brain, hormones, internal organ functions.

"What were you trying to achieve?" I asked, analyzing the image.

"It turned out the molds respond well to certain types of radiation," Herman began to explain. "But they're initially tuned to a specific spectrum. I shifted it slightly into the neutral zone. If we find similar radiation sources..."

I looked at my assistant in surprise, and he fell silent, probably starting to doubt himself.

Seeing my silence, he became even more nervous. But I wasn't angry or disappointed with him.

"Once we resolve some of our current tasks, I'll talk to Vens," I finally said. "Maybe some of his people will agree to help you."

For the next hour, we refined the boy's work. His approach was extremely unconventional, and I couldn't believe that an ordinary boy from a wild village in a primitive world had come up with it. Where had the thousands of scientists in the Confederacy before him been looking?

Tunnel H4U6 activation recorded

I stopped my calculations and activated the communication link with my warriors.

"Squad, ready in five minutes."

On the surface, I was met by five foresters in traditional green clothing. Swords, bows, and familiar leather pouches slung over their shoulders. Only Ditras and George were carefully adjusting their loose garments. Small emitters were attached to the belts of both.

"Just in case," Ditras said. "We remember your command. In combat, we'll use only bows and swords."

"Get up on the carts," I said. "I'll explain the plan on the way."

Node 213

13 miles away from the former Wolf's camp

"Raul, good to see you!" A robust gray-haired man, one eye covered by a black patch, easily jumped off the transport platform and casually walked towards his worst friend.

Raul was sitting in the shade of a tree, chewing on a blade of grass as he waited for Pirate to approach him. Pirate once had a different name, but no one remembered it, and he himself wouldn't admit to it. No one knew who or when had deprived the leader of Node 216 of his eye. Pirate never talked about it, and people weren't particularly interested anyway.

Neighbors and friends were more concerned with the fact that Pirate was a vicious dog who bit hard if anyone touched something of his, or something he considered to be his.

Raul, the leader of Node 215, stood up as Pirate approached. "Hello to you too, Pirate!" They were of the same rank, their strengths were roughly equal, and they had little to fight over. There was no reason to escalate things. The men exchanged a firm handshake.

"Baka isn't here yet?" Pirate asked, looking around.

"That jerk is never in a hurry," Raul grimaced.

At these words, Pirate burst into loud laughter. "Still can't forgive him for that unfortunate chick?"

"Chick?!!" Raul was enraged.

Unlike Pirate, Raul was young, tall, strong, and fiery. He got his dark skin from his ancestors, along with his explosive temper. Neighbors feared Raul because he was truly terrifying when angry. He was also an excellent fighter. The only things that kept him from seizing neighboring nodes were the Masters and, surprisingly, his own weak band.

His fighters were decent, but their equipment was mediocre. Raul was always short on exchangeable goods. In the absence of money, barter thrived in this world, but nothing valuable stayed in Raul's hands for long. He wasn't cut out for commerce or management. Moreover, the Regent had expressed dissatisfaction several times when Node 215 repeatedly failed to meet its energy quota.

"I had plans for her! And that bastard turned her into a junkie, willing to do anything for a fix!"

"Alright, alright, calm down. Karsa was a good, honest trader, I'm sorry about what happened to her. So yes, I partly share your grief, but be careful with Baka, you know."

"I know!" Raul said, irritated. "Everyone's been buzzing in my ears! Baka exceeds his quota! Baka is highly regarded! Baka this! Baka that! But he's gone too far!"

"Alright," Pirate smirked. "What's the time?"

Raul checked the system message. "You came almost at the last minute, but you had the farthest to go. And that bastard is still not here. Seventeen minutes, then we move out."

"Shouldn't we wait?" Pirate frowned. "We're allowed to wait up to four hours past the deadline."

"Screw that," Raul said. "We'll go ourselves and get more of the reward. And as for him, he can catch up if he wants."

Pirate also reviewed the system messages, particularly the part about the Regent's reward, which would be divided among those who completed the task.

"Agreed," he nodded.

Exactly seventeen minutes later, they set off in the required direction. After a few hours of marching, they reached scorched earth, with a massive crater gaping where Wolf's camp used to be.

"Well, damn!" Pirate shook his head. "Have you ever seen anything like this?"

"No," Raul said. "What happened here?"

"No idea," Pirate said, giving orders to his scouts to search for survivors.

The two raider commanders cautiously moved forward to get a closer look at the destruction, though there wasn't much to see. They approached and stopped at the edge of the melted crater that had once been the underground area beneath Wolf's camp. Like all others, it had housed the system's equipment, plus the facility for extracting and storing energy.

"Damn," Pirate muttered. "Nothing left." He listened to his senses and frowned. "Is your System working correctly?"

"No, it's not working at all," Raul shook his head. "There's no System here."

"Boss!" Two scouts called out to Pirate as they dragged a filthy and partially burned man across the ground.

"Who are you?" Pirate asked, examining the prisoner, who looked utterly deranged.

"A god! A god from ancient tales descended to

punish the sinners! Ha-ha-ha!" The toothless mouth opened, and the madman burst into a hoarse laugh. "He killed everyone! Everyone!!! And he'll kill you too! And the Regent!"

"What nonsense are you spewing, you freak?" Pirate slapped the madman twice across the face, breaking his nose and drawing blood. This had no effect. On the contrary, the prisoner started yanking at his burnt beard, pulling out clumps, smiling, and babbling incoherently.

"God! He will come! He will come, and kill all of you! He's immortal! Immortal!!!" The madman's final words turned into hysterical screams, drawing unnecessary attention from the other raiders who were listening in. Pirate pulled out a knife and slit the madman's throat.

"We need to report this to the Regent," Raul said. "I don't like any of it. Not at all!"

He looked around, his gaze lingering on the distant edge of the forest. A strange feeling overcame him. Used to considering himself invulnerable, he felt a threat emanating from that direction. A strong threat, if not to say deadly.

Chapter 10

May my Faith be deeply rooted in my heart,
May steadfastness and strength always be by my side,
May fear not overcome me in my sacred battle,
I will pass through the darkness and bring light to my Kin.

"Book of Hope"
Prayer of the Warrior of Humanity

Tunnel H4U6

NAUM LOOKED AROUND grimly. He had never been on the paths of the wild foresters and would never have gone to this place willingly. His gang was one of the smallest in the area, not having so much as its own fort. There was just an ordinary village next to the Regent's node, where raiders lived alongside peasants.

In essence, Naum had long been entirely dependent on Fat Spat. He had accumulated so many debts that he'd never repay them. Spatus didn't pressure his neighbor and continued to help, even sending his own people to protect Naum from the attacks of other gangs. Without any hints or compromises, simply out of the goodness of his heart.

The painful collection of resources for the Center was draining Naum's territory, and he increasingly thought about officially coming under Spatus's wing. Why not? His neighbor had established a good life for all the residents, not just for himself, as all the other leaders did. It was a rare case where ordinary peasants spoke the name of the territory's master with respect. People actually fled from other lands to join Spatus. They had to be returned, of course, but not always and not everyone.

"Mother of God!" Naum shuddered at the latest scream of the horrific monsters. "Is it always like this?"

The question was directed at one of the guides. A group of four grim men had come with Spatus's son. Pierce had conveyed his father's proposal to Naum. Very lucrative and interesting. Perhaps this was Naum's chance to prove himself and move from being a debtor to an ally. And then he could slowly transfer his territory to Spatus.

"They cannot get onto the path," one of the foresters replied calmly. "No need to worry."

"No need," Naum grumbled in response. "There's no need to come here at all. How does one live here?"

The guide didn't answer. The squad, which consisted of almost all of Naum's men, had been moving through the green corridor for about thirty minutes. He didn't know what awaited them on the other side, but he didn't care. The roar of the monsters was constantly growing. It seeped into their minds, making everyone turn their heads desperately in all directions.

Spatus's request was extremely simple. It was surprising that such a generous reward was offered for it. All they had to do was go into the forest and find the madman who dared to defy the Regent. Naum had enough men for that, all of whom had been tested in battle many times before. It was a simple task.

The only thing that troubled Naum were the rumors about the death of Wolf. Supposedly, this very rebel had killed him. But Pierce didn't say anything about it but did share some good news — they didn't have to kill the stranger hiding in the forest. If they could, it would be great, but getting his description would suffice.

"We're leaving the path," the guide in the front said, quickly glancing at the other foresters as if to ensure everyone knew what to do. "Three, two, one!"

The raiders found themselves in an ordinary forest. The howling of the monsters had long since faded, and Naum felt confident in his own strength again. A pair of guides went off to the sides, while two others came up to him.

"Attention, everyone! Stay alert!" Naum commanded, drawing his sword from its sheath. It was the only artifact from the old world in his band, and the leader protected it with everything he had. "We need to go a few miles into the forest to get to the location. We're looking for a tall, half-dressed man. Move out!"

"You shouldn't have come here," a powerful voice boomed from the forest. It sounded like a bear growling. "Get lost! This territory is mine now!"

"And who the hell are you?" Naum barked in response. "Come out of your hole and let's talk like the men we are!"

All he heard back was loud laughter. The bushes ahead rustled, and a muscular barbarian with a sword in his hands stepped into the open. He looked just like the man Pierce described earlier, and a sinister smile appeared on Naum's lips.

"Looks like we won't have to go any further," he said. "Well, well, did Achilles himself come out to play?"

"That is me," the man replied sharply. "Leave now! Or else..."

"Fire!" Naum shouted, without waiting for another ridiculous threat. Half of his men were carrying bows, just waiting for the command.

Book Two

Arrows whistled through the air. The half-dressed savage swayed oddly from side to side and then charged forward, his sword glistening in the sun. One arrow sliced the skin on his arm, another stuck in his side.

"Dead man walking," Naum thought with satisfaction.

"Forward! Finish him off, slackers!" He roared. And then something happened.

A couple of archers beside Naum jerked and fell to the ground, each with an arrow sticking out of his chest. Several more archers fell soon after.

"He's alone!" Naum managed to shout. "There are ten of you! The first one to stick a sword in this bastard's gut gets the reward!"

"Five," came the voice of one of the guides.

"What?" Naum asked.

"Now three," added the second.

Naum turned to face the savage and saw him finishing off the last of his men. He severed the leg of one and snapped the neck of another with his bare hands. Blood streamed down the madman's bare chest, the arrow still protruding from his side. He roared like a wild beast and charged forward. Naum raised his sword. One of the guides on the right was doing something, but the raider saw only the approaching enemy.

On the last step, the savage stumbled and fell forward. Naum shifted his blade slightly to the side and felt its impact with the body. He saw his sword sink into the enemy's body, and then the green walls of the tunnel reappeared around him. Naum stared incredulously at his bloodied sword. He was the only one of his warriors to survive. Beside him, silently stood the two guides, who had forcibly yanked Naum out of the dangerous predicament.

"I wounded him," the raider whispered. "Did you see that?"

"We saw," one of the foresters replied. "Now we need to go. The path won't hold for long."

"Of course," Naum nodded and almost ran down the tunnel. He had fulfilled Fat Spat's task and wanted to report back as soon as possible.

* * *

A flash of the path activation blinked in front of me, and I immediately switched to the Brist signal. The guides were leading Naum in the opposite direction. The bandit was running so fast, he nearly forgot about the guides at his back.

"Regen," I said.

Energy: 643/1000

Minor energy matrix Regeneration activated

"Achilles!" Ditras shouted out of the thicket.

The warrior was rushing towards me with some rag in hand. I winced slightly from the unpleasant sensations of my muscle tissue pushing the arrow out of my body.

It took quite an effort for me to ensure the desired effect. The raiders were terribly bad shots. To run into Naum's sword, I had to exert extraordinary skill, barely refraining from guiding his trembling hand to ensure that his sword wounded me. But I managed...

The abrasion on my shoulder healed almost instantly. Fresh skin had already appeared at the site of the arrow wound. By the time Ditras covered the twenty yards separating us, the puncture wound on my thigh was crusted over with dry blood. My body carefully returned everything usable right back through the skin.

"Let me treat your wounds," Ditras said, slightly out of breath, and handed me the rag. The warrior's gaze was fixed on my side, from which the arrow had been protruding just a few seconds ago. He hesitated, standing there with his outstretched hand.

"Thank you," I calmly said, taking the rag from Ditras. I used it to wipe the raider blood from my skin. The energy matrix didn't absorb it. "You did an excellent job."

I had long stopped considering raiders to be serious opponents. There were only ten of them this time. And they seemed to be mostly rookies. I didn't even bother using combat matrices.

"You didn't mention you were supposed to get wounded!" Ditras grumbled.

"I wasn't wounded," I smiled. "It was just for show."

The other fighters rose around the perimeter of the clearing. The guides, who had retreated at the beginning of the fight, approached from the right and left.

"What did the dukuna say?" I asked.

"The negotiations went well, Achilles," one of the foresters answered. The name "Roman" glowed above his head. Judging by his condition, he hadn't participated in the support of the transition and had conserved his energy. "Spatus accepted the gifts but didn't want to verify Valentina's words himself. Instead, he sent his debtor — Naum. He's the leader of a small gang. You could say he's been under Spatus's control for a long time. Almost all his warriors came with us. About ten fighters remained in the village. If you want, we'll escort you there."

"There's no need for that yet," I said. "How did the raiders receive you?"

"Fat Spat is a good leader," Roman said. "Not like the others. He has a large territory and many resources. They gave us a place for a temporary settlement near his fortification. Provided us with food and a piece of land, assigning local folks to teach us how to work the land."

This information was quite interesting to me. Until that moment, I genuinely believed that all raider leaders were the same, like the scales on a Lirdag's ass. It was extremely difficult to believe that any of them weren't out for themselves. But verifying the guide's words was fairly easy. The main goal of all the leaders in the area was to collect resources from the population and feed the living relays of the system. So far, I had only seen the vilest solutions to this issue.

"Does Spatus have the Regent's equipment on his territory?" I asked. "Special places where outsiders are not allowed or where prisoners are kept?"

"Spatus doesn't keep prisoners," the second guide, Irga, said with confidence. "If you mean places where ordinary residents have no access, then Spatus has two of them. One was originally there, and the other he took along with his neighbor's territory. He might take a third. Naum has no resources left to defend his lands."

"You've learned a lot in a couple of days," I said.

"I lived in Spatus's main city for almost a year," Irga shrugged. "He hired me and several other guides to escort his caravans. He paid us in grain for each day and even gave us a bonus when we led his people out of another gang's trap."

"Interesting. Quite an unusual behavior for local bandits. What else can you tell me?"

"Spatus has the largest gang south of the forest," Irga said. "He sends out grain caravans three times more often than anyone else. His personal squad travels on flying machines that Spatus bought in the Center. He's wealthy, owns many items from the old world and understands them. He imposed a double tax on all residents of his territory. One is weekly, and the other is annual."

"What kind of tax?" I asked with interest. Apparently, the dukuna went to this leader for a good reason. Irga's speech seemed artificial and more like an advertisement for a new product on the network. If even part of it was true, I might one day reconsider the necessity of eradicating all the

Lirdagi lackeys in this world.

"I can't really say," the guide shook his head. "I've seen it happen several times, but I never understood why it's done. I even asked the locals, but they don't know either. They said they've been doing it for a long time and don't see anything unusual about it. They just feel a little weak the day of the tax, but it's manageable once a week. Everyone gets an extra ration of food and a cup of good wine after."

"Describe what you saw," I asked. It seemed I had indeed stumbled upon an exception to the general rule. The only question was how accurate Irga's words would prove to be.

"Spatus's people drag a shiny cube on a flying cart down the street," the young man began, squinting slightly to concentrate and not mix anything up. "It's guarded by many warriors in ancient armor. Ten or more. One always sits on the cart and shouts out people's names. Each person whose name is called approaches and touches this cube. Not for long, but no one could do it for long anyway, because people weaken quickly. Some of Spatus's warriors help them down to the ground and wait until the person can walk on their own. Then they give them food from a special cauldron, pour some wine, and move on."

"You saw this yourself?" It was very hard for me to believe the forester's words. Almost impossible.

"Many times, Achilles," Irga said. "Every week for a whole year. You can ask Roman. We were just leaving when that cart appeared."

I looked at the second guide, and he calmly nodded. I pondered the situation for a few minutes, adding new data to the psychographic profile of Fat Spatus, who was turning out to be rather extraordinary. Maybe even suitable for collaboration.

"Let's move back!" I ordered. By this time, my warriors had already taken everything valuable from the dead. Today, it was mostly weapons, and not even all of them. The raiders' equipment was so bad that even the foresters refused to take some items.

All the valuable findings were carried aboard our transport. When the guides saw the vehicle, they were speechless. My warriors just smiled and acted as if they had been riding on such machines for the past twenty years, not just the last two days.

"Ditras, add Irga and Roman to the team," I ordered. "I'll find them some gear, but you will train them yourself. You know the capabilities of your people better than I do."

"Understood," the warrior nodded and turned to the stunned guides. "Get in. I'll brief you on the way."

"To the settlers?" George asked, taking the driver's seat.

"To the settlers," I nodded.

On the way, I barely listened to the conversation of the foresters. Ditras vividly described the events of our recent raids, while the others added their thoughts. I was completely immersed in my thoughts, only occasionally catching the astonished glances of the new squad members. According to Ditras, I was a true god of war and an invincible warrior. My former reputation was catching up with me even in this primitive world.

For some time, I had been troubled by the question of further developing my territory. A base in the forest was good. Having some transportation and modest equipment was also a significant benefit — I was no longer the naked savage who had come into the forest. But I knew that I would soon need to move forward.

A couple of sets of armor and a few emitters were not enough, much like the number of warriors on my squad. The energy source was also weak, and I wouldn't get far on my own reserves. I needed to level up, but I didn't yet understand how to do it.

The ideal option was to attract new allies. For now, only Fat Spatus fit this role, even if conditionally. I'd have to run multiple checks and talk to him myself. If the raider leader survived the upcoming events.

The meeting with the settlers went as usual. The guys habitually handed over the trophy weapons. Vens thanked us for the help. At this point, a hundred residents of the new village already had a full arsenal, something not every raider gang could boast.

Construction was also progressing steadily. People were hurrying to fulfill my orders and worked without rest. Several houses already had smoke rising from the chimneys.

"There's something we need to discuss," I said once the pleasantries were over.

"My people are at your disposal, Achilles," Vens replied. "Just give the order."

"And you're not even going to ask what I need and why?" I asked with a slight smile.

"For me and everyone else, it doesn't matter," Vens said. "You gave us a chance at a new life and saved us from a painful death. We're ready to repay that debt at any moment."

"I need five people," I said. "Strong men who can handle weapons."

"I can give you twenty men right now," Vens responded immediately. "We have weapons."

"I need five. They'll be back by nightfall."

Chapter 11

In our hearts, the spark of Hope still burns,
The strength and will of Humanity will be reborn,
and the Ideals will return.
The finest Protectors of Humanity will stand guard
once more,
And may the mistakes of the past be lessons for us
in a bright future.

"Book of Hope"
Verse II

WE MOVED TO THE BASE right away. Vens called out, and half the villagers responded — at least, those who were nearby and heard his words. I selected five of the strongest men and told them to get on the platform.

"I'm bringing volunteers," I said, activating

my earpiece.

"How many?" Herman asked eagerly. It sounded like he'd been waiting for my message the whole time.

"Five," I replied.

"We can change..." Herman began, but I interrupted him.

"No need to change anything," I said. "For now, we'll only conduct the second test according to your plan. Don't touch the rest of the hounds."

"Then two and the leader," the boy said.

"The leader?" I asked, frowning.

"Well," Herman sounded a bit guilty. "We need complete statistical data, don't we?"

I didn't respond. The modification of the pack leader wasn't part of the initial plan, because it was unknown how a more complex hound would respond. The rest could be stopped at the boundary of the designated area, but the leader was different. I and some volunteers would have to go as backup.

"I can reconfigure the defense system," Herman quickly added, sensing the tension. "Or divide the test pack into parts."

"That will disorient the Hass-Arss," I replied. "They've already accepted the leader."

"Oh..."

"When we get to the site, separate the couple of the hounds that haven't been modified," I ordered after a moment's thought. "Try to send them to the other end of the territory."

At the base, I dropped off all the foresters and

went to the lab to get the medical kit. It was unclear how the tests would go, and I didn't want to lose people. The guys immediately went off to show the newcomers around the base and their equipment. I got behind the wheel.

"You're staying here," I said when one of the settlers decided to follow my team. "Who's in charge?"

"I am, Achilles," one of the men said. His dark hair was heavily streaked with gray, and an old scar pulled up the corner of his mouth, giving him a perpetual smirk. "I'm Joker."

"Fitting," I smiled. "What weapons can you use?"

"Whatever's available," Joker replied calmly, running his hand along the shaft of his weapon. "But nothing beats a spear."

"The others?" I asked.

It turned out there were two more spear enthusiasts and one swordsman among the settlers. The last man, who had a feral look, preferred a club.

"Who are we fighting, Achilles?" Joker asked.

"For now, only ourselves," I answered. "Let's go."

On the way to the test site, I told the volunteers about the purpose of our journey. No embellishments or secrets. I needed to understand how ready these people were to face the alien creatures. In my experience, a charge from a Hass-Arss could cause panic even among well-coordinated Junior units.

Book Two

Tired and traumatized people could behave unpredictably. I also couldn't rule out a counter-attack by a handful of people against massive monsters. It turned out that the local residents were generally indifferent to any monsters. For them, unfortunately, the most terrible enemies were humans.

"There's no creature scarier than Wolf, Achilles," Joker said. "Any monster is only looking for food or the death of its enemies. Monsters won't take pleasure in the suffering of their victims. If you say we only need to stand there, then we will stand there. Even if we are being eaten alive."

The last part was likely an exaggeration. I didn't demand such sacrifices from my subordinates even in the harshest periods of the war. Everyone's loyalty has its limits. For some, it's the painful death of loved ones; for others, it's as little as poor armor and bad weapons. The latter didn't stay long in the Confederate army.

The territory of the needed pack was marked by a thin line on the Brist's map. For my passengers, the surrounding forest was the same as the forest they were used to, which surprised them. I didn't know what they expected to see — maybe piles of human remains or a terrifying dead wasteland. Fortunately, such signs of the hounds' presence existed only in my memory.

"We're disembarking," I said. "We go on foot from here."

Without any questions, the men got off our transport and lined up in front of me. Joker looked around carefully and sniffed the air.

"Something bothering you?" I asked.

"No. Must be my imagination. The smell seemed familiar."

I looked at the former prisoner with interest. Maybe Herman wasn't so far off in his assumptions. Over the centuries, people had changed significantly under the influence of the Lirdagi system. In the past, no ordinary civilian could smell a Hass-Arss.

"What's the status of the hounds, Herman?" I asked.

"About a mile away from you," the boy responded. "I've split the pack and am leading a couple to the far border. The rest are heading your way. They'll be there in two minutes."

"Why so fast?" I tensed up. In their normal state, the monsters patrolled their territory much slower, conserving energy. They could only reach such speed when they had already seen or smelled prey.

"I don't know!" Herman replied nervously. "I'm trying to figure it out. One of the blocks I set up has malfunctioned. Achilles! Get out of there! I don't know how they'll behave. Achilles!"

There was panic in the boy's voice, but I still didn't respond. Herman was facing a situation where his experiment was out of control for the first time. If I had sent the settlers to the test site alone, they would have had no chance of survival.

We heard a powerful thudding sound coming from the forest. Far ahead, bushes shuddered and disappeared under the massive bodies of three monsters. The settlers behind me let out a frightened gasp. However unpleasant, the experiment had to be aborted. Then more time and resources would need to be spent on restoring the battery population.

The first of the trio of hounds was the pack leader. He would need to be taken down first. There were only a few seconds left before the clash. I didn't have time to send the volunteers back. Nor could I take the brunt of the hounds' attack myself. At the last moment, Joker pushed me aside and stepped forward. His thunderous roar echoed through the forest: "Sit!"

And then the unbelievable happened. The two ranking creatures skidded to a halt, whimpered, and lay down. The leader hesitated, twitched, but continued to run. I didn't want to kill it. Even if something had gone wrong, I was sure it could be reprogrammed. A lot of resources had gone into its creation. In my situation, their value couldn't be overstated. It was created and grown with very limited energy resources.

So, I slid forward, shielding the people behind me, and struck the leader on the skull with the hilt of my sword just as it tensed its hind legs for a lethal leap. The creature yelped and was flung aside, tumbling several times but quickly getting back on all fours and shaking its head in bewilderment.

"Achilles, let me," I realized with surprise that it was Joker, who had stepped forward and started chanting a mournful song or melody. The words were definitely not human. They didn't resemble the hissing of the Lirdagi language, either.

"CES, analyze the situation," I said automatically, and data began streaming in immediately.

Individual Joker included in the authorized connection list... Protocol HRO234-07

Preliminary analysis shows tendency for interaction with lower Lirdagi creatures...

Request received for information packet, according to the identified tendency...

Information packet "Controller" uploaded...

I smiled reading the alert. It had been so long since I'd heard that chant that, honestly, I had just forgotten. Back at the dawn of our conflict with the Lirdags, our scientists tried to understand how to control their simplest creatures and developed a "Controller" course that taught our fighters to control the creatures.

The only problem was that it required an extraordinary amount of energy. Some of the Seniors were able to partially control the enemy's monsters, but it was akin to shooting sparrows with a cannon. A Senior could apply their abilities in a much more complex and massive way than simply controlling a few creatures. In other words, a Senior could have easily destroyed this pack without batting an eye, rather than taking control of a couple of its members. Moreover, I had never heard of a Junior managing to handle even one such creature.

In fact, this packet was taken up by a few of the Ideals. Personally, I didn't need it, as I always relied on pure destruction. But Aphrodite — the ever cheerful and vibrant Ideal No. 55... She mastered and developed this skill to the highest level. I witnessed her simply "shut down" the Lirdagi Queen, giving our Army the time to destroy the enemy invasion fleet with much smaller forces than the enemy's.

Once again, I was overwhelmed by a human emotion of sadness, which was unusual for us Ideals. Was Aphrodite still alive? Were the rest of my comrades?

"CES, analyze the compatibility of the individual Joker with the enemy system," I commanded.

Lines of data scrolled in front of my eyes.

Analyzing individual connection to System @#&%@@&...

Individual Joker has a direct communication channel with the System...

Level of interaction — highest...

Communication channel — stable...

Number of available connections at the moment: 15...

Options to enhance individual's potential. Ready to receive information?

"I'll receive it later," I waved it off, smiling even more.

That's what it was. People had tried to control the creatures without stepping outside our human system, using only raze-energy, which was common to both species. However, if raze-energy could be compared to primitive fossil fuel, then the human system and the Lirdagi system could be seen as two different machines. Yes, the fuel is the same, but the construction and, most importantly, the software were entirely different.

But now, Joker effectively had direct access to the alien system, and the "Controller" information packet integrated in a completely different way, exponentially increasing its efficiency while drastically reducing energy costs.

Joker's initial energy reserve was 4 units. But now, after the information packet had been loaded, the "gates" had opened. No wonder the CES mentioned preliminary analysis and identified tendencies. One's real potential could be determined based on similar studies conducted under much less extreme conditions. Right now, Joker's raze-energy reserve had jumped to 40 units — equivalent to an average recruit who could eventually develop into a Junior. This man certainly had potential.

Joker had spent one unit of energy to subdue each of the two creatures and was now trying to take control of the leader.

All of this flashed through my mind in an instant. The Hass-Arss and Joker were slowly walking towards each other. The chanting intensified, and unlike the other monsters, this one didn't lie down but sat on its haunches, breathing heavily and hypnotically staring into the approaching man's eyes.

"Careful!" I shouted.

But Joker had already extended his hand, gently stroking the creature's head. When his palm reached its mouth, a bit of poisonous saliva dripped onto it. Hissing in pain, Joker jerked his hand back. It was a delicate moment when I thought the creature might break free from control. But Joker surprised me once again. He didn't sever the mental connection, hastily wiping the saliva on his clothes, which also started to melt.

Unable to wait any longer, I jumped forward, and cut away the smoldering part of his shirt with my knife. Then I took the flask from my belt, grabbed his hand, and generously poured water over it, rubbing it feverishly. The saliva and a layer of Joker's skin, washed away, leaving half his palm raw.

"You were a bit hasty there," I said.

At that moment, Herman's voice came through my earpiece: "Sorry, Achilles, I've reconfigured the system and can take back control of them now."

"Do nothing," I commanded.

"What?" The boy asked.

"Do nothing but be ready. Take them back under control on my command."

"Got it," he said, clearly surprised.

I looked at Joker, still holding his wrist.

"And now what?" I asked with interest.

"I can control them for about half an hour," the man replied.

"And after that?"

"After that, I can't control them anymore," he

said, shrugging.

I was taken aback by his straightforwardness.

"Understood. Herman, take them back."

"Got it," the boy replied.

Visually, nothing happened, but the creatures jumped up and began shaking their heads. They looked like they wanted to run away, but something was holding them back. They whimpered and looked at Joker.

"Achilles, I don't understand. I see that they are back under my control, but they're not following commands," the boy said, sounding deeply worried. He was sure he was making a second mistake, and I needed to calm him down. He was already working at the level of an experienced operator, but he was still just a boy.

"Wait a minute," I said and turned to Joker. "Let them go."

Joker nodded, the creatures shook themselves off, and then quickly ran away, disappearing among the trees within a few seconds.

"Oh! It worked!" The boy exclaimed. "I'm sorry, Achilles, I..."

"We'll talk later, over and out," I said curtly, then turned to Joker and added, "Wait."

I then ran to the cart for a medical kit. When I got back, I took out a healing spray.

"Sit down on the grass. Now, tell me what that was and what kind of a relationship you have with animals."

Joker complied and began telling his story, glancing occasionally at the bubbling foam as I treated his hand.

It turned out that Joker, his father, and his grandfather were farmers who kept livestock. They lived much farther South, where there were no forests but beautiful pastures where their sheep and cows had plenty of food and a good life. They also raised and trained riding lizards for the Regent.

"Riding lizards?" I asked.

"Yes. Eight feet at the shoulder. When they stand on their hind legs, they reach up to fifteen meters. We raised and trained them for the Regent. Our former master specialized in preparing lizards for the Heir's army. But then," A grimace of pain crossed the man's face. "The old master died, and the new one... well, they executed my grandfather and father, but my mother and I managed to escape. We found refuge with Wolf. Or so we thought."

Everything clicked into place. Ssarak Maru, or riding lizards, were a type of mass cavalry used by the Lirdags that caused our troops a lot of trouble. Their armored heads and chests could withstand several hits from standard Confederacy emitters. Sharp teeth and strong jaws could easily bite through a Junior in infantry armor. Their riders, depending on the tactics, used either spears or firearms.

I remembered those "mounted" lizard attacks. Beyond their combat effectiveness, they had a significant psychological impact. These creatures were unmistakable. When a wave of armored beasts came at you with terrifying screams, many young Juniors couldn't handle it. And like all artificial Lirdagi creations, the lizards were connected to the system. If Joker and his family interacted with them, they already had the necessary communication channel.

This was a very interesting discovery that allowed me to see the situation in a new light. Previously, I thought I could only use the Hass-Arss as passive defense, but now it was a different picture all together. Joker could already control 15 creatures simultaneously, which was a significant asset to my still small armed forces.

Chapter 12

Once we soared in the skies, and distant stars became our home.
We created worlds, crafting wonders with our own hands.
The fire of the Divine lived within us, and some of us were nearly immortal.
May this ancient light burn within us once more, turning to ashes all evil around us.

"Book of Hope"
Verse VI

Node 234
Spatus's Camp

"YOU SET ME UP!" Naum shouted at Spatus.

As soon as the guides led him out of the tunnel, he ran straight toward the village, leaving them far behind. Horror and anger propelled Naum forward. Adrenaline surged through his veins, and he only realized something was not going his way when the broad barrel of a hand-held emitter gun pressed against his forehead.

"Are you sure about that, son?" Said Spatus in a cold, menacing voice.

"They're dead, they're all dead. That outsider..." There was no sign of adrenalin in Naum, he was empty and devoid of emotions. He dropped his hands and sagged to the floor. "He cut everyone down. There were archers with him. He got an arrow in his stomach, but didn't die. I stabbed him," Naum perked up a bit, looking at Spatus with hope. "Maybe he'll die from that wound? But I don't know. I..." He fell silent.

"You ran away?" Spatus smirked. "Don't worry, buddy," he patted Naum on the shoulder and sighed. "You did the right thing, but I'm disappointed."

"I did everything I could!" Naum said. "All my people are dead! I have nothing left to defend my node."

"We'll handle that, don't worry," Spatus said. "And no, it's not you who disappointed me. It's the outsider. If he managed to get shot by your clumsy fools and take a sword to the gut from you, Naum, it doesn't speak well of him as a great warrior. How useless must one be to let themselves get wounded like that?"

Naum tried to protest, but his fire had completely gone out. There was nothing left to argue.

"Honestly, I expected more. And if everything is as you said, it changes our plans significantly," Spatus turned to his eldest son. "Sound the general assembly, Graham. We're moving out."

"Yes, Father," Graham nodded and went to carry out the order.

"Moving out where?" Naum asked cautiously. He didn't want to move out anywhere. All he wanted now was to drink himself into oblivion and wash away the sticky horror that seemed to have seeped into every part of his body.

"You'll see, buddy," Spatus patted him on the shoulder. "You'll see."

Everything was going according to Spatus's plan. The guides were supposed to leave the battlefield anyway. That was their order: observe from the sidelines, escape, and if possible, take Naum with them.

They managed to get Naum, which was good, as he provided valuable information. It all suggested that this outsider couldn't have done what they say he did to Wolf. That or he got lucky. Naum mentioned archers in the forest. Perhaps this unknown Achilles had gotten together a small army.

Fat Spat had lived so long because he was very good at gathering and analyzing information, and he estimated that the foresters could field around fifty archers, half of whom were absolutely useless in close combat, while the other half might pose some threat.

But fifty foresters definitely knew how to handle a bow and hit their target. Perhaps Wolf had simply underestimated his opponent, as he always did. In any case, based on the available information, Spatus decided to intervene. The promised reward far exceeded the potential risk. Besides, he already knew that three raider commanders had answered his call.

Spatus looked at the guides. "Can you work?"

They exchanged glances, and one answered for both: "We could use some rest, we're exhausted."

"Let's try this." Spatus put on a glove, carefully took a case out of his pocket, and opened it. Inside was a small silver cylinder — thin and long. With his gloved hand, Spatus took it out of the case and extended it, nodding to the guide. "Grab it from the other side. Yes, go ahead, don't be afraid." He smiled encouragingly.

The guide didn't dare disobey and took it with two fingers, as if it were something dangerous or disgusting. At first, fear flashed across his face, then surprise, and finally, a smile.

"You've had enough," Spatus pulled the cylinder away and handed it to the second guide. "Now you."

Seeing that nothing happened to his companion, the second guide wasn't afraid. A look of satisfaction quickly appeared on his face.

"You're full now," Spatus pulled the cylinder away. "If needed, I can recharge you both. Can you work now?"

"We can," the guide nodded. "But it won't be enough, esteemed Spatus."

"Don't push your luck," Spatus snapped.

The curious device was purchased from the Regent for a fortune a while ago. It was an energy accumulator that didn't require a huge transformer for energy transfer. The small battery released energy upon touch. Its capacity was astonishing: 100 units. Among all the people Spatus had met and had information on, he had never seen anyone stronger than himself, with his own reserve being a full 42 units. The bandit leader did not plan to deplete the artifact completely.

"That's not the issue," the guide replied. "We appreciate your help and want to repay your kindness. You shouldn't go through the forest. Your group is too large."

"I don't have time to detour," Spatus said. Any other leader in his position might have punched the insolent commoner, but not Spatus. The fat man knew how to derive benefit even from the most hopeless situations.

"We understand," the second guide spoke for the first time. "And that's why we want to offer you a quicker and safer route. If you help us with energy, we'll lead your army to the desired point twice as fast. We don't usually use the fast path for large groups, but we'll make an exception for you."

Spatus looked intently at the forester guides, then slowly nodded.

"If you keep your promise, you'll each get a sack of grain."

In the remaining half hour, Spatus descended

into the operations room, stepping aside on the way to let a group of workers pass. They were pushing carts loaded with slaughtered bovine, meant to feed the mysterious Heart of the Node, which was overseen by the semi-mad Operator.

Spatus smiled, recalling all the jibes from his neighbors, who fed their hearts with the bodies of thoroughly drained humans. They even suggested trading the corpses of their "herds" for Spatus's bulls, pound for pound, claiming it would be more beneficial. But Spatus refused; he had certain principles, and he stuck to them.

He also sent a message to the Center, stating that he was joining the Regent's mission, and waited the required fifteen minutes. No objections returned, which meant he had done everything correctly and it wasn't forbidden. After that, they set off.

Five guides spent a long time fiddling around at the forest's edge. Spatus had to give them his precious battery, but the result was worth it. The foresters opened a tunnel to lead Spatus's eighty fighters directly to Wolf's node.

The big man went himself, along with his younger son, Pierce, leaving his disgruntled elder son to manage the estate. Fat Spat was a pragmatist and knew anything could happen, so his heir never accompanied him on military campaigns. Honestly, Spatus had been avoiding going anywhere himself lately, too. Why bother when he had two strong young sons and more growing up? He had been spending money on equipping his fighters — possibly the best elite force around — for a while now so he didn't have to go anywhere. But this situation was too interesting to miss.

Fully charged, the guides quickly led the entire unit through three tunnels. And now they were emerging in the forest, already within Wolf's node.

There, Spatus felt something strange — there was no system, which meant only one thing: the heart of Node 213 had been destroyed. This also confirmed Wolf's destruction. Just like all the other hearts, this one was located in the most protected part of the camp or fortress, depending on the strength of the raider clan.

At that moment, Spatus's famed intuition screamed at him to turn around and leave, but it was too late. He had declared his intentions, and the Regent had accepted them. If he backed out now, there would be consequences, no doubt about it. Maybe, just maybe, Spatus could come out unscathed. But probably not.

At the edge of the forest, two scouts came forward to meet them. They introduced themselves as Raul's men and were quite surprised to see an entire army of raiders.

Spatus was initially surprised, as well, but then he understood what had happened. Without access to the system, the scouts likely didn't know about the new participant in the hunt. There were no problems, though, because many knew Spatus. Soon they arrived at a temporary camp on the edge of a scorched field, where Pirate and Raul were already waiting.

"Greetings, wanderers!" Spatus smiled politely, receiving equally polite greetings in return.

Spatus was respected and feared. He treated everyone with marked neutrality and friendliness because tension in relationships was bad for business. On the other hand, Raul's raiders were pleased to see the newcomers. Everyone in the area knew that Spatus had the strongest army, and the well-equipped fighters behind him only confirmed this.

"Hello to you too, Spatus," Pirate nodded equally politely. "As you can see, the rumors were true. It looks like Wolf and all his men have gone to hell, where they belong."

"What do you intend to do next?" Spatus asked. "Have you informed the Regent?"

"Yes," Pirate said. "It's all very strange."

"What exactly?" Spatus inquired.

"Well, first of all, you've probably noticed that there's no system here, and Raul had to travel to the border with his node to send a report."

"Yes, the absence of the system is hard to miss," Spatus said.

"And the second thing... The nameless are on their way here."

Spatus felt a chill run down his spine. He hadn't met a single person who remained indifferent to those emotionless beings that looked so much like humans. People's reactions to them were split into two categories: either utter terror or reverent awe.

Spatus belonged to the latter group; having

firsthand knowledge of their power and authority, he respected their strength.

"We've been told not to disperse."

Spatus quickly calculated the distance to the Center in his head.

"That means we have two or three days. What shall we do?"

"No, you don't understand. This is the third strange thing," Raul said. "They're not coming on lizards. They'll arrive on gliders."

That was strange, indeed. Spatus had seen those flying contraptions, but only the Regent used them. He knew that the consumption of valuable energy for the gliders was extremely high, and they were never used frivolously. That meant something truly extraordinary had happened here.

"Any ideas?" Spatus asked. Raul and Pirate shook their heads.

Of course, Spatus expected as much — lazy, dumb fools. He had his own theories but didn't get a chance to voice them. A high-pitched whistle sounded from behind them, and they all turned. Three small dots, rapidly growing larger, moved toward them.

"Strange. I've never seen such small gliders," Spatus said. "And why are they coming from Baka's direction? The Center is the other way."

Within a few minutes, three small, elongated speeders approached and landed, kicking up a cloud of dust. Two creatures sat one behind the other on two of them. The third glider was occupied by only one.

They generally looked like humans, but they probably weren't. If you looked closely, one creature had visible armored scales starting at the neck and disappearing under the armor.

The second mutant was extraordinarily large for a human; he just barely fit on the glider alone, taking up all the available space, while the two pairs of the smaller nameless fit two to a glider. The Regent's other guards looked ordinary from a distance. They could be mistaken for humans until you looked into their eyes. The vertical pupils and cold gaze were hypnotic and terrifying.

Spatus turned to the giant, assuming he was the leader, but it was the other, the one partially covered in scales, who spoke.

"Raul, who gave you the right to pass judgment without the knowledge and approval of the Regent?"

"What?" Raul sounded genuinely surprised.

The nameless one paused for a moment, then pressed a button on his bracelet. A holographic image appeared before them: scattered, naked bodies as viewed from above. The camera descended, zooming in on Baka's ridiculous vehicle, which lay on its side. His idiotic, pompous throne was unmistakable. Right on the throne sat Baka himself — unnaturally slumped with his throat slit. He stared into the distance with dead eyes, his severed member stuffed in his mouth, Raul's name carved into his forehead.

"It wasn't me! I've been framed!" Raul yelled, jumping back.

"Guilty," the nameless one nodded shortly.

His giant colleague moved with unnatural speed for such a large body, blurring through the air. With a sound of a popping cork, he tore Raul's head off with his bare hands.

The nameless one turned unemotionally to the tensed Spatus and the raiders.

"Now listen to me, monkeys, and follow my orders exactly," he said. "I don't have time right now to find out why you allowed one of your own to disobey your Lord's command, but we will return to this issue. For now, what have you learned?"

The scaled face turned toward Pirate, who was the only remaining leader from the original trio assigned to reconnaissance. Pirate knew he had to speak up, but at the same time he also knew that Raul couldn't have killed Baka, if only because he had been with them the whole time. Moreover, Raul never knew how to keep his mouth shut and would have spilled his beans if he'd killed Baka. But Pirate didn't dare share these conclusions.

"Almost nothing, sir," mumbled Pirate. "We saw massive destruction, found one survivor, and immediately reported to the Center."

"Where is this survivor?" The nameless one asked. His companions had already disembarked and scattered in different directions, each holding various instruments that looked expensive and rare.

"The thing is," Pirate stammered, desperately

trying to find a way out of the situation, "the thing is, the survivor went mad. He was babbling nonsense, and…"

"Where is he?" The nameless one's voice lashed at Pirate like a whip.

"Raul interrogated him!" Pirate said, glancing at the blood-soaked body of his colleague. "He killed the prisoner when he realized the man had nothing useful to say. That's it! I don't know what he told him. Raul said he would report it to you."

"He probably tried to buy his life after breaking the truce," the nameless one sneered. "Pathetic bastard."

"I have some information," Spatus began, but quickly realized it wasn't the right moment. One of the nameless ones approached their leader and said something quickly in an unknown language.

"Completely destroyed?" The senior guard asked in surprise. "Do you understand what it would take to do that?"

Instead of replying, the nameless showed his leader something on a device he was carrying. Spatus craned his neck to see the image but couldn't make out anything but a tangle of lines.

"Hmm…" the nameless chief mumbled. "Report to the Center. We will continue the search until the identity of the perpetrator is established and he is eliminated."

"May I…" Spatus said.

The nameless chief shot him an annoyed look. "I'm starting to get tired of you, fat man," he said. "Did you join this mission to hinder my work?"

"I joined the mission, esteemed warrior," Spatus replied, freezing at his own audacity, "to provide you with important information about the person you're looking for."

"Speak," the nameless one said, his dead eyes never leaving the raider.

"The person you're interested in, who, along with a small number of assistants, destroyed the camp of my colleague and close friend, Wolf," Spatus carefully chose each word, feeling that he was beginning to sweat, "is now in a territory that doesn't belong to the raiders and is considered a neutral zone. I have reliable information about his condition and abilities. For a modest reward, I will immediately share everything I know."

"I like your nerve, worm," the nameless chief smiled. A wave of cold ran down Spatus's spine looking at the dozens of sharp spikes that were the chief's teeth. Then he received a reward system notification sent to him by the Regent's representative and his eyes widened in surprise.

"Continue," said the nameless chief.

"Eight miles from here, the forest begins," Spatus said. All his calculations had paid off completely, and this was even before receiving the overall reward for completing the mission. "A small community of guides lives there. They came to me for help because they were driven from their land. The outsider, named Achilles, along with a handful of assistants, attacked Wolf's camp and treacherously killed him. Our enemy is now wounded. He may not be able to fight effectively. I know where the entrance to the foresters' territory is. Some of them came with me."

"That's not relevant," the nameless chief said. He waved his hand, calling his warriors over. "What do you think?"

"He has nowhere else to hide," the giant rumbled in a deep voice.

"A dead zone," one of the more human-like guards grimaced.

"We'll have to leave the gliders behind," the second continued the thought.

"Verification is needed," the last one stated.

The chief listened to this fragmented report and pondered the situation for a while.

"Hey, you bastards!" He finally shouted, turning to Raul's fighters, who were standing off to the side. "Choose a leader among yourselves. He will become the leader of your node if he survives. You will go first. We need to test something."

Chapter 13

*There is no salvation from the vile creatures that
have gained great power,
Mixing abomination and infernal strength
With Human cunning and intelligence.
There is no enemy more terrifying than the mutant
half-humans who serve our Enemy.*

*"Book of Sorrows"
Verse VII*

"NOW YOU HAVE A REAL refuge," I said, emerging from my thoughts. "But it will take a lot of work to make it safe to live in. If you're willing to work with these monsters, I'll be glad to have you on my team."

"I can't do it alone, Achilles," Joker said. "If you don't mind, I'll recruit some help. Even these guys here."

Joker gestured toward the grim-faced refugees. The situation with the Hass-Arss was quite tense, but none of the men had fainted or fled into the forest, which meant we could work with them. I'd need to fully equip them first. There should be enough of the Alive sets for everyone. We could deal with weapons later.

"We need to inform Vens that you won't be returning today," I said.

"He already knows," one of the refugees unexpectedly replied. "Vens told us to join your force to help protect our shared home. If we return, he'll know that we can't be of any help to you."

"And if you die in the forest, where I took you?" I said. "Who will bear that responsibility?"

"We agreed to come with you, Achilles," Joker replied. "We knew what we were getting into, you told us everything on the way. If we had wanted to or were afraid, we would have left. We had the chance."

"Then let's head back to the base," I nodded.

My tiny unit had doubled in size in less than a day. At this rate, we would soon have to open the underground levels of the base to accommodate everyone. But that could be dealt with later. For now, the fighters could share their quarters, and my room was almost always empty anyway.

When we returned to the lab, I saw something that amused me quite a bit. When we left, Ditras was explaining the features of the underground shelter to the recruits and showing them samples of armor. I expected to see the fighters training or doing demonstration shooting, but I was greatly mistaken.

The guys were engaged in a more practical task, trying to reinstall the cover of the entrance hatch that I had removed, albeit without much success. The lock mechanism was hopelessly damaged. If it weren't for Herman's help, they wouldn't have made any progress at all.

The kid had somehow acquired a portable terminal and was now trying to explain to the five burly men why the locking rod needed to be replaced rather than just bent back and slotted in.

"Achilles, you tell them!" Herman shouted when he saw me approach. "They've been trying to shove it in for ten minutes! They're going to tear up the whole socket and we'll have to replace that too!"

"Replace it," I said as I walked by, and Herman gave a triumphant look to the others. His joy was short-lived. "Herman, you're coming with me."

"But..." the boy mumbled.

"Now!" I said.

"Coming," he sighed.

The five former refugees didn't dare to speak, still unable to believe they had been accepted into the unit and fearing I might send them away. That was certainly not my intention, especially considering Joker's abilities.

"We're changing the structure of your research," I said as soon as Herman and I entered the workroom. "From now on, all experiments with the Hass-Arss will involve Joker. Joker, this is Herman. He'll be the voice that accompanies you everywhere and assists as needed."

"Hello," the boy said shyly.

To my surprise, Joker approached him and extended a hand the size of a shovel. "Glad to work with you, little seer," the warrior said.

I had never heard that term before, but Herman blushed to the roots of his hair.

"Issue protection sets to all group members," I ordered. "How much will it cost us to replace two hounds from the test pack with modified versions?"

"Around 100 RE," Herman said. "We can reduce the cost if we herd them back into the replicator. Or we could feed them in parts. Simply disabling and destroying the subjects seems wasteful."

"Risky," I said. "Run a test first. If Joker can command the ordinary hounds through the leader, then take them for processing. If not, disable them. Take George with you. He knows how to butcher carcasses and handle transport."

"What will you be doing?" Herman asked.

"Waiting," I replied and sat down in an empty operator's chair, taking over the boy's workstation.

There was no point in double-checking all the preparations. I already knew they were in order. Instead, I brought up the Brist signal on the central monitor. Both guides sent with Naum had markers, making it easy to track the raiders I was interested in.

Book Two

Everything was going very well. A quite impressive squad had gathered around the foresters. I hadn't seen such high-quality equipment in these parts before. The information about Spatus and his leadership style was partially confirmed

The squad was moving toward the forest. At one point, I even thought that Spatus had decided to deal with the problem himself, which would have disrupted some of my plans. However, I quickly realized that I was mistaken.

System request to open peripheral transport tunnel 4U3R registered

Exit point at tunnel 3S8P requested

Response time: 3 minutes

The Savannah module at operational power

Initiate intervention program?

Yes/No

I replied no. While such a scenario was part of my calculations, I hadn't expected any of the foresters to have the strength to activate the peripheral system, let alone guide eighty armed raiders through it. It had to be the portable accumulator Spatus was carrying. For the locals, such an item would be of immense value.

The exit point was in Wolf's territory. As soon as the raider group left the transport tunnel, I immediately removed the markers from the guides. The last thing we needed was our enemies questioning the dukuna's people.

Nothing really happened over the next couple of hours. The raiders almost reached the rally point, giving me a chance to assess the preparation of the other bandits. Compared to Fat Spatus, they looked quite unimpressive.

During this time, Herman had equipped our monster handlers and sent them on their first mission. Out of the corner of my eye, I saw the new recruits awkwardly adjusting their unfamiliar armor, but they didn't complain.

"It's starting," I said, noticing distortions on the Brist display. Spatus had just reached the rally point when three powerful distortion sources appeared from the other side. They were approaching at incredible speed, ignoring the terrain and other obstacles. "Gliders."

This moment was one of the most delicate in my plan. The aliens' domes had a different nature and interacted with their system on another level. Essentially, the interior of the perimeter was an energy depleted zone. The field of the relays spread thinly at the perimeter, making it less dense. At the time of the Lirdagi landing, the dome operated in the same mode. This was necessary for the lizards to block the effects of our system. Now, their technology was working to my advantage. But there was always a chance for error.

If the gliders had a standard structure and autonomous power sources, the Lirdags could continue their journey on them. In that case, I would face an air attack, for which I was not prepared. However, if their transport fully depended on system power, that would be a different story.

"Perfect," I smiled as I saw the enemy forces

advancing towards the forest border on foot.

Two hundred heavy infantry men and five high-level Lirdagi system users. These were most likely the nameless ones sent from the Center. Unfortunately, I couldn't perform a deep scan on these entities, because there was a high probability they would detect targeted work by the Brist, revealing my capabilities. It was still too early for that.

The enemy units stopped at the perimeter border. For about five minutes, nothing happened, and then four small detachments broke away from the main group. Each had a dozen people in it, led by the nameless, heading toward different entrance points — predictable and according to my plan.

"Increase power to the Savannah module," I ordered. "Display the breach schematic on the main screen."

The ideal scenario for me would be to eliminate the nameless leading the reconnaissance groups, but that was nearly impossible. The envoys from the Center were not eager to push ahead of the raiders, which was to be expected.

Forced activation of tunnel 5G4H with admin rights registered

Savannah module acceleration initiated

All I had to do was monitor the unfolding of events. Intervening now would be too risky, and there was no need for it. The paths had to appear natural, with all the changes I made seeming like minor malfunctions.

I watched intently as the first group traversed several hundred yards through the stabilized path created by the nameless. They reached the first disturbance point and moved on, then the tunnel began to deform. It didn't collapse like it would under direct influence from the Savannah module. Instead, one of the walls melted away and vanished. A second later, the markers representing ten of the raiders went dark.

Tunnel 5G4H closed and sealed by order of administrator

Forced activation of tunnel 2B8U with admin rights registered

The second nameless opened the path as soon as the first one closed. They were a couple of miles apart, meaning their communication was functioning well.

The second tunnel was somewhat longer. The disturbance point was farther, and the raiders didn't get to it, because a breach in the upper wall of the tunnel activated before. Immediately, I got a signal that the first canister of liquid gas was released and empty. Delivery took less than a minute. The second group perished. The tunnel closed.

I leaned back in my chair and stared thoughtfully at the screen. My defense system lacked variability, so the enemy might try to bypass the established obstacles or conclude they were facing resistance. For that, they needed to...

Forced activation of tunnel 1P9A with admin rights registered

Forced activation of tunnel 8D1U with admin rights registered

"Activate two tunnels simultaneously," I smiled with satisfaction.

Managing an active defense system required constant monitoring of each section, unless a specialist with Herman's gift was involved. However, I doubted the nameless ones knew of the existence of such people, especially on their planet.

Another twenty raiders fell victims of this test. They perished almost simultaneously, and only then did the attack leader come to the necessary conclusions. It was time to move to the second phase. I activated my earpiece and said: "General assembly at the lab entrance in ten minutes. Full combat readiness!"

Forest's outer border

The nameless chief stared indifferently at the wall of trees about twenty yards from the raiders' camp. He had been standing like that for almost an hour. His subordinates had long since dispersed in different directions with their reconnaissance teams. The raider leaders were wary of disturbing this important person and pretended to check their men's readiness. None of them dared to ask why the chief had been staring into space for an hour.

And it was good that they didn't, because they wouldn't have liked the nameless one's reaction had they disturbed him. He was very angry. Enraged, in fact. The test groups were dying one after another, and there was no understanding of what was happening.

Each incident appeared to be a system failure, which was nothing unusual. The neutral zone had been established by the Masters many centuries ago. Such blind spots existed all over the world. They were protected from the herd's penetration and served as unloading points for the Masters' system. Without them, unpredictable disturbances would arise in the homogeneous field, interfering with the even collection of energy.

It was not surprising that this system had partially failed. It was performing its function better than expected before. But this was of no comfort to the nameless chief, because the dome was also functioning oddly. He'd spent almost an hour analyzing the situation and searching for a solution, which was an incredible amount of time given his capabilities. Yet he still hadn't found an answer.

When reports from all his subordinates came in, the chief realized he needed to search for the solution elsewhere. The final straw was the simultaneous activation of two passages. It was a tried-and-true method to rule out external interference with the dome's operation. But it didn't help.

The nameless chief decided to study the issue more broadly and connected directly to the dome's system.

"Anything?" One of the other nameless asked after ten minutes of waiting.

"Yes, Eighty-Five, but you won't like it," the chief replied quietly. "Look."

Each of the guards received a message showing the internal structure of the dome. A chaotic jumble of dots and a tangled mess of breaches made the diagram incomprehensible.

"It seems the Masters overdid it on the protection of this dome, Eleven," one of the guards snickered. "It'll take us days to unravel this."

"Isn't anyone curious how the locals can move through these tunnels?" Said one of the nameless twins.

"Great thought, Thirty," the chief said and beckoned one of the guides who had come with Spatus. "Open a path, worm."

"I have no strength, sir," the man bowed low. "We used up everything on the way here and even borrowed energy from the honorable Spatus."

"How do you travel through your paths?" Thirty asked the forester cautiously. This manner of speaking often misled people, making them think the nameless ones were uncertain or doubtful. By the time they realized otherwise, it was too late.

"No more than eight people per one of us, sir," the guide replied. "Otherwise, the path breaks. It can only be opened once every few days. Sometimes it can't be opened at all, and we have to find another way."

"Pathetic meat..." Eighty-Five sneered. "They use depleted paths, Eleven. That's not suitable for us. There are too many of these fools and they're heavy."

"Look who's talking," Thirty-One, the other

twin, said.

"Quiet," the chief said softly, and his subordinates instantly fell silent.

It would be too costly to untangle the knot of anomalies. The guard knew that depleted sections remained active for a couple of days. Then, the floating defense system of the dome would close the breach and create a new one elsewhere. Predicting where exactly that would be was almost impossible.

"You!" Eleven pointed at Spatus after considering the situation. "I have a lot of questions for you, fat man. Time to earn your reward."

"I'm ready to tell you everything I know, sir," Spatus said.

"Better hope it's enough," the nameless one said. "When did you get the information about the Regent's enemy?"

"Today, sir," Spatus replied with a pale smile. He liked the situation less and less, but it was too late to back out. "As soon as I learned all the details, I accepted the Regent's task and hurried to the rally point."

"Six hours ago," Eleven said, cross-checking the data. "Who brought you this information and where is this person now?"

"He stayed in my settlement, sir," Spatus said. "His name is Naum, the leader of the neighboring Node 237. He decided to try his luck and complete the Regent's task. He asked for my help in the form of some guides. I told the boys to save Naum if something went wrong. They went..."

Spatus trailed off as the nameless one raised a hand and spread his fingers wide.

"I hear this much, but I want to hear this little," he said, bringing his fingers close together, leaving a barely visible gap. "Where is the tunnel this loser used to enter the forest?"

"In my domain, sir," Spatus replied. The nameless one's gaze grew distant, as if he was seeing something beyond the mortal realm. Spatus sensed his help was no longer needed but didn't dare to leave.

Eleven slid along the dome's schematic to the desired location and found an active depleted tunnel. With the right approach, he could stabilize it and turn it into a gateway to the enemy's lair.

"We move out," the nameless chief said after a couple of minutes. "We need to secure the tunnel before the discharge point changes. Thirty."

Thirty turned to his chief, ready to fulfil any order.

"Announce the Great Hunt," Eleven said. "I want every scum within a forty-mile radius to come and work off the Regent's favor. Let's see how great this Achilles is."

Chapter 14

Let the voice of Greatness be heard, let the Human Spirit rise.
Within it lies the power and steadfastness of titans.
Go forth, in search of our lost Ideals,
And then Humanity will once again become godlike, proud, and free.

"Book of Hope"
Verse XIX

THE HURRIED FOOTSTEPS and voices of people could be heard outside the workroom. It was a too familiar pre-battle situation — there were always those who forgot something. Anar burst into the room, hastily setting spare batteries on charge. I needed to go to the surface and brief my warriors. An Ideal must be an example for his subordinates.

Being late was unacceptable. But I couldn't move.

I was glued to the terminal, watching the enemy's actions. They had only two options left. I was prepared for both, but I preferred the first: a slow advance of the invading forces through the forest to the point of interest, without using the tunnels.

In this case, presumably, the nameless ones would have to disable or scare off the Chucklers encountered along the way to prevent them from devouring their loyal "herd". Something told me the Regent's envoys had such capabilities. This was the situation that suited me best. Part of my traps lay in wait within the general field of the perimeter. They weren't tied to any one path and could create deadly distortions at specified points in space. Aerial breaches permeated the entire dome, and I could use them at any moment. With good timing, I could eliminate a significant portion of the raiders, and the nameless ones wouldn't be able to protect them.

The second path was to return via the bypass tunnel to Spatus's territory. From there, the enemies could follow the well-trodden path of Naum's gang, which I had already destroyed. I had measures planned for this scenario, as well, but the risk to my people increased significantly. However, it would allow me to study the capabilities of the nameless ones in practice before the battle began.

Soon, I realized that the enemy commanders had decided to take the second option. Numerous enemy points simultaneously moved toward the perimeter border.

System order to open peripheral transport tunnel 3S8P registered

Exit point set at tunnel 4U3P starting gate

"Switch the Savannah module to pulse mode," I ordered. "Create discharge points within standard deviation along the entire length of peripheral tunnel 3-S-8-P."

Savannah module switched to impulse mode

Calculation of number of discharge points initiated

Sequential activation of discharge points initiated

The long caterpillar of the enemy unit shuddered all at once. My intervention went unnoticed, but I could clearly see the reaction of the nameless. Unfortunately, they lived up to my expectations.

A series of probing pulses ran along the tunnel walls. Ninety percent of the disturbances were detected within seconds. Another eight percent — within the next minute. The remaining ones posed no threat to them.

I didn't cause any damage to my enemies, but I definitely made them nervous. They also had to expend a significant amount of energy to stabilize the passage. I got away with using just ten RE from Amina's reserves.

Operational information could be received remotely, and I was about to leave the control panel and begin preparations, but something held me back. It seemed my famed intuition had kicked in.

I smiled, recalling the old days. Back then, the era of high technology was in its full glory. The incredible System, capable of calculating any scenario, sometimes even frightened operators with how accurate its predictions were. My so-called intuition seemed ridiculous then. There was no scientific basis or proof for this feeling. But the famous "intuition of Achilles" awed not only the regular units of the Confederacy's forces, but even Ideals equal to me. Millions of Juniors and Seniors comprising the Confederacy's army were glad to know that I would be commanding them in the upcoming battle.

Statistics are relentless and hard to argue with. A rather interesting picture emerged when one looked at the statistics of the army of Humanity. The average casualty rate of army units under the command of an Ideal, given, for example, a tenfold numerical superiority of the enemy, was 53.433%. For all Ideals except Ideal #003, codename "Achilles."

For me, that rate was 32.975%. A 20% difference is hard to attribute to a statistical error, especially since this figure hadn't changed over many years, from battle to battle.

Now, this inexplicable feeling made me stay by the screen. I scrutinized the holographic map, specially displayed for me by the lab system. I was trying to understand what had caught my attention.

"Conduct an analysis of the information

exchange among the five nameless ones," I ordered the Brist while tagging them with the weakest identifiers for better interaction with the system. "Scan all the nodes available and list all suspicious activity."

Analyzing. Time to completion: 1 hour, 12 minutes, 43 seconds.

The countdown had started, and I couldn't just sit around waiting for the results, especially when all my fighters had already gathered on the surface. So, I headed to the base's entrance shaft.

In the next hour, I assigned tasks and went with the squad to the future positions. We checked armor and weapons, equipped Joker's group with the remaining emitters, and allocated fire sectors. We even devised command options and actions for various situations. I appointed George as the transport chief. Given the number of enemies, our battery supply definitely wouldn't be enough, and George had to handle the delivery of ammunition.

One hour and thirteen minutes later, the first reports came in. By then, I had returned to the base and resumed the operator's chair.

The CES had done an excellent job. The responses were vague and fragmented but detailed. I immediately began asking follow-up questions, and the map was updated with new points.

I shook my head. I had underestimated the enemy, assuming they would use the two available options I had left for them. But the Regent's servants had come up with a third option, which involved calling for reinforcements.

Book Two

As the Brist showed, eight more raider squads were currently forming in the nodes adjacent to Spatus's territory. The total number was about three hundred people, and that was only within the radius I could detect. Along with the forces already moving through the tunnel, this made for about five hundred armed fighters against my ten civilians-turned-warriors and me, with nothing left of my former power but my name.

There was no considerable choice for me. The idea of fleeing, leaving civilians to be slaughtered by raiders, and starting over somewhere else was repugnant to me. Though the five hundred markers on the map made me question the wisdom of my decision, I concluded that I had about four hours before the attack began, and I needed to use that time wisely.

I was almost right. The attack began four and a half hours later. During that time, two of the six raider groups arrived and, joining part of the initial group, began their assault.

I didn't leave anything to chance and had been on the positions for an hour. The guys were a bit nervous, but that was normal. Without my presence and the experience of past victories, their nervousness might have already turned into panic. But we were ready. The next move was the enemy's.

Spatus's Node

Spatus was nervous. No, not just nervous.

Spatus was scared. Probably more than he had ever been in his life. The reward he received was extremely useful — a fifteen percent markup on the sale of goods from any three caravans initially filled him with excitement. But no reward was worth his life. When the squads passed through the tunnels and arrived in his home territory, a messenger from his eldest son came up to Spatus.

With great difficulty, avoiding the nameless ones' sight, Spatus gave short and clear instructions. His eldest son was already excited and wanted to join the army, but the experienced father did not grant such permission. Moreover, he gave an unequivocal order: under no circumstances was he to come here; he must stay in the settlement. If Spatus could, he would have sent his younger son to the village, as well, but he was sure the nameless would not allow that. The number and composition of the squads were under their strict control.

And then there was this Great Hunt. As the head of a node, Spatus knew of an existence of such a protocol, but he had never seen it in action. He had only heard that it was used once during his father's time, likely for entertainment purposes. Back then, one of the raider leaders had taken over two nodes without being sanctioned to do so. He thought he could deal with the Masters after the fact.

He couldn't. The Regent announced the Great Hunt, and all the surrounding bands united to give him a public thrashing, earning well-deserved rewards from the Regent, as well as the three nodes, which were given to the lucky chosen ones.

Only now, this protocol was most certainly not being used for entertainment. Spatus didn't fully understand the decisions or actions of the nameless, but he wasn't a fool. He knew that something was clearly wrong with the greatest warriors of the planet. This shattered all of Spatus's notions about the existing order. He had seen a single nameless wipe out several dozen armed raiders. In his view, five of the Regent's servants could slaughter the entire population, yet they called for reinforcements. Who was this Achilles, who opposed them now, that four hundred eighty-three men in addition to the five nameless were summoned to eliminate him?

Spatus had already regretted ten times over that he had been enticed by the rewards. Especially when the nameless ones began forming the first wave of the attack. Catching the evaluating gaze of their scaly leader, Spatus suddenly wished he could just fall through the ground.

But he and his men weren't chosen. He guessed that what saved them from participating in the first wave was his well-known industriousness and prosperity. These qualities had allowed him to equip his fighters at the highest level. Spatus watched silently as the nameless ones send forward the obvious riffraff. Pirate and two other ragged leaders were driven into the tunnel like cattle. Realizing this, Spatus perked up a bit. He knew all the bands who would come today. He also knew for sure that his band was the most numerous and best-armed among them.

The nameless stood still like stone statues. It was an unpleasant and very annoying ability, highlighting their alien nature compared to ordinary humans. No human could stand motionless for two hours without blinking.

Then, the Regent's servants sprang to life as suddenly as they'd frozen. The chief started to give out short orders, and two more squads were formed from the newly arrived fighters. Once again, Spatus was left in reserve. But the most surprising part was that, after a brief command, the giant known as Eighty-Five followed the last man into the tunnel. The fate of the first scouts was unspoken, but it didn't take much guessing. Most likely, Pirate and the others were already dead.

Spatus relaxed a bit. Eighty-Five gave the impression of a formidable and powerful warrior. Something told him that there was nothing in the raiders' arsenal capable of piercing his reinforced skin and heavy armor. Would Achilles have the necessary weapons?

* * *

I was surprised by the counter move of the Regent's servants, because it was rather foolish. They had split their forces and sent three groups through the stabilized tunnel. I thought I knew why they did that, though. They had checked the passage's safety and were confident there were no traps — that there would be no accidents. According to their initial plan, the nameless aimed to conduct a reconnaissance in force. I would have acted differently in their place, but I wasn't in their place.

As a result, there was a real slaughterhouse. Coming out of the tunnel, the fighters entered a cloud of poisonous gas, and then my snipers picked them off one by one. Yes, I only had five hastily trained fighters and five emitters. But they had plenty of spare batteries and were in good positions. It wouldn't have been easy to get to them.

To their credit, the enemies tried to organize a resistance. Those at the back realized their comrades ahead were being attacked and, instead of retreating, simply accelerated and rushed out of the tunnel. Some even managed to run through the gas cloud and avoid the deadly beams, though they still inhaled some poison and were very disoriented.

I had to use my high frequency sword and Acceleration to avoid moving my fighters from their positions. Ninety-three raiders fell at the exit. Twelve who hesitated in the tunnel couldn't handle the pressure and were now fleeing back.

Attention: Forced deactivation of tunnel H4U6

Really? That wasn't me.

The tunnel didn't collapse or deform; it simply ejected the fleeing dozen right into the middle of a field of Chucklers. It seemed their nameless commanders, like me, didn't have much tolerance for cowards. The deserters died very quickly.

Attention: Repeated activation of tunnel H4U6

"Achilles, one of the nameless is coming with the second wave," Herman said. The boy was managing the flow of system information so I could focus on commanding the battle.

"Thank you," I replied.

His comment was a bit late, but I didn't mention it. It was hard to miss something like that. They were sending in the heavy artillery. This time, there were only seventy-two fighters, but the nameless one following behind the raiders made me both tense and excited. Finally, I would see the fully-fledged mutants, and I had something to compare them to. Had the Lirdags come up with anything new during my creo-sleep, or were they still following old patterns?

I decided to save the remaining gas for the next attacks, and the guys had only one battery left each — George was rushing as fast as he could, but he couldn't teleport. Besides, I figured the presence of the Regent's warrior on the battlefield would have an effect on the raiders. And I was right — they immediately surged forward. It was time to use my secret weapon.

The nameless didn't wait for all his minions to perish and rushed forward. The mutant ran out right behind the raiders, kicking somebody's corpses out of his way in annoyance. Or perhaps it was intentional, as the body flew 30 feet through the air and knocked over a dense bush on the edge of the clearing. It was show time.

"Joker, begin. Cease fire!" I ordered. Joker didn't reply, but immediately, powerful thumping thundered from far to the right. The crowd of raiders began to halt, none of them understanding what was happening.

Seconds later, five Hass-Arss burst into the open space. Screams of terror filled the air. The raiders were unprepared for this and staggered back, but it was too late to do anything. Seventy enemy warriors instantly turned into a frightened herd. Swords and spears couldn't inflict significant harm on the Lirdagi creatures. The Hass-Arss stormed into the crowd and commenced their bloody feast. Joker would be able to hold them for a few minutes. The rest of the raiders would have to be finished off by Ditras's fighters. By then, George would return with the batteries.

I noted all this only at the edge of my awareness because I was fully focused on my opponent. The huge creature standing in the middle of the empty space couldn't be called human. The nameless one moved his head left and right. It seemed he wasn't at all concerned about the death of his companions. They didn't matter to him. Fixing his gaze on me, the monster stretched his lips into a wide grin.

I was not surprised by what I saw. This was a "Cyclops" — a type of Lirdagi modifier named by some funny scientist and created to counter our Seniors. A modifier designed for physical power and speed. He had excellent armor and monstrous resistance to most types of radiation.

An unpleasant and powerful opponent, but I had an advantage — the enemy had no idea who I was. I, on the other hand, knew exactly who I was dealing with. And I knew the best way to kill him. A similarly menacing smile appeared on my face.

Chapter 15

Evil creatures pose a threat to the Humankind.
At the core of the Human Enemies lies hatred for
Humanity.
But cursed forever will be those who, willingly or
unwillingly,
Destroy their own brothers and sisters, serving the
Enemy.

"Book of Sorrows"
Verse XXVI

"SR THREE, ACCELERATION THREE," I gave the mental command to the CES and activated my high frequency sword. It was fully charged, but the charge wouldn't last long.

Energy: 706/1000

Minor energy matrix Skin Reinforcement,

level 3, activated

Energy: 616/1000

Minor energy matrix Acceleration, level 3, activated

A wave of blue light rippled across my skin, and the monster opposite me raised his massive eyebrows in surprise. I saw the activation of his response matrices. His outline glowed with a putrid green tint.

The third level of Skin Reinforcement consumed much more energy, but it was the obvious choice for the current situation — this matrix had a longer duration and better protection. The same went for Acceleration, but I would have to pay a price for that one later. Without a connection to my native system, even my body couldn't handle such overloads without consequences.

The nameless one assumed a combat stance. Cyclopes almost always disregarded conventional weapons, relying solely on their strength. This one was a bit smarter than most and wore armor.

To everyone else, we simply vanished into thin air. One moment, two beings stood motionless in the middle of a corpse-strewn clearing — a twelve-foot-tall scaly monster in power armor and a half-naked man with a glowing sword in hand. And the next they were gone.

I understood that my enemy was less prepared than me right away. I was a long fraction of a second faster than the nameless one and struck with my sword at the junction of his breastplate.

"Impulse."

My sword became a conduit. The strike was calculated perfectly. The surge of energy knocked out part of the systems in the alien's armor, turning it into a heap of metal. I was fully aware that the mutant, as we had become accustomed to calling them, possessed analogs of the skills of our Seniors and could fully control his armor. I wasn't going to give him the chance to use that ability.

Energy: 586/1000

Minor energy matrix Impulse activated

A blue flash lit up the air. The massive body of the nameless lifted off the ground, momentarily visible to onlookers as a dark blur. I darted after him. It took less than a second to cover fifteen yards. My muscles screamed from the overload, but I could still endure the pain without much effort. However, soon I would need to use regen to continue the fight or even just walk.

The second attack was aimed at the armor's energy accumulator. The model chosen by the mutant had many advantages and only one flaw. Its energy source was positioned in such a way that, upon detonation, the explosion was directed inward — if the attacker had the strength and experience to exploit this.

The air shook with a monstrous roar. The Cyclops lost the last veneer of humanity, revealing his true face. He began to rise with me standing on his back.

"PA two," I commanded the CES, simultaneously concentrating all the power of my sword at its tip.

Energy: 541/1000

Minor energy matrix Physical Augmentation, level 2, activated

I sent the blade into his body, and it cut through the fortified metal like warm butter. The mutant's jerk only sped up the process. I felt a slight vibration from the power source and leaped aside.

The directed explosion was an unpleasant surprise even for the Cyclops. The blast embedded the enemy two feet into the ground. The rear of his armor turned into shreds of metal. Among them, I saw bits of flesh and the creature's pale blood. But the enemy was still alive and not planning to give up.

I saw the light of a new ability activation during my jump. The mutant was disoriented but remained conscious. I knew he would stay conscious even if he were cut into pieces. These monsters felt no pain. That was their strength, and their weakness.

A series of lightning-fast strikes turned the nameless one's spine into separate bone fragments. I struck at the bones and nerves that ran parallel to the spinal cord. The only way to kill this monster was to completely incapacitate him.

I worked the sword relentlessly for another five seconds. Nearby, the leader of the Hass-Arss was eagerly devouring a raider. I kept striking until my sword's reserve was depleted. Pain from overstrained muscles surged through me. Inside the enemy's armor, there was nothing left but finely chopped meat. Yet, the mutant was still alive.

"Impulse," I said, shoving my hand into the enemy's body and grabbing the remnant of his spine.

The energy surge scorched my skin. I directed it where it needed to go and only then allowed myself to briefly collapse to the ground.

Energy: 511/1000

Minor energy matrix Impulse activated

Energy: 630/1000

Attention: Absorption of raze-energy is limited without full deployment of the System.

22,451% of the enemy's raze-energy absorbed.

"Regen," I croaked. Pain surged through my body in waves. I knew I had to hold on for ten seconds for the matrix to kick in and start healing me. Eight, seven, six, five...

Energy: 600/1000

Minor energy matrix Regeneration activated

The CES message was slightly delayed. This meant the damage was deemed significant enough for the system to fully focus on matrix activation. By the tenth second, I could stand, and by the end of the matrix's effect, I felt fairly decent.

"Achilles!" Ditras screamed. "Herman says he can't reach you! The main enemy force has entered the tunnel. They'll be here in twenty minutes."

"What else?" I asked. The activation of slightly more powerful matrices had predictably fried the

Juniors' equipment. The boy claimed he had improved the earpiece, but I knew I was left without communication.

"He says the Brist lost the markers of two nameless ones," Ditras replied, clearly trying to relay the boy's message word-for-word, though he only partially understood what they meant. "Two hundred raiders are moving ahead. Behind them, a couple of the nameless ones. It seems someone else is heading to the rally point. What are your orders, Achilles?"

This was bad, though predictable. The leader of the nameless ones had to react to the death of his subordinate. For the locals, the Regent's servants were gods-like. No one ever thought they could be killed, especially by some forest savage. And this reputation of mine had to be maintained. By killing the Cyclops, I likely signed the death sentence for all the bandits in the attacking squad. They didn't know it yet, but none of them would return home, even if they survived the day. But something else worried me more.

The Brist could lose the mutant signals in only two cases: if they died or if they were Shadows — nasty Lirdagi spawn that were nearly impossible to detect. I'd lost a countless number of Seniors to them during the war. These creatures lived for a single strike and could stand next to their target for hours, waiting for the right moment.

"Joker, get the hounds out of here," I said. "Ditras, take everyone and fall back to the base. Seal the entrance and wait for my command."

"You don't have a communicator!" Ditras said. He realized that such a sudden change of plan could only mean we had serious problems.

"I'll inform Herman through the Brist," I replied curtly. "Quickly! You have three minutes to evacuate! Conduct a roll call!"

We weren't going to make it. I could feel the impending danger with my very skin. There were still five minutes until the main enemy force arrived, but I had no idea when the Shadows activated their camouflage.

"One," Ditras was the first to respond.

"Two," George called out from far to the right.

"Three," shouted Anar.

"Four," said Bers.

Cat was silent. I waited a few seconds, then ordered: "Everyone to me!"

I felt a movement of air against my back. Adrenalin forced me to drop to the ground and strike with my sword from there. A green veil of alien camouflage flared before my face. Mere inches away, I saw the hateful expression on the face of a creature in a gray jumpsuit. Blood trickled from the assassin's mouth in a thin stream. My sword protruded from his abdomen, yet he still tried to reach me with a hooked knife.

Energy: 721/1000

Attention: Absorption of raze-energy is limited without full deployment of the System. 21,451% of the enemy's raze-energy absorbed.

Shadows had always been very fragile. Due to their specialization, they had to sacrifice armor and health in favor of speed and camouflage. Three of my fighters sprang from their positions and rushed towards me. Bers stood up to his full height, staring intently at the spot where Cat was supposed to appear.

"Bers!" I barked. "He's dead! Move!"

But Bers didn't react. Or rather, he reacted in a way I hadn't counted on. Bers slowly raised his emitter and began firing at the surrounding thickets.

"Damn you!" I snarled and yanked Ditras's weapon from his hands. "Give it here!"

I automatically switched the fire mode to a wide beam. A pale streak of energy shot out from the emitter's barrel, and the battery quickly drained. The Shadows moved in peculiar jerks, pausing periodically for a couple of moments. I stayed still, searching.

"Another battery!" I roared, throwing the empty one to the ground. Someone handed me a spare, and I reloaded the emitter. Bers had emptied his own and hesitated for a second. The air rippled next to him, and a I saw a knife plunge into Bers's throat. The shadow's blade easily penetrated the protective film of the armor, and we'd never found helmets. This was the nameless one's last victory.

Then I burned a hole in his chest a few inches in diameter. He was already dead, but George and Anar still fired more shots for good measure.

Energy: 834/1000

Attention: Absorption of raze-energy is

limited without full deployment of the System.

20,451% of the enemy's raze-energy absorbed.

"Everybody back to the base," I ordered, returning Ditras's weapon to him. "Fast!"

No one dared to argue. I quickly snatched the communicator from Anar's ear and put it on.

"Herman, change the territory borders for all the packs," I commanded, not doubting that the boy could hear every word. "In ten minutes, all the Hass-Arss must be here."

"But we can't control them!" The boy exclaimed in fear. "Joker has no energy!"

"Follow your orders, operator!" I snapped back. "Do not leave the workroom until the main forces return."

I had only a minute left to remove my squad from the path of hundreds of raiders. I could already see them running in the distance, with less than a hundred yards left to exit the tunnel.

"Accelerate!" I roared and rushed towards the entrance to the path.

Within seconds, the specialization of the fourth nameless one became clear. The front rows of raiders merged into a single organism — mindless dolls obeying the Controller's mental commands. This modification was much rarer, mainly because their influence was quite easy to counteract. You just had to have a damn helmet, which was standard issue for all Juniors.

My movement didn't go unnoticed. Arrows flew toward me, which were now released by an operator with perfect aim. Since I had no other armor, my high frequency sword turned into a blurred streak, slicing through the arrows midflight. Three seconds, and I crashed into the first line of raiders.

The CES immediately shut off the notification stream. Energy trickled in from each fallen bandit and was spent on activating more and more matrices. Ordinary bandits, even those guided by the Controller's hand, couldn't stop my onslaught. Each puppet I killed affected the state of the nameless. I knew this as well as I knew the limits of my own strength, which was coming to an end.

"The hounds are a minute away," Herman reported, sounding like he was nearly crying.

"Well done, boy," I rasped, then activated second-level Acceleration and bolted out of the tunnel.

A massive heap of corpses lay behind me. I would never know how many I killed in those few minutes, nor did I want to. Most importantly, I saw a dozen bandits dropping dead for no apparent reason before I retreated.

This was the signal I had been desperately waiting for. It was how the forced disconnection from the Lirdagi mutants affected ordinary people. The Controller couldn't withstand the multiple deaths of his puppets and burnt out. For any modifier, this was tantamount to death.

The raider army halted briefly but was quickly forced to run forward again, right into the clutches of the Hass-Arss. I sped past the hounds and stopped only beyond the clearing. The creatures were too excited by the powerful scent of blood pouring from the tunnel's orifice to be interested in me.

Unfortunately, only the best of the enemy fighters remained, and as they rushed towards their prey, the Hass-Arss were met with emitter fire. The creatures were dying one after another but managed to reap a bloody harvest, nevertheless. At some point, a powerful force blast swept the remaining five hounds out of the passage. The nameless chief had joined the battle, though he hadn't revealed himself yet. I still needed time to devise a combat strategy.

That time was granted by the gas. The raider squad was hit from all sides by what was left of the smoss. The hundred and fifty raiders were well protected from conventional weapons, but not all could handle chemical attacks. Some of the warriors began to choke. Others cranked their shields to full power and scattered in different directions. Only two people remained by the tunnel entrance.

One was a fat man encased in heavy armor, and the other, a Lirdagi modifier covered in dark scales. I sensed interference in the dome's perimeter. The mutant was drawing power directly from it and within seconds had blocked almost all breaches. This was the level of a true Operator, a Controller of Enemy Systems. The ultimate warriors, to whom the Lirdags gave full access to their structures. They were the most loyal in the Lirdagi army.

"You've created a whole lot of problems, Achilles," the Operator said, shaking his head. "And to think, at one point, I actually believed the dome system failures were natural. You surprised me."

There was hardly a more foolish waste of time than a pompous speech in front of a defeated enemy. The remaining raiders broke into groups and quickly began setting up a perimeter. The nameless chief looked at me with superiority, and I looked back indifferently.

The mutant made two mistakes; both were fatal. He gave me time and revealed his specialization. That was more than enough for me. Lines of the Savannah's report scrolled before my eyes. The module responded to the new task and started building the necessary sequences.

Enter reverse mode

Creating interaction points

Activating the field based on the specified parameters

Begin?

Yes/No

"But now it's time for you to…"

"Yes," I smiled broadly, and the mutant stopped mid-sentence. He couldn't speak anymore. All he could do was stare at me and try to force out a few words.

The Savannah had created a reverse field around the chief administrator of the protective perimeter. The module was pumping all the energy reserves of our transformer into him, causing the Operator immense pain. The strike had paralyzed his nervous system, effectively turning him into a vegetable.

"Fat Spatus, am I correct?" I said coldly looking at the fat man. The raider leader could have given the order his master had been about to, but he didn't. For this, he had condemned himself and his men to a painful death.

"You are correct, Achilles," he replied slowly.

"I'll ask you this only once," I continued, nodding towards the mutant. "Who do you want to die next to? Them or people?"

At that moment, the nameless began to wheeze in pain. Despite the Savannah's efforts to immobilize him, his right hand started to rise. I accelerated and darted forward, but couldn't stop the suicide attempt. The nameless one's finger touched an invisible panel, and the Lirdagi protective dome above us ceased to exist.

I didn't expect that. The lizards never entrusted their minions with access to the self-destruct system. Trust always had its limits.

The forest around us came alive. I heard numerous hideous screams of the Chucklers. It seemed as if demons had burst from the very depths of hell to tear every living being to shreds.

"Achilles!" Herman's panicked message flashed before my eyes. "The protection is gone, the restrictions are lifted, and the Chucklers are uncontrollably leaving their places of habitat! They are all moving towards you! And me! And the settlement! Achilles! What should I do?!"

There was that little boy once again. His

achievements were undoubtedly remarkable, but he was still too young. Despite acquiring a wealth of knowledge and skills, his psyche hadn't changed. The child was in a state of panic, and I didn't blame him.

The entire population of creatures in the "gray zone" was on the move. The dying nameless had managed to sour my victory. The "Rakha" protocol couldn't be canceled. The Lirdags used it when they had no chances of victory left.

All the dome's energy was transferred to the Chucklers' fields. The creatures gained the ability to reproduce uncontrollably and were no longer attached to specific locations. Their first target was the inner part of the perimeter, and they were now moving in search of victims — living people. First, they would kill everyone in the forest. Then they would move beyond it, spreading like a cancerous tumor across the world.

To stop them, we had to destroy every last creature. In the age of the Confederacy, we used special Cleaner units for this. I was alone now, which meant I was the cleaner.

For the first time since awakening, my reserve was filled to the brim. But I knew all too well that it wasn't enough.

"Transformer reserve level," I said, ignoring Spatus, who was nervously shuffling his feet next to me.

The raiders began to gather around their leader. Many looked fearfully in the direction of the approaching monstrous howl. I had very little time left. A minute, maybe two. The Amina had only two hundred RE left, which should have been enough, if we were lucky.

"Full energy extraction!" I commanded clearly. "Initiate the 'Last Bastion' protocol."

"What's happening, Achilles?" Spatus asked cautiously, but I didn't answer. I was closely watching the lines of the CES report.

Phalanx modules switched to interaction mode. All current connections removed

Amina module switching to support mode

Brist module set to mode 0

Savannah module ready for operation

Energy: 1300/1000

Sufficient energy for deploying the "Last Bastion" protocol

Confirm deployment?

Yes/No

"I confirm! Deploy!"

Warning: In the event of deployment, you will become the primary System node and will require a constant supply of raze-energy. If the reserve is depleted, you will die!

"Deploy!" I growled, angered by the foolish delay.

Panic broke out among the raiders. Spatus tried to calm his subordinates, but with little success.

Meanwhile, a faint message appeared before my eyes.

"Last Bastion" protocol activated

You are the primary System node

Current/number of connections 0/180

Personal energy reserve: 300/200

100,000 RE required to complete the first stage of primary System node stabilization

Duration of stage 1: 72 hours.

Do you wish to exit autonomous mode and connect to the System?

"Yes, damn it!" I snarled, causing another bout of anxiety among the bewildered raiders.

Extraction of RE from the primary node system initiated. Current rate: 1 RE/2.55 seconds

Personal energy reserve: 299/200.

I had delayed this for a long time, but I could delay it no longer. My lips stretched into a grim smile. Now, the rules of the game became very simple. To survive, I had to kill. Again and again…

Chapter 16

*The Glory of the Ancestors will light my path and
guide my soul,
I will overcome all hardships, showing the World
my resilience,
The Enemy of Humanity will not shake my faith,
I will walk through the darkness and bring the Light
of Justice and Honor!*

*"Book of Hope"
Prayer of the Warrior of Humanity*

THE RAIDERS RETREATED. Fifty armed fighters
suddenly felt a threat more serious than the approaching horde of monsters. Each of them understood that a naked savage couldn't stand against
an elite squad armed with the most advanced ancient weapons their world had to offer. Yet, their

hands were trembling with fear, because they had seen what I was capable of.

They had witnessed the deaths of the legendary nameless. All five of them! The Regent's envoys were dead, and I was still standing. Thanks to Regeneration, my body had no wounds. And now, I was finally connected to the native system, though this connection was draining my energy and could kill me.

Personal energy: 298/200

I still had about five minutes before the system started to tap into my personal energy reserve. It was inevitable, because the system needed energy to establish the necessary connections. And I had to provide it, even at the cost of my life.

"Run," I said quietly. "You'll have a slightly better chance to survive in the central part of the forest. If I find out that any of the foresters died because of you, you will all die too."

"You are the reason we may die," Spatus said in a surprisingly calm voice. "The Regent won't let the death of his best warriors go unpunished."

"You signed your death warrant when you decided to take part in the Center's mission, Spatus," I said. "Think about that. What would the Regent and the nameless do to someone who brought them information. To someone, who was the reason for the death of the Regent's envoys. Someone who watched them die at the hand of an ordinary human."

Personal energy: 297/200

Spatus stared at me for a couple of seconds,

then pointed a thick finger in my direction.

"It was you!" He shouted. "You lured me here! You deliberately let Naum go!"

He'd finally put the facts together. After the massacre, even a complete idiot wouldn't believe that Naum had managed to escape from me.

"There's a mountain about six miles north of here. On it are the remains of a human base from the distant past," I said, not responding to the accusation. I saw no need. "There, you can wait out the most dangerous time. Then we'll meet again, and you'll answer my question."

"What question?" Asked Spatus in an angry voice.

Personal energy: 296/200

"Right now, only one question matters," I said, striding toward the approaching wave of Chucklers. The raiders quickly stepped aside as I walked through their ranks without slowing down. "People or the Masters."

Soon I would be blind and deaf. The base's power supply was depleted. There wasn't enough energy to even turn on the emergency lighting. The Brist had switched to supporting the deployment process. The Savannah was disconnected from the laboratory's security system and tasked with other things. The CES was ninety percent consumed with the process of energy control and transfer.

I was alone, and it reminded me of a day many years ago, when it was just me, my sword, and a horde of monsters storming the research base on Kilras IV. It was my first battle after body modification. A trial the Lirdags arranged to celebrate my second birth. This time, I had far fewer resources.

A hundred RE of my personal reserve had to remain untouched. Even the basic energy matrices would be inaccessible in the red zone. And I won't be able to go above two hundred. The fact that I was above that number now was a gift to let me find my first enemies. Fortunately, I wouldn't have to go far.

My connection to the human system was still purely nominal. Without the Phalanxes loaded, the external reserve was inaccessible to me. Until the first stage of deployment was complete, the system was in its embryonic state and would only consume energy. There was a slim chance that I could accumulate the necessary amount of RE to transition to the second day of deployment ahead of schedule. Then things would become much more interesting. But I had to survive until then and gather forty thousand units of energy, which seemed almost impossible.

"Achilles!" Spatus shouted after me. I slowed my pace slightly and turned to him. "I'll wait for you on that damn mountain, if I can find it. Kill all those monsters! Good luck!"

I nodded to the fat man and gave out the mental command: "Acceleration two. Freeze. Scan."

Personal energy: 251/200

Minor energy matrix Acceleration, level 2, activated

Personal energy: 201/200

Minor energy matrix Energy Freeze activated

Personal energy: 171/200

Minor energy matrix Scanning activated

As I took off, the air snapped shut behind me with a faint pop. The surroundings changed under the influence of the Scan matrix. The mass of barely noticeable movements in the thicket along my path took on volume and meaning. The Lirdagi monsters weren't moving fast enough, but that had never been a problem for them. They relied on sheer numbers.

Every mound, every stump, every shrub — all objects within sight revealed their true form, and I could see the outlines of the Chucklers despite all their camouflage. The chosen skill combination allowed me to operate for more than twenty seconds, which was enough to make up for the lack of RE. Every bit of energy beyond my reserve would go into the system. The next three days promised to be very eventful if I followed the protocol. But I had another plan.

Personal energy: 200/200

Attention: Absorption of raze-energy is limited without before full deployment of the System

45,342% of the enemy's raze-energy absorbed

I split the first monster in two without stopping. The air contracted, but I felt only a slight breeze. The Energy Freeze matrix stabilized any energy within half an inch of my body, so the

Chucklers' main weapon simply didn't work. And they had nothing else in their arsenal except for energy fields. But this skill had its drawbacks because I couldn't use external matrices, either. They got stuck in the freezing field and shattered into free energy.

In a normal state, using Energy Freeze would be foolish. No Ideal would deprive themselves of their main weapon in the middle of a fight. But right now, I had nothing but my sword and speed.

The second drawback of Energy Freeze was its vulnerability — it could only be activated when there were no enemy fields around. As the practice of war had shown, it was nearly impossible to find yourself in a situation, when all these conditions are met. Hence, I rarely used this skill.

Personal energy: 200/200

Attention: Absorption of raze-energy is limited without before full deployment of the System

45,342% of the enemy's raze-energy absorbed

I raced through the forest, destroying everything in my path. Dozens of monsters tried to stop me, but they couldn't do anything, and the trickle of energy turned into a full-fledged stream. I counted the seconds until the Energy Freeze effect ended and prepared for a new sprint.

Five seconds before the imaginary timer expired, I made a circle through the forest, clearing everything within fifty yards. For a couple of seconds, I would be completely defenseless, because it was impossible to activate a skill the second time before the first activation expired. Any mistake could cost me my life. Without armor, my chances of surviving under the monsters' field were slim.

The first run went smoothly, and the reserve was holding steady at maximum. It was too early to talk about results, but the goal no longer seemed impossible to reach. I paused for a moment and reactivated all the matrices.

Personal energy: 155/200

Minor energy matrix Acceleration, level 2, activated

Personal energy: 105/200

Minor energy matrix Energy Freeze activated

Personal energy: 75/200

Minor energy matrix Scanning activated

Attention: Personal energy levels below critical! Access to minor energy matrices temporary restricted.

Warning! If personal energy drops below zero, you will die.

"Great news," I smirked, quickly scanning my surroundings.

The Lirdags created their creatures for one sole purpose — to kill humans, mostly civilians. They had a clear order to move towards the center of the dome to destroy their Masters' enemies. By this time, there were often no Lirdags left alive. Now, the Chucklers were crawling toward me from all directions, as I was the only available target.

Personal energy: 114/200

Attention: Absorption of raze-energy is limited without before full deployment of the System

45,342% of the enemy's raze-energy absorbed

Access to internal energy matrices was restored. However, I understood that this wouldn't always be the case. The mob population had its limits. Given a few days, their numbers could double, but I couldn't allow that. The high frequency sword sliced through the shells of one creature after another; calculations clicked in my head.

The foresters' territory perimeter stretched for several dozen miles. The Brist's map was firmly ingrained in my memory: the average width of the protective perimeter was about six hundred yards.

Personal energy: 151/200

Attention: Absorption of raze-energy is limited before full deployment of the System

45,342% of the enemy's raze-energy absorbed

The barrier field was thinner at its edges. With any luck, there'd be over two thousand monsters crawling through the forest. I really hoped it would be over five hundred at least. Otherwise, the energy balance wouldn't add up.

The waterfall of system messages had long ceased: the CES was conserving resources and my attention. Only the messages about falling into the red zone kept appearing with annoying regularity. This forced me to act more aggressively, which nearly cost me my life.

Book Two

I couldn't use third level of Acceleration to increase the clearing zone of the next cycle, because I was already working at my limit, killing about ten creatures every twenty seconds. I constantly fell into the red zone and only climbed out after killing the next monster. The mass of Chucklers moved towards the center of the perimeter. Any deviation from my chosen strategy could end things quickly. I would simply die of exhaustion.

The Bastion algorithm was relentless. Every two and a half seconds, I lost one unit of RE. The system didn't care how much energy I had left. My muscles were already screaming from the overload, and for the first time in twenty minutes I decided to use Regeneration.

Almost six hundred creatures had already given their energy to the system. I didn't know the exact number, I just hoped that the daily cutoff would kick in soon and the drain would slow down.

Constant acceleration dulled my reflexes. My brain was stalling from overload and chaotic streams of information. During the three-second rest intervals between matrix activations, I saw only a red haze before my eyes. My capillaries had long since burst, but I couldn't stop. Another hour at this pace, and no regeneration would help. Even my body had its limits.

It was only a matter of time before I'd start making mistakes. But I hadn't expected it to happen as soon as the next phase.

I was deliberately destroying monsters in only

one direction. It was impossible to return, because I wouldn't make it back to the starting point. So I decided to begin the clearing towards the refugee village. If I didn't eliminate the threat to the residents, there would be no one to connect to the system, which would stall the second stage of deployment indefinitely.

I didn't want to think about what was happening near the base. I believed that my subordinates had followed my orders and were now underground. In about ten minutes, the wave of Chucklers would pass over the territory above the lab. If anyone came to the surface or just opened the entrance hatch, that would be the end.

These thoughts threw me off balance. I was too exhausted after the endless thirty minutes, which felt like an eternity. And I made my first mistake of retreating a hundred yards back to avoid clearing another patch in the middle of the horde. I secured myself, but I didn't account for the movement of the tightening ring of monsters. The Chucklers moved away, and I was left in a vacuum. There were no enemies around, and I had already refreshed the matrices.

Personal energy: 72/200

I had no access to the map. The visible radius around me was empty. I had long lost my sense of direction and no longer understood where I was — a mistake that could cost me my life.

Five precious seconds I spent trying to make my tired brain function. I needed a direction. Any direction. Otherwise, the next minute could be my last. And here came the sun.

A warm ray brushed my cheek, and the image in my mind clicked into place with a deafening snap. I pinpointed the center of the foresters' territory and took off. After six seconds of running, a glowing silhouette of another enemy flickered in front of me. A moment later, energy extraction began anew for a full five minutes.

I made another stop. A distinct smell of burning appeared in the air, and I thought I even saw a grayish haze between the trees. I no longer risked straying from the enemy path — I was afraid I wouldn't find my way back. My sword had turned into a heavy rail. I wielded it with great difficulty, sometimes just letting its tip drag on the ground, using the momentum of my run to kill the next enemy.

How many Chucklers had it been? A hundred? A thousand? The fifty-yard circle gave me a couple of seconds of respite, but it had long been insufficient. And the circle turned out to be seven yards shorter than I'd anticipated. I realized this when I saw the blurred outline of something flying toward me. It was a stump, or a clump of earth.

Personal energy: 186/200

"SR two," I croaked out, and in the next second, my entire body was squeezed by the grip of a hostile field. I lost my main advantage — mobility. Several more projectiles followed the first, and the pressure from the fields increased. "Freeze."

Personal energy: 155/200

Minor energy matrix Skin Reinforcement,

level 2, activated

Minor energy matrix Energy Freeze unavailable. Excessive number of active fields in activation zone.

Even in this state, I didn't dare use the third level of the matrix. Ninety RE was an unattainable amount for me at the moment. I still had a chance as it was. Predictably, Energy Freeze didn't work. To stabilize the space, I had to be in an empty zone. In any other situation, this wouldn't have been critical. Any other, but not mine.

Chucklers aren't intelligent creatures, they could interact with each other in only two ways: creating joint fields and using the Throw matrix. I had miscalculated the size of the cleared area, it turned out to be insufficient, and a couple of monsters had managed to use it for an attack. The others joined in. Some of them had already turned around and started to crawl toward me.

I moved my sword with great difficulty. My arms almost didn't respond, bound by the monsters' traps. The first monster was a few feet away from me and now crawling away. The tip of my sword scraped the side of another Chuckler.

Personal energy: 154/200

"Impulse!" I commanded mentally, no longer being able to speak. There wasn't enough air. Skin Reinforcement successfully held off the enemy's attacks but didn't save me from the overall pressure.

My sword flared with blue light. A stream of energy scorched the flesh of the alien creature, and the air filled with the stench of burnt organic matter. The SR matrix had worked for half its duration. The number of monsters around me continued to increase. My brain was overwhelmed by the chaotic roar and numerous voices.

"You'll die! You'll die! You'll die!"

"Pathetic creature! Nasty creature!"

Energy: 153/200

Attention: Daily system limit reached

Energy consumption recalculated considering the remaining time

New energy extraction from primary node System 1RE/4.27 seconds

Access to intermediate external energy matrices of 1 level granted

Attention: Before full deployment of the system, external energy matrices are activated using the primary node System

I read the message and couldn't help but smile, despite the screaming monsters around me and the crushing grip of the force fields on my body. Finally!

"Destruction!" My mental command was filled with hatred and triumph.

Chapter 17

With the fire of good and the strength of faith, Warriors of Humanity will shine,
Their valor, their courage are unbreakable.
Let Humanity rise from the ashes once more,
And reclaim its place under the Sun, striking down our Enemy.

"Book of Hope"
Verse XXI

Forest

SPATUS HAD NEVER SEEN or heard of anything like this. All his preconceptions about the world and the Masters had shattered in an instance. First, Eighty-Five died. Then Spatus saw with his own eyes how all the best raiders in all the gangs were killed within minutes. And finally, one by one, all the nameless fell.

Fat Spat was no fool — he noticed the beam fire from the few shooters in the forest. He even saw the hounds fighting on the enemy's side, but the only real opponent was the half-dressed man, covered in blood from head to toe. Using just his sword, Achilles had orchestrated this entire massacre with incredible speed and brutality for a human.

When Achilles appeared before him and asked a reasonable question, everything inside Spatus turned upside down. He didn't want to die, and his brain was working faster than it ever had in his life. He was trying to figure out what to do next. The man standing before him, holding his sword seemingly casually, looked like such an easy target.

Spatus was wearing heavy armor, the best he could get from the Regent. The cost of it alone could outfit several dozen men. Hanging at his waist was an ancient kinetic blaster, which could blow up a house or shatter a huge boulder with a single shot. It seemed simple enough — there stood a half-dressed, seemingly defenseless savage, just draw the weapon and pull the trigger.

Spatus's eyes darted back and forth until they caught sight of Eighty-Five's corpse lying nearby. In peaceful times, Spatus enjoyed lobster with homemade beer brewed by his wives. The lobster had a hard shell, under which hid tender and delicious meat. The formerly powerful nameless lying there looked like a large grilled lobster, with its neck slit open so you can get to the juicy white meat. His spine was missing, as if it was ripped out. Spatus glanced at Achilles's hands, which, besides being covered in red blood, also had the whitish blood of the nameless. He had heard that the Regent's servants had different-colored blood, but now he was fully convinced.

He was deeply terrified. On the other hand, he still had nearly fifty of his fighters left. Maybe, if they attacked all at once, they had a chance. Spatus finally stopped his frantic scanning of the clearing and looked into the eyes of the man named Achilles. Unwillingly, he seemed to fall into those strange eyes, the color of which was hard to determine.

Inside them, Spatus saw death and destruction for all who stood in Achilles's way. There was inevitability, as well — none of his enemies had a chance against this man. And yet, deep within those eyes, there was a hidden hope. Hope that Achilles would help free humanity from the rule of the Masters and their minions. For within those eyes, it was clear that he was not humanity's enemy, but its protector.

Achilles moved toward the terrifying creatures emerging from the forest. He walked as if he were heading for a leisurely stroll, despite the howls and screams of the monsters that made the hair on Spatus's body stand on end. Spatus watched his men step aside to clear the path for Achilles and fought his own feelings.

This was the feelings he always buried deep within his soul. As the leader of the raiders, he couldn't admit his doubts to anyone. He was even afraid to admit to himself that he had always thought of the Masters as disgusting creatures, parasites that had latched onto his race and were sucking it dry. And then he'd made his decision.

"Achilles!" Spatus shouted after the departing man, who turned slightly in his direction. Spatus still hesitated, but managed to overcome himself and continued, "I'll wait for you on that damn mountain, if I can find it. Kill all those monsters! Good luck!"

He had made his decision and intended to follow through no matter what. And Achilles simply vanished. Spatus didn't understand how that happened. The air just collapsed in the spot where the savage had stood a second before.

"What now, boss?" One of his commanders asked. The other fighters were looking nervously toward the forest, where some kind of madness was unfolding. Screaming creatures choked on their howls one after another and fell silent forever.

"We head North, Borcha," Spatus replied, not taking his eyes off the thicket, trying to catch a glimpse of Achilles among the forest shadows. Sometimes he thought he saw the warrior with his sword, but he couldn't be sure. "Six miles. Let's move!"

He shouted the last order at the top of his lungs before taking off, setting an example for his warriors. For him, this sprint was especially grueling. He had plenty of physical strength, but his endurance wasn't what it used to be. Fortunately, his expensive armor compensated for some of his excess weight.

The raider squad took off. Spatus ran at the front for only a couple of minutes before Borcha and another commander overtook him. They always tried to shield their leader from unnecessary risk. Even the regular raiders understood that if Spatus died, the lives of everyone in his territory would change drastically and for the worse.

Three more men surged ahead, they were the most enduring ones in his squad. Without stopping, Borcha ordered them to keep an eye on the surroundings and signal if they saw anyone or anything. No one knew what they might encounter in this cursed forest.

After just ten minutes of running, Spatus was breathing heavily, sweat pouring down his body in streams. He couldn't remember the last time he exerted himself so much, but it was clearly worth it — the roar of the monsters gradually grew quieter. The squad was moving away from the main direction of where the Chucklers were heading. Achilles hadn't lied, even though he could have easily set up the raiders, who had come to the forest to kill him.

Then the sounds shifted slightly, as if the raiders were running parallel to the monsters. Suddenly, through the haze of sweat, Spatus saw one of the scouts, who was clearly waiting for them. But it wasn't an enemy the scout had seen. If it were, there'd already be a fight breaking out.

"Speak," Spatus wheezed, trying to catch his breath.

"There's a village ahead, boss," the scout reported.

"Avoid it," Spatus said. "We shouldn't get involved with the locals. Otherwise, the next encounter with Achilles might be very unpleasant."

"There aren't any serious opponents there," the scout said, clearly uneasy.

"I don't care," Spatus growled. "Avoid it! Don't mess with the locals."

"They're preparing for a fight, Spatus," the scout said.

"What?! With us? How did they know about us?"

"No," the raider shook his head. "Not with us. With those creatures."

"What are you talking about? Where?"

"The edge of the village is a hundred yards away. Over there," The scout pointed, and Spatus quickly walked in that direction. He could no longer run.

A couple of minutes later, Spatus reached a dense thicket. The undergrowth was so thick that he had to force his way through to reach a tiny village. Only five newly built log houses, with just as many unfinished ones. The residents had clearly been in a hurry building them. Now they looked like they were preparing for their last stand.

On the other side of the village stood about

thirty people, men and women, each holding a weapon. Spatus had never seen anything more absurd. Dressed in rags, these people were preparing to fight monsters with rusty swords and home-made spears. Any one of Spatus's fighters could easily disperse this crowd by himself.

"Idiots," Spatus muttered, shaking his head. By and large, he didn't care about these people. They were strangers to him. He could easily continue on his way and wait for Achilles at the agreed spot. In the distance, he could already see the beginning of the rise that would lead his squad to the mountain.

"Achilles has given us a second chance!" A man's voice reached them. He was standing in front of his people, holding his sword high. "Right now, he's still fighting for our new home and for our right to call ourselves human. He told us to stay in our homes, but I will never forgive myself if I don't try to help him."

"You idiot!" Spatus snarled. "Who's going to look after the women and children if you all die?"

"What should we do, Spatus?" Borcha asked. "The villagers will hold off the monsters, and we can safely reach our destination. They're just strangers. Ordinary people that mean nothing to us."

The suggestion was logical, reasonable, and very timely. Spatus appreciated Borcha for his cool head and clear thinking. But right now, he couldn't follow that advice.

"And what are we?" Spatus asked,

unexpectedly even for himself. "Whose side are we on? The side of humankind or monsters?"

"Orders?" Borcha asked.

"What weapons do we have left?"

Borcha didn't hesitate: "Fifteen emitters, five explosive artifacts. The rest have swords and cutters. Half the batteries are drained."

Spatus quickly calculated his options and began issuing orders: "Shooters to the front line. No close combat. The rest, evacuate the villagers. Achilles said the mountain is safe. Get everyone there. I'll lead the shooters."

The fat man hurried towards the thin line of village residents. Just a hundred yards from the village, the forest was already buzzing and howling, having turned into a place of horror and death.

"Everyone back!" Spatus yelled as he ran. "Get out of here, you idiots!"

People immediately turned towards him, most raising their weapons.

"Who are you?" The man, who looked like the village elder, asked.

"Achilles sent me," Spatus replied without hesitation. "He said to take you to a safe place."

"You all heard him!" The elder barked. The mere mention of Achilles's name silenced all questions. "Follow these people. Ron, Dihma — get our folks out of the houses."

Most of the village fighters stayed put, but Spatus had no time to persuade them to leave. Shadows began to move in the distance. It was unclear what they were, and Spatus didn't know what the monsters were supposed to look like, but they were clearly getting closer.

Fifteen of Spatus's shooters spread out before him. They were the best fighters of his node. And at the moment, they were completely clueless about what to do.

"Boss, who do we shoot at?" One of the warriors shouted, constantly swinging the barrel of his emitter back and forth.

"At anything crawling towards us!" Spatus snapped, pulling the kinetic blaster from his belt and firing at a stump that appeared for a second behind a bush. "Burn everything that shouldn't be moving!"

Spatus's shot left a huge crater where the bush had been. The result of the attack was unclear, but he wanted to believe that the monsters' chorus had become one voice quieter. Maybe it hadn't, but otherwise, this whole crazy endeavor lost its purpose.

A dozen-and-a-half emitters fired a coordinated volley. The forest was shrouded in a strip of smoke. Dry grass caught fire with cheerful flames.

"Again!" Spatus growled, shooting at any movement indiscriminately.

The second volley finally revealed part of the monsters. In some places, force fields appeared, visible only because of the smoke from the budding fire. Once the enemy's location was clear, the fighters began to fire more accurately. The ghostly films of force fields dimmed and went out from the overload.

The villagers stood in tense silence behind Spatus and his men. Far behind them, the nervous voices of retreating people could be heard. The forest warriors already realized that they wouldn't have managed on their own, but they still didn't leave.

Spatus didn't understand what they'd been hoping for until he heard the raspy whisper of one of the women.

"He will come," she chanted like a mantra. "He will come if we are strong enough and save all who remain faithful. Those who stay human even in the darkest hour."

"He will come," her neighbor nodded. "He will show us his power, as he has done before. He will stop the dark creatures, just as he stopped the fire — with his will and great strength."

Spatus looked at these strange people in amazement and shook his head. Their words seemed like complete nonsense to the seasoned raider. It was as if these people believed in long-forgotten tales of great beings who could help mortals in their time of need.

Spatus knew very well that no such things existed in the world. Only people's own decisions shaped their fate.

All his life, he had tried to make decisions that allowed him to live in peace with his own conscience. He had taken control of his node for that reason because he saw what was happening around him and wanted to change it, at least partially.

"One battery left!" The nearest shooter shouted. "Who has more?"

Someone shared a spare. The shooting paused briefly. The fighters peered into the forest, trying to determine if they had managed to stop the monsters.

"Soon," one of the villagers whispered, and Spatus glared at the speaker. The man was unfazed and smiled back. "You just don't understand yet."

At that moment, the fire in the forest abruptly extinguished. In its place appeared a single field, a hundred yards long. It looked thick, even to the eye. Ugly faces and strange symbols could be seen on its surface. The sight was utterly horrifying.

"Fire!" Spatus barked. "Throw the crackers!"

Five of his men pulled out thick tubes and aimed them at the field. Compressed air whined as the five projectiles flew towards the field, but they exploded a few feet short. Spatus's main weapon had misfired.

"What is that?" One of the shooters said. He had a scope for long-range shooting on his emitter. "Can anyone see that? To the right. A hundred and twenty yards."

"He has come," the same man from before calmly smiled at Spatus. "Do you see?"

"Give me that!" Spatus snatched the weapon from his subordinate and glued his eye to the scope.

Something was indeed happening in the

forest. The monsters' fields flared beyond the barrier line, but his fighters weren't shooting there. Spatus's gaze swept past, then jerked back.

"What the hell?" He whispered.

In the middle of the forest, stood the motionless Achilles surrounded by the force traps of numerous monsters. The savage held his sword at arm's length, seemingly indifferent to the creatures around him. It was as if he was waiting for more of them to gather.

The monsters desperately tried to tear the defiant man apart but couldn't.

Spatus adjusted the scope and saw a sinister smile appear on Achilles's face. The savage dropped his sword as if it was no longer needed. As if he intended to tear the enemies apart with his bare hands. And then a ghostly light radiated from his figure in all directions.

The light swept through the forest, reaching the energy field in front of the village defenders. The dissonant roar of the creatures turned into a unified howl of pain and terror. Achilles was enveloped in the same light and slowly rose into the air. The warrior calmly spread his arms and threw his head back. Then, the monsters throughout the forest began to die.

Spatus watched as the most unexpected objects exploded into clouds of foul-smelling smoke — mounds, stumps, even patches of grass. The wind carried an unbearable stench of rot. But Spatus only noticed this peripherally because he couldn't tear his eyes away from the scope. This couldn't have been happening, but it was. He saw Achilles glowing with an unknown light with his own eyes.

"I see," Fat Spat croaked. "Now I see."

225

Chapter 18

*Seek the weaknesses of our Enemies, reveal their
vulnerable sides,*
Unite and with your unity, repel the foes,
*Let the fire of freedom burn in your hearts; ignite the
flame of truth.*
*You, Children of Humanity, will be the shield and
sword of our people.*

"Book of Hope"
Verse XXIX

> **Personal energy: 3/200**
> **Intermediate energy matrices "Destruc-
tion", level 1, activated**
> **Attention: Personal energy levels below**

critical! Access to minor and intermediate energy matrices temporary restricted.

Warning! If personal energy drops below zero, you will die.

A WAVE OF DESTRUCTIVE RAZE-ENERGY spread out for a hundred yards around. In the past, I could have covered this entire planet with my Destruction matrix, but now I only had enough power for a miserable patch. I had to force myself to limit the attack radius to avoid burning out completely. Fortunately, it was enough. My three remaining energy units would last for seven seconds. That would be enough to see the results of one of my favorite close-combat matrices.

I had almost forgotten the pleasure that came from streams of raze-energy leaving my body. Any user of the humanity's system felt an indescribable euphoria during these moments. No one knew exactly why this happened, but it was especially intense in critical situations. Perhaps one of the system's developers thought that such an effect would help humanity in its war against the aliens.

They were a thousand times right, because every single fighter in the Confederacy used their strongest skills in moments of mortal danger without hesitation. There were rumors among the Seniors that this was the final gift to humanity's best warriors. I was inclined to believe them.

Personal energy: 41/200

Attention: Absorption of raze-energy is limited before full deployment of the System

43,382% of the enemy's raze-energy absorbed

Personal energy: 80/200

Attention: Absorption of raze-energy is limited before full deployment of the System

44,042% of the enemy's raze-energy absorbed

Personal energy: 119/200

Attention: Absorption of raze-energy is limited before full deployment of the System

40,641% of the enemy's raze-energy absorbed

Personal energy: 159/200

Attention: Absorption of raze-energy is limited before full deployment of the System

45,342% of the enemy's raze-energy absorbed

Personal energy: 200/200

Attention: Absorption of raze-energy is limited before full deployment of the System

45,352% of the enemy's raze-energy absorbed

A stream of system notifications filled my entire field of vision. Nearly three dozen Chucklers turned into smoldering chunks of dead flesh in an instant. The creatures boiled alive in their shells, filling the forest with wild howls of pain and terror.

In reality, they felt nothing of the sort, as they lacked the necessary receptors to experience any sensation. The energy matrix simply activated part of their systems until they overloaded and burnt out. This caused a strange effect, as if the chunks of Lirdagi biomass were in extreme pain.

My feet touched the ground and the light around my body faded, as the second feature of Destruction ceased to function. Part of the enemies' energy was automatically used to restore my body, which was a huge advantage of all higher-level matrices. Many allowed multiple tasks to be accomplished simultaneously.

For instance, Destruction lifted the user into the air and provided a three-second shield because many alien creatures exploded upon death, like acid bombs. But it was quite difficult to explain this to the regular warriors. They only saw the external effects, which led to more and more rumors about the true origin of the Ideals.

Such skills were available only to the Ideals and the strongest of the Seniors, but the latter received only the offensive and healing effects. The Ideals were the only ones who received protection from the Destruction matrix because it interacted with our energy system on a deeper level.

I picked up my high frequency sword, which had fallen from my hands at the moment of greatest weakness, and took a fresh look at the forest around me. It took one hundred fifty units to activate the matrix, which was quite a lot, but I was confident I could integrate my new capabilities into old tactics.

There wasn't a single monster left in sight, but that wasn't so detrimental to me now — I was full of energy and could take my time to look around and continue the cleanup a bit later. I no longer doubted I'd manage to kill them all.

The CES was still overloaded. I expected it would return to its main functions after the system's second-day reserve was replenished. For that, I needed about forty thousand RE, maybe forty-five.

Personal energy: 199/200

Partly due to the lack of the usual support system, and partly due to overall fatigue, I noticed the crowd of people in the distance only then. I recognized the surroundings, but we usually approached the settlers' village from the other side. This meant my calculations and the initially chosen direction of the sweep were correct. Among Wolf's former prisoners, I saw many other people, who were wearing armor and holding emitters in their hands.

The origin of the smell of burning and the bluish haze around became clear immediately — I saw scorched patches of ground and trees slightly to the right. I even spotted a few dead Chucklers.

Heading towards the crowd, I stepped into the open space. The villagers looked at me with excitement. Vens broke away from them and quickly walked towards me.

"We're glad you found the time to visit our village, Achilles," he said, struggling to contain his emotions. The others kept their eyes fixed on me, as if trying to memorize this moment as precisely as possible. Among them, only Spatus's sullen face stood out.

"You deviated from the course," I said calmly.

I already knew what had happened having seen the traces of shots and explosions, but I wanted to hear Spatus's explanation. A decision to protect civilians was quite unusual for a raider.

Personal energy: 198/200

"This man came to us right before the monster attack, Achilles," Vens said. People are so fickle — a minute ago, every villager was sincerely grateful to the raiders who saved them. But now, barely sensing my doubts, they reached for their weapons.

One word from me would have been enough for them to pounce on the raiders, who drew back towards Spatus, trying to protect him as much as possible. This also spoke volumes about the immobile fat man.

"He said you ordered them to help us," Vens added, grimly pointing at Spatus.

"That's correct," I said, nodding slightly without taking my eyes off Spatus. "I didn't think he'd get here before me, though. Why didn't you go to the mountain?"

The last question was directed at Spatus, who frowned in displeasure. When he made the decision, everything was obvious to him, but now he clearly didn't want to talk about his motives, especially in front of so many strangers.

"The people," he said, looking at the forest, avoiding meeting my eyes. Then he as if gathered his thought and looked directly at me. "Your people have crappy equipment, Achilles. They were going to get heroically killed."

"We only had the weapons received from your raiders," I smiled. "Maybe in the future, we can arrange for supplies of something more decent."

Personal energy: 197/200

"If anything is left of my territory," Spatus smirked. "There's a record in the system of my involvement in the Regent's mission. He'll soon find out I'm alive and that everyone else is dead. The ways the Regent's servants ask questions won't leave me a chance. If I'm lucky, I might manage to warn my sons. Maybe they can stage a rebellion and seize power. But a node had never passed to the heirs of the old leader before. My people won't go for it, either. There'll be a lot of blood."

"There won't be," I shook my head. "The Regent won't risk losing three nodes at once. It's too big a blow to the system. If done right, you'll get a few days' respite."

"Why three?" Spatus asked.

"Naum," I said, and Spatus slowly nodded.

"You can't know that," he said. "No one knows what the Regent and Masters will do. No one knows how their system works."

Personal energy: 196/200

"You are mistaken there," I said with a broad smile. "Send a trusted person to your sons and wait for me on the mountain. I'll finish my current tasks, and we will continue this conversation. Vens, you may resume construction, but don't venture too deep into the forest for now."

With these words, I turned and walked back into the woods. Behind me, Vens began giving out orders to the villagers, who were happy to get back to their routine.

"Achilles!" Spatus called out. "About your question..."

"I've already seen and heard enough. In fact, you've already answered it," I said, smiling as I glanced back. "I have a lot of interesting stuff for you, Spatus."

"Do I really need it?" Spatus muttered to himself. Though I heard him, I didn't respond.

Actions speak volumes about a person's character, much more so than words do. Imagining someone like Baka in Spatus's place, the outcome of this entire situation would have been obvious. But I couldn't really imagine myself dealing with such a low-life like Baka. Spatus turned out to be quite different.

I returned to the forest and continued the cleanup with renewed vigor. The fact that energy was constantly taken from me to maintain the first stage of deployment forced me to keep moving forward. According to my calculations, after eliminating the entire population of Chucklers, there would be enough energy to take care of other matters. At least, I very much hoped so. Worst-case scenario, I'd have to use the raider squads that hadn't made it to the main assault and would be undoubtedly stationed at the forest's edge.

I broke into a run, activated the Scan matrix, and focused on finding the enemy. Of the full ring of monsters closing in around the forest, a little more than half remained at this point. I had dealt with the first part in an hour, but back then, I didn't yet have access to the intermediate matrices.

The skills of the Ideals were divided into four levels. The internal matrices could not be taken from us under any circumstances. They were closely tied to our bodies, becoming an integral part of them. But our basic skills were significantly less effective than all others.

The second level allowed me to affect real space within a small radius of my body. The arsenal was extensive enough to feel confident in battle with most of the Lirdagi creatures, but not with the Lirdags themselves, nor with their strongest mutants.

Unfortunately, only a few intermediate energy matrices were available to me at the moment. The two hundred RE forced me to constantly weigh my actions, but I was glad even for that. One day I would regain all my abilities, but for now, I had to work with what I had.

For almost an hour, I ran through the forest, exterminating hordes of Chucklers. The monsters stubbornly trudged toward the center of the territory, and if left unchecked, they would have been able to establish themselves. In a day, dozens of replication nests would have appeared. In two days, the reverse movement would have begun, which would have been nearly impossible to stop, even for me.

Personal energy: 200/200

Attention: Absorption of raze-energy is

limited before full deployment of the System

45,772% of the enemy's raze-energy absorbed

Attention: Daily system limit reached

Energy consumption recalculated considering the remaining time

New energy extraction from primary node System 1RE/24.84 seconds

Access to intermediate external energy matrices of 2 level granted

Attention: Before full deployment of the system, external energy matrices are activated using the primary node System

CES functions partially restored

Equipment testing initiated

Preparation for second stage of deployment initiated

Access to basic functions in the deployment zone of the primary node granted

I paused briefly to review the notifications, most of which were irrelevant to me. I couldn't activate the intermediate second-level energy matrices yet. Equipment testing was also of little importance and was worth paying attention to only if something went wrong.

However, the reduced energy extraction rate was a great relief. I even slightly exceeded the plan for the second day. If I pushed a little more and requested a recalculation, I could get some rest. The reduction in the CES load was expected, but no less pleasant because of it. And then there were the basic functions.

Essentially, this meant that the system could already utilize the features of the connected modules to operate properly. This allowed me to stop running blindly through the forest and initiate a targeted search.

"Display enemy markers in the system deployment zone," I ordered.

A map of the area appeared before my eyes. The underground lab, where all the modules were concentrated, became the notional center of the new node of the human system, but the coverage was sufficient to show me the entire forest.

I sighed heavily looking at the seven Chucklers crawling half a mile away from me. Then I quickly crossed the distance between us and killed the last monsters as efficiently as possible. I could congratulate myself on successfully clearing the area. Unfortunately, there weren't enough Chucklers to sufficiently replenish the reserves. I had a rough idea of where to get another ten thousand RE, but that could be dealt with later.

A large group of enemies was still waiting for their commanders at the edge of the forest. They glowed less brightly and were my backup option. Filling the second day's limit provided another definite advantage, which wasn't reflected in the report. The percentage of enemy raze-energy absorption should have increased by another quarter. After completing the first stage, I would finally be able to absorb ninety-five percent of the enemy's RE. The remaining five percent would be used for the system's needs. In this situation, even ordinary bandits seemed worthy of my attention.

I was near the site of the battle with the nameless, trying to decide if I should proceed to close out the third day or take a break

Personal energy: 199/200

Yes, I could afford to take a little break. Even the basic functions of the newborn system completely changed my perception of the surroundings. It was strange that I hadn't thought of this sooner.

I didn't need to initiate the CES for every little thing anymore. Even pieces of equipment had their own markers, and I could see real-time information about the enemy. At the moment, there were no living enemies nearby, but there were plenty of markers for potential loot.

The system displayed everything that had any value. Later, I would need to configure the techno-complexity filters. Every product of the Confederacy's factories had a certain index of utility and complexity, composed of numerous characteristics — from the value of the alloys used to the size of the production batch. To simplify perception, all items were divided into four categories.

Simple items — household junk and basic weapons that cluttered all human worlds — had white markers.

Complex items — equipment and gear capable of using raze-energy in volumes accessible to Juniors — were marked in blue.

Ultra-complex items — Seniors' armor, heavy combat equipment, serious shields and barriers;

anything that could interact directly with the system and didn't rely on built-in batteries, or only partially depended on them — were marked in purple.

The latest developments were the best examples of human technology. Mostly, this was equipment for Ideals and their subordinate Senior units. Each such item had a monstrous utility index, mainly because it could withstand the full power of Ideals without falling apart. They were marked by red markers, which I almost never encountered among the loot on battlefields.

The entire area ahead was littered with the bodies of slain raiders. The leaders had indeed brought their best fighters to the Great Hunt. There were so many white markers that nothing could be seen underneath them. The strip where the tunnel had been located was especially densely packed. Protective suits, plasma cutters, some household vibrational knives. The bandits considered any junk from ancient times to be unique weapons. Considering the quality of their own products, they weren't far from the truth.

"Remove markers with utility index below five hundred units," I ordered, and the space before me instantly changed. Only Seniors' items had an index above this level. The result of this simple check surprised me so much that I couldn't contain myself. "Now this is interesting!"

Chapter 19

The greatness of Humanity's past had lost its allure,
Only memories of glorious days remain.
In this ruthless world, where suffering reigns,
The thirst to survive clashes with the weight of destiny.

"Book of Sorrows"
Verse VIII

TO THE RIGHT OF ME lay the Cyclops I had killed earlier. The system had highlighted his armor a very pale purple. Theoretically, the armor could be restored, if someone could clean it of the mutant's innards and find a proper power source in this backward world for replacement. The other nuances of the alien armor could be ignored. During the battle, I assessed the nameless one's equipment and concluded that it was too inconvenient for me. Otherwise, I would have tried better to keep it intact.

There was another purple marker a bit to the left, and its exact copy farther beyond the main field of battle. The perfect vision of Ideals allowed me to detect the slightest shades of system markers. For all other users, purple remained just purple. I, however, could determine the potential of an item down to the tens on the complexity index scale. These two items glowed identically, which wasn't surprising, considering they belonged to two almost identical creatures.

.HFsK 12/11
Condition: Fit for use
Status: Fully operational
Inner reserve: 50
Potential conductivity: 300

Excellent piece of equipment. The field operatives of the Ideals Support Service were equipped with the best human technology. This applied to weapons above all. I was pleased to see the conductivity potential in the item description again. This parameter influenced the amount of energy the item could draw from the human system without damaging its own structure.

Shadows used these knives to their full potential. Among the Regent's nameless, these two guys were possibly the most effective killers of armored targets. The main advantage of the HFsK knives was their ability to penetrate armor. The weapon automatically adjusted the necessary energy impulse and, if the requirements were below the conductivity potential, pierced any personal barriers like a thin sheet of paper.

Personal energy: 198/200

My current blade once belonged to some sergeant or major from the Juniors. It didn't have the capability to interact with the system at such a level. I had to charge it constantly, just like all other equipment with a lower complexity index. It was a pity that the knives were a bit short, which didn't matter under Acceleration, but in regular mode, I would prefer something more interesting as my primary weapon.

Still, I would keep the knives for myself. None of my subordinates could use them effectively and to their full potential. But I would finally have a pair of blades that wouldn't melt if I poured some of my energy into them when my reserve became more than disgustingly modest. Right now, I couldn't even use one knife to its full potential. I would die of exhaustion.

This was another issue that needed addressing. The internal reserve of the Ideals served for interacting with the system. Many higher-order matrices, especially those that operated over a long distance, required control threads. The expenditure was minimal — something around one RE per minute. Considering the replenishment rate of the internal reserve, there were never any problems.

Now, I faced a very unpleasant fact that I had

to constantly use my internal reserve just to survive. When I underwent modification, a biological energy source with a capacity of a thousand units was the pinnacle of human science. It was simply impossible to fit more into a living being. No one anticipated that this energy would be used in such a barbaric manner. I winced, recalling the hundreds of Accelerations I had used to clear the forest. How terrifyingly primitive!

This was a serious miscalculation on the part of the human scientists. Ideals were created with the expectation of a constant energy surplus. We could draw so much RE from our enemies that the concept of scarcity lost its meaning. Even during the worst periods of the war, myriads of users were connected to the human system. Ideals always had priority for receiving external energy. Entire factories could halt operations, but any Ideal always received the necessary amount of RE.

We were always at the forefront of the fight against the aliens; always in direct contact with the enemy. No one ever anticipated a situation like the one I found myself in — where there was no system, and drawing energy from an external source was impossible. When there were so few enemies that I physically couldn't engage in full combat. Sometimes I expended more resources than I gained from the entire fight, which was beyond unreasonable.

I was far from scientific work, but even I understood that this oversight needed to be addressed urgently. I couldn't rely on always having an infinite energy supply from the system nearby. What had happened once could happen again.

Personal energy: 197/200

The Shadows had nothing else of value. I was surprised that they even had decent weapons. Things had changed a lot while I was sleeping. In the past, these mutants served as disposable tools for the aliens. On a few occasions, I had seen naked creatures with sharpened metal scraps in their hands fall out of their camouflage. It looked like in the new realities of this world, Shadows could live significantly longer because their opponents were much weaker, allowing them to survive an attack.

I walked to the center of the clearing and bent over the nameless chief. This creature had too many physical modifications for an operator. Scales like his all over the body were only necessary for fighters. The Lirdags had a vast array of genetic enhancements for their warriors, and scales were one of them. It was always easier to work with existing material than to create something from scratch. For humans, however, such a mutation was quite painful.

The system placed a purple marker over the entire body of the nameless chief, as if it couldn't pinpoint the exact location of the item. The description field was also blank, which was rare and could only mean one thing — the found item was somewhere inside the creature's body and interacted with it directly.

I drew my knife. The Regent's servant

commander wore mediocre armor, much simpler than the Cyclops, but it was a complete set with uniform markings. I didn't want to ruin such a find and had to remove it first. Fortunately, the situation ended up being resolved sooner than I'd expected.

Personal energy: 195/200

The energy system of the human body is extremely stable. The production of raze-energy can just stop if there's significant interference. For example, I don't emit any RE at all. None of the Ideals do. This is our price for the ability to wield colossal amounts of power. With other humans, it's much simpler.

The Lirdags have always been meticulous in their approach to collecting valuable resources. If an individual can be of use, they will be, even if that's not what they want. The Lirdags almost never tampered with the energy system of their subjects. The main core remained in place, just below the solar plexus.

It was precisely in this spot that the nameless operator had a physical implant — a glass sphere the size of a man's fist. I requested a detailed analysis from the CES and prepared to extract it. I had to be careful not to damage anything.

Experimental sample detected

Multi-channel accelerator for interaction with virtual structures AnCS-00004

Condition: Fit for use

Statues: Fully operational, one active connection

Inner reserve: 100
Potential conductivity: 10

This was an extremely rare find. Although the system marked the item in purple, I could clearly see that it was on the very edge of the red zone. Such devices were common among operators of all human systems, and even strong Juniors could use them. They allowed ordinary people to gain a shadow of the capabilities of true operators. However, only gifted Seniors could fully utilize the potential of the accelerators. People like Herman.

"Prepare to disconnect active link," I said, touching the sphere.

Remote disconnection of active link impossible. Carrier is dead.

"Display emergency equipment shutdown map," I ordered, and a network of purple lines spread across the body of the nameless chief. Each line had its own designation — depth, power, and connection points. I couldn't avoid getting my hands dirty.

It took me five minutes to get the sphere out. I wiped the knife on the grass and cleaned the recovered artifact with a piece of cloth found nearby. The bundle of semi-transparent threads instantly retracted into the clear sphere, and the system reported that the device was ready to form a new link.

Personal energy: 180/200

The system deployment continued to consume my energy, and I couldn't spend too much time going through the loot. I still had one more marker that needed to be examined, so I headed toward the pile of bodies at the site of the protective tunnel.

On the way, I requested the current status of all modules. Since I could partially use their capabilities, there should be something good for my people, as well. More precisely, for the underground lab where they were located.

I didn't have enough resources to activate all the equipment in the lab, but there was enough for the bare minimum. A series of commands activated emergency lighting and connected one of the terminals to the transformer.

"What's your status?" I wrote. I had no doubt that my dispatcher was in the operations hall. There was no way Herman would miss the fact that the lights went on and the terminal was activated.

"Achilles!" Herman replied a second later. "We thought you had long perished! I barely stopped Ditras from opening the entrance to the lab and go to help you! Joker was on my side, lucky me."

"Did everyone make it to the base?" I asked. I couldn't keep track of my subordinates' movements, nor did I have the technical capability to do so during the Chucklers' cleanup operation.

"Everyone's here," Herman replied. "Only George got a bit hurt. He was on guard at the entrance shaft, and something tried to saw off his arm. We dragged him into the operations hall and patched him up. For a long time, we heard the monsters screaming in the corridor, calling us out for a fair fight, but we didn't go."

"Good job," I said with a slight smile. "You can come out now. Tell Ditras that the surface is clear. We need to sort and organize the loot at the battle site."

"Umm, we have a slight problem," the boy replied after a brief delay. "We didn't go for a fair fight, but the guys hit the corridor hard with emitters. Something broke near the entrance hatch. I'll try to fix it, but we can't get out right now."

"You can use the second corridor. Through the bio-replicator," I suggested. "It's currently offline."

"It's currently dead," Herman said. "I mean completely. The monsters managed to reach it from the surface and sawed off the upper part. I'm not sure we'll be able to use it again. But thanks for the exit suggestion. We'll give it a try."

I pushed one of the bodies, and a pile of corpses toppled to the side. Beneath it was the last of the nameless. Controllers were not suited for close combat and used puppets to fight for them. These were monsters or captured humans, depending on the modification. The one I was looking at was a human controller.

Armor hindered this modification. Sometimes they didn't even carry weapons, preferring to move under the protection of a couple of zombified puppets. If the puppets were prepared in advance, controlling them required almost no energy. However, to effectively use their power in combat, the mutants needed support. Even in death, the nameless one I was looking at was clutching such support in its hands.

Influence power amplifier Status 2M
Condition: Fit for use
Statue: Fully operational
Inner reserve: 30
Potential conductivity: 100

The device looked like a small scepter. Initially, it was supposed to have only markings near the handle, but one of its owners had decided to embellish it. A metal head of a screaming man was mounted on top, and a couple of spikes were welded near the handle. Perhaps for intimidation, or maybe to further motivate the puppets.

For me, its status held no value. I always preferred to kill enemies rather than control them. The question of control never arose with allies either — I couldn't stoop down to acting like the Lirdags did. But I wasn't alone in my work against the alien enemy.

If I managed to restore the bio-replicator, I could return to experimenting with the hounds, which had performed excellently in combat. With proper training, Joker could significantly strengthen my army, and this device would help him. It would just need to be recalibrated for the new task.

Personal energy: 175/200

For now, I needed to focus on finishing the current tasks. I checked the reconnaissance data and assessed the potential of the remaining enemy group. There were about two hundred raiders left outside the forest. I was confident they would stay put until they received their next orders. While this wasn't enough to solve the energy deficit problem, I could still get something from them. Maybe I was underestimating the bandits, and there would be some valuable specimens among them.

Valuable in terms of energy, raiders remained raiders. Exceptions like Spatus were anomalies in the local society. Therefore, my opponents couldn't be considered full representatives of humanity. They were just human-like creatures.

I moved towards the edge of the forest, walking slowly and contemplating my next actions. Was I really so different from my enemies, considering that I now easily equated people with mere resources? When in war, anything could happen. There were times when the human system was stretched to its limits — when Lirdagi ships were stationed on dozens of inhabited planets. Back then, everything was both simpler and more complicated.

I knew exactly what I was fighting for, then and now. The global matrices, which were extremely difficult even for Ideals to maintain for long, consumed monstrous amounts of RE — hundreds of thousands of units in just a few seconds of operation. The system provided us with the required resource on demand. Sometimes this meant increasing RE production in individual users. For some, this ended in death.

I never questioned whether my actions were righteous or not. If it was necessary to destroy an alien queen, I did it by any means available to me. Because I knew what would happen if I didn't complete my task, if I doubted myself.

Then it wouldn't be just five thousand people across the Confederacy who would die from overload. Every breach by the lizards cost humanity millions of lives. This was the damned rule of the lesser evil in all its ugliness. The Ideals' psychological control department avoided this topic, but we knew. We knew everything.

And now, I was approaching the forest edge, where two hundred people were stationed. Yes, they were complete scumbags — I was almost certain of that. But I didn't want to just kill them for a few thousand RE, like I would any Lirdagi creature. Every person should have a chance to change their life. We had fought for this for many years, and I saw no reason to deviate from this rule.

I emerged from the forest. The rays of the evening sun fell on my bare shoulders. Ahead, many people were sitting on the ground, none noticing me. In ones and groups, the raiders rested after a long march. Some were chatting, while others were gazing into the sky or taking a nap.

Personal energy: 170/200

Finally, one of the raiders noticed me. The man stared at me in surprise for a couple of seconds, then took off running somewhere. Soon, five people emerged from the other side. By their behavior and superior equipment, I could tell they were raider leaders.

"And who do we have here?" A tall man with

a heavy hammer at his belt said. The name Hammer was glowing above his head. "Lost, are you? Or just taking a walk?"

I calmly looked at the raider leaders. Each of them had their own squad. Each controlled their own node. This meant each supplied energy to the Regent in one way or another. Perhaps among them, there were even some who followed Spatus's ways, which could be a decisive factor.

"Your masters are dead," I said quietly. "You still have a chance to leave alive if you tell me how you feed the creatures in your underground lairs."

Chapter 20

Do not retreat before the darkness and perils that surround us.
Your resolve and courage will crush the infernal creatures.
March boldly forward; our sacred mission is to restore Humanity.
Children of Men, unite, and victory will be ours once more!

"Book of Hope"
Verse XXI

Edge of the forest.
Great Hunt participants' meeting point.

THE FIRST TWO GROUPS arrived at the gathering point a few minutes after the tunnel was closed. They even managed to see a faint green light in the distance, but they couldn't do anything about it. Exhausted from the march, the fighters were already at their limit. Two leaders met at the border of Spatus's territory and continued together.

They covered almost fifteen miles in three hours. If it weren't for the high-priority order, the raiders wouldn't push themselves so hard. But they had no choice.

"Think we're in trouble?" Trunk asked, breathing heavily. He stood with his hands on his knees, barely keeping himself upright from exhaustion. Hammer, in contrast, looked fresh.

"We didn't make it on time," Hammer replied. "We arrived an hour early. It's not our fault that the Hunt has already started."

"I think we're in trouble," Trunk shook his head. "If even Fat Spat went with the nameless, then it's very serious. Spatus would never jump into the fire if there was an option to stay out."

"Like with the cows?" Hammer sneered. "That fat bastard is so afraid of losing the herd's support that he's completely lost his mind. I don't understand why the Regent tolerates this."

"You should keep it down," Trunk muttered. "You never know…"

Hammer grimaced but nodded. All the neighbors knew that Spatus cleverly went around the Center's orders. That he had devised his own method of energy collection, on which he had spent an exorbitant amount of exchange funds. None of the neighboring band leaders could afford such expenses. They also knew that Spatus paid generously for any information related to him or his territory. And then he dealt harshly with those who dared to speak ill of him.

The squads settled at the forest's edge, precisely at the point indicated by the Regent's orders. None of the raiders even considered going further. The orders were clear: they were to arrive at the location and await instructions from the Regent's representative. The rest didn't concern them.

The leaders ordered a fire to be made and sprawled on the ground. About thirty minutes later, the next squad arrived.

"You didn't rush much," Hammer said mockingly to the freshly arriving raiders.

"I was feeding the node's heart," said the leader of the new group grimly. "Everything okay on your end? My consumption spiked. Had to put some workers to the knife to meet the demand right away."

"Everything's fine with me," Hammer replied and looked at Trunk.

"Mine increased too," Trunk said. "Fortunately, a convoy had just arrived with the tribute. Replenished the warehouse and spared my workers. Unlike some."

The trio of leaders laughed loudly as if it were a funny joke. To them, the residents of their nodes had long ceased to be human. How else could you regard beings that you regularly sent to feed the Regent's equipment?

An hour later, two more leaders joined the combined force. This was already a full-fledged army by local standards. Considering that a battle was already underway somewhere in the forest, all the leaders were convinced they would soon head home. It couldn't go any other way if Spatus was in the forest with his elite fighters. As much as the neighbors hated the prosperous fat man, they all recognized his strength. There were also the Regent's nameless there, so any threat to the established order would quickly be eliminated, no doubt.

It was all the more surprising when a disheveled man appeared at the leaders' campfire. The bandit hesitated for a moment, unsure how to deliver his news. Should he go to his master, or speak in front of everyone?

"Speak, Spark," Trunk said with a serene smile. "We're all friends here."

"Some guy came out of the forest," Spark said uncertainly. "Almost naked. Just a sword and a couple of knives at his belt. He's just standing there, watching our camp."

"And you ran off to warn us instead of killing him?" Hammer said lazily, reluctantly getting up from the ground. "What kind of fighters do you have in your squad, Trunk?"

"Better than yours!" Trunk snapped and looked at Spark. "One more mistake and you'll lead the next batch of fodder."

"If it's for the common cause..." Spark bleated, instantly turning pale.

There was indeed a tall, burly man at the edge of the forest. He was standing there, thoughtfully observing the raiders' army. Hammer smirked. Such power could impress anyone, but most likely, they were dealing with some local hunter. It was unlikely he was a warrior. Although, anything was possible in Fat Spatus's lands. So Hammer decided to show some courtesy.

"And who do we have here, wandering around?" Hammer said. "Lost, are you? Or just taking a walk?"

The man looked coldly and indifferently straight into Hammer's eyes, as if he were making a major choice. Or maybe he just didn't know how to respond to someone important.

"Your masters are dead," the stranger suddenly said. He spoke quietly, but everyone heard him. "You still have a chance to leave alive if you tell me how you feed the creatures in your underground lairs."

"Are you confused, kid?" Hammer asked. "These are respectable people you're talking to. Masters of nodes. And over there are our fighters. If you don't want to be flayed into ribbons, at least introduce yourself. I'll take my complaints to Spatus later, for his herd forgetting the rules."

"My name is Achilles," the stranger replied calmly. Out of the corner of his eye, Hammer saw Trunk twitch nervously. "You can answer first."

"That's *the* Achilles," Trunk hissed into his colleague's ear. "The one we are hunting. His name is in the assignment. He must have escaped from the battlefield."

"Achilles, you say," Hammer smiled broadly.

He fully understood that participating in the Great Hunt was a huge risk. But the reward was astronomical even just for participating. If he personally killed the main target of this whole affair, the prize would be exponentially greater. "A beautiful name... Since you 'allow' me to be the first, I'll take the honor. In my Node 147, it's simple. We feed the Node's heart with the sick and outsiders. Usually. But I also have a special squad for outstanding individuals, so to speak."

Hammer waved his hand. Most of his men were already alert, watching him closely, waiting for the signal. They jumped up from their places and hurried to their leader.

"If someone really annoys me," Hammer continued, "or doesn't show enough respect to my friends, I send them to the live bait group. We drive them into a caged walkway and prod them with spears to keep them moving, making sure they reach the end of the walkway alive. Does that answer satisfy you, Achilles?"

"Quite," the stranger replied indifferently, shifting his gaze to the next leader. "Your turn."

"Have you lost your mind, bastard?" Hammer growled. "Or do you not understand that you're only alive because of my patience?"

"You," Achilles repeated briefly, not taking his eyes off Trunk.

"We all do the same," Trunk grinned. "Only the idiot Spatus coddles his herd. Come on, Hammer! How long are we going to play around with this idiot?"

The leaders stepped aside, revealing five shooters with emitters — Hammer's main asset. But the stranger seemed unimpressed. He simply nodded to some thought of his own, and a wave of spectral energy radiated from his body in all directions.

* * *

"Destruction," I commanded the CES without the slightest hesitation. I didn't see a single human before me. Only hideous alien parasites that preyed on my race.

Intermediate energy matrice Destruction activated

Personal energy: 100/200

I didn't often see this skill used on ordinary humans. When a large number of civilians fell under the control of the aliens, other units handled their neutralization. While most Lirdagi monsters boiled from the inside, humans died from shock. Unlike bio-replicants, humans could feel pain, and the connection burning out in their heads caused them immense suffering.

The energy matrix field enveloped the enemy squad almost entirely. I had calculated everything correctly. During my conversation with the leaders, most of the bandits had overcome their laziness and came up close enough. These bastards were used to intimidating their opponents with their sheer numbers and thought that standing a few feet away from me would make me think twice about fighting them.

Notifications about the killing of nearly two hundred enemies merged into a continuous stream and automatically dimmed. I only noted the increased energy extraction from the first few kills. This was enough to predict the effectiveness of my sortie.

After the first activation, only fifteen raiders were left standing. The rest of their comrades lay silently on the ground. I saw each of the remaining enemies as I hovered two feet above the ground. Ten were foolish enough to try to punish me for the death of their leaders. The others ran away. Fortunately, all in the same direction.

I quickly stepped forward and grabbed one of the emitters from the ground. The weapon had been poorly maintained, and this was probably its last fight.

Personal energy: 200/200

Attention: Absorption of raze-energy is limited before full deployment of the System

72,382% of the enemy's raze-energy absorbed

Personal energy: 200/200

Attention: Absorption of raze-energy is limited before full deployment of the System

73.042% of the enemy's raze-energy absorbed

Personal energy: 200/200

Attention: Absorption of raze-energy is limited before full deployment of the System

71,641% of the enemy's raze-energy

absorbed

Five shots merged into a single wave of light. I didn't even need the help of the CES. The escapees were outside the energy matrix's range, but the distance between us was no more than seventy yards.

My reserve was filled to the brim. One after another, new surges of energy were being used to deploy the system. The near-instant death of the five raiders cooled the ardor of the remaining ten survivors, but they couldn't flee. They just stood there, unsure of what to do next.

I did know. The emitter fired ten pulses with intervals of less than a second. By the time I was done, the gun was practically boiling. Without proper maintenance, the beam capacitor had turned into a lump of fused metal. The killing power had already been halved, and the last shot, instead of creating a hole in the enemy's chest, left a deep burn. The victim rolled on the ground with wild screams for another minute before falling silent forever.

Personal energy: 200/200

Attention: Absorption of raze-energy is limited before full deployment of the System

71,641% of the enemy's raze-energy absorbed

Personal energy: 199/200

"Recalculate the remaining necessary energy, considering the current reserve," I said, tossing aside the now useless weapon and heading back into the forest. The new realities of this world had been accepted.

Energy consumption recalculated considering the remaining time

New energy extraction from primary node System 1RE/165.6 seconds

I could now feel more relaxed and move on. There were no enemies near the forest, but I had the energy to calmly wait for the next wave. The Great Hunt — that's what the leader named Trunk had called the big raider gathering.

For me, it only meant a constant supply of energy. The raiders couldn't oppose me. Without their masters, they were merely resources. But I couldn't forget about the Regent and his nameless ones. They wouldn't ignore such a slap in the face. All the Center's forces would be mobilized to eliminate the threat that was I. But that would come later. Right now, the enemy only knew about the death of their minions. Some were less valuable, some more, but they were all just pawns in a larger game.

Everything would change once the first stage of the human system deployment was completed — that couldn't be hidden, the threat couldn't be ignored. The Regent would have to respond as harshly as possible to nip the problem in the bud. The most serious measures would be used.

To eliminate the problem quickly, the enemy would have to use transport. I doubted the ruler of this backward world had anything serious at his disposal, but a couple of dozen gliders were likely. There might be something larger but less swift.

At the edge of the forest, I turned and started to run. I could wait on distributing the loot to my guys. I needed to prepare for what was yet to come, first.

"The trophy collection zone is expanding," I informed Herman. "Tell Ditras to take all the vehicles and first visit the exit of the old tunnel outside the forest. There's a chance that new enemies will appear there soon."

"I'll relay the message. What happened there?" Herman asked. "I thought the fight was only on our side."

"Not just on our side," I said. "Have you gained access to the Brist?"

"Yes, but it seems different. It's like it's become more intelligent," Herman said. "And I see signs of a complex algorithm at work. The program is almost complete, but it's stalled. Probably because there's not enough energy."

"Exactly," I said. "About fifteen hundred units of energy remain to be collected."

"How much?!" Herman was extremely surprised, and I didn't need to be nearby to sense it. "One and a half percent! Achilles, that's insane! That means ninety-eight thousand RE were needed for the part that's already been completed. That's impossible! Where can you get that much energy?!"

"Killing enemies," I replied. "Use the Brist to monitor the forest's surroundings. Warn Ditras about incoming raider squads in advance so they can retreat. The bandits won't venture into the forest."

"What do you mean 'killing enemies'?" Herman asked, ignoring my last message.

"Read about energy extraction features. There should be war chronicles in the database," I replied. "Did you hear my instructions?"

"Monitor the surrounding area with the Brist. Inform Ditras about the enemy. Retreat without engaging," the boy repeated. "Already in progress, Achilles."

With that, I temporarily disconnected from the base's communication channel. I needed to think. Until the system was fully deployed, I could only see what was happening near my base. The rest of the world was shrouded in the fog of the unknown. I understood all too well that one node was too little to contend with the Regent. It was no time to think about extensive conflict. But no one was going to give me time for long-term preparations.

The Lirdags had likely not forgotten their defeat. This world had been in their possession for a very long time, which meant that the main forces of the lizards were far from here. The reaction to the appearance of the human system in one of the distant worlds would be unequivocal — they would try to cleanse this planet. And that wasn't entirely bad. More lizards meant more energy. However, there was just one snag.

I was the primary Node of the human system. This meant my identifier would be reflected in its structure during the initial scan. This data would be transmitted further, and the enemy would learn that an Ideal had awakened on their territory. I did not overestimate my own importance. It wasn't about an inflated ego or a huge sense of self-importance.

It was just that I was one of those who had cleansed the lizards' home planet to the point of complete sterility. Such things aren't forgiven or forgotten. If the Lirdags found out that there was an Ideal on the planet, they would destroy it. The question was when? And what could I achieve before their arrival?

Chapter 21

Forgotten are the Power and the Might that were once bestowed upon us,
And the light of distant stars now brings only longing and sorrow.
Under the dominion of darkness, we perish in suffering and despair.
And the final Fall of Humanity draws nearer and nearer.

"Book of Sorrows"
Verse III

Arkutak-Kuru (Mountain Nest)

TAKING ADVANTAGE OF THE OPPORTUNITY, the Regent delved into economic calculations. He thoroughly reviewed the food supplies and then moved on to energy collection. All individuals connected to the info-network contributed a small amount of energy naturally. This amount varied depending on the strength of these individuals and was collected at different intervals. On average, one member of the herd provided the system with 1 unit of energy, which was insufficient. The masters waged endless wars to expand their territory, and even with trillions of beings in the network meticulously controlled the expenditure of this valuable resource.

Which is why the process of gathering food was secondary, necessary only for the herd's survival and its continued energy generation. The primary task was energy collection, which was mainly carried out through forced extraction of RE. The only way to meet the norms set by the masters was through human destruction and death. The herd was lazy by nature, in every respect. The law of conservation of energy had not been repealed, so if the herd were left alone, fed, and watered, it would provide only the small and insufficient energy contribution to the system.

The herd reproduced quickly enough, and the number of permitted forced extractions from each of its members had been mathematically calculated long ago. Each node leader had a quota for energy collection and delivery. Those who failed to meet the quota were punished, and repeat offenders were destroyed. Those who exceeded their quotas were rewarded and, with continued growth, were given a node previously managed by a less competent counterpart.

The Regent noticed with dissatisfaction that

the individual Baka, responsible for Node 214, had been eliminated. He quickly skimmed through the information and saw the report from the nameless chief — Eleven, whose squad was currently dealing with the issue. The report indicated that Baka had been killed by another leader, but Eleven had already handled it. The Regent saw with satisfaction the note next to Raul's name: "Eliminated for violating the truce and the Regent's orders." This idiot had succumbed to his human emotions and killed his neighbor without the Regent's sanction.

Kalamar Arku shook his head in dissatisfaction. He had big plans for this Baka, who had been exceptionally good at extracting energy, far surpassing all his neighbors. Perhaps, if the Regent had been more attentive and shown his favor earlier, he could have preserved this valuable servant. As it was, he lost two node leaders at once. But then again, the system existed, and the system worked. What would happen if one went against the system? Pure chaos.

So, the Regent moved on and summoned data from the central station, which showed that the capacity of the giant accumulator was at 73%. With satisfaction, the Regent looked at the planetary data. He was still ahead of the other Regents in how fast he collected energy. The Masters would be pleased.

At this moment of great satisfaction, he was disturbed by the commander of the nameless. Maraktar Uru was supposed to be overseeing the operation involving his subordinates, much like he always did. It spared the Regent from having to personally verify the outcomes. Nothing had ever needed to be cleaned up or corrected after Maraktar.

Maraktar entered the hall using precise, perfectly measured movements, his gaze cold, eyes not blinking at all. Only the Regent, with his modified perception organs, could notice that Maraktar was quite nervous, which was bad. Certain parts of Maraktar's brain had been artificially dulled, making him unable to experience fear. The Regent realized that any other being would now be in a state of utter panic.

"What do you want?" The Regent asked.

"I have come to report on the outcome of the operation, sire," Maraktar Uru replied almost indifferently.

"Then report!" The Regent barked back, his massive body leaning slightly toward his subordinate. "Or do you have no desire to share this information with me?"

"Eighty-Five has been destroyed. Additionally, two hundred forty-three members of the combat group assembled by Eleven were also destroyed," Maraktar began to speak monotonously, staring into space. The more he spoke, the more astonished the Regent's rough face became. "Thirty and Thirty-One have been eliminated. Another hundred fighters from the combined detachment followed. Forty-Three died from overload. Eleven was the last to die. Currently, the entire Araknat Eru combat group has been destroyed.

The remnants of the local militants are scattered throughout the forest. New groups are converging on the scene."

"What?!" The Regent roared. "When did this happen?!"

"Five hours ago, sire," Maraktar replied grimly.

"And why am I only finding out about this now? Have you forgotten the laws, Maraktar?"

"I was verifying the information, sire, as per protocol," Maraktar replied and obediently bowed his head, expecting inevitable punishment. For such a mistake, the penalty was his life.

With a wave of his hand, the Regent sent all economic data to the buffer and switched to the consolidated report on the recent operation, which had been lingering in the corner of his vision for some time. He immediately frowned because what he saw was very strange.

First, the five nameless ones had spent several hours circling the gray zone before beginning active operations. Their initial attempt had ended catastrophically, which wasn't surprising. The tunnels within the zone were unstable, and Araknat Eru decided to take a detour. There was a stable tunnel on the other side of the gray zone.

This was a reasonable and balanced decision, but then something went wrong. In the first stage of the assault, over two hundred raiders and the Araknat Eru modificant number Eighty-Five were killed.

"How did this happen?" The Regent asked

just out of order. If the system hadn't provided him with the cause of death, then his commander wouldn't have seen it either.

Maraktar had been working with the Regent for a long time and knew him well, so he understood that the Regent wasn't expecting an answer, and he couldn't provide one anyway. Or rather, his answer wouldn't satisfy the master.

"Eighty-Five's armor power source failed, sir. As a result of the detonation, my subordinate died."

The Regent meticulously reviewed every second of the battle. The remaining nameless launched their attack. And then things got strange again. The event density was off the charts. Within a few seconds, one nameless was lost, followed shortly by the second. With a gap of a couple of minutes the third modificant, with the ability for total herd control, died from overload.

"What was happening there?!" Kalamar Arku exclaimed. The dry data of the summary did not give a clear picture of the actual events. The bare numbers of damage and losses only added more questions.

Maraktar Uru looked at his master with a mix of fear and surprise. In his memory, this unemotional creation of the Masters had never been so agitated.

The Regent reviewed the report twice more before he noticed, at the bottom of the summary, a strange symbol, which only he and more powerful system users could see. He was reluctant to press it, but its very presence indicated a rather unpleasant and dangerous situation. The Regent hesitated for almost a second before deciding to touch the symbol unseen by others. In response, green system messages suddenly filled the entire screen. They kept moving until they froze on a shocking message:

Activation...
Attention!
Warning!
Personal notification confirmed
Protocol "Cleansing" activated...

If the Regent could sweat, he would be sweating now. This was his oversight. He hadn't forcibly blocked the capabilities of the first twenty of his nameless, who in turn were commanders of fives.

He hadn't cut down their functionality because it was impossible to disable the unnecessary features while keeping the important ones. This was why his first twenty were probably the best warriors on the entire planet.

Other Regents had modificants that were prohibited from activating any master protocols. Kalamar Arku had left this capability deliberately, not envisioning a scenario where his loyal war dogs would exercise this right. But one of them had.

Sweeping away all notifications with a roar of rage, the Regent began mentally manipulating the map, sending system requests at an enormous speed beyond human capacity. He awaited the appearance of the gray zone on the map, but the delay of three seconds felt endless. The entire territory should have already been covered in red spots, considering that the fight happened five hours ago.

Soon, the redness would cover the gray node and spread beyond its borders. Considering that all fighters capable of combat were now dead in this suicidal attack, the five adjacent nodes and the herd were in danger.

Without hesitation, the Regent began sending signals to his servants. Troops were being pulled from all nodes across his continent to simply establish a defensive line against the advancing creatures of the Masters.

The Regent ground his teeth. In effect, Eleven had unleashed a local Armageddon. His intent was clear: to free the creatures and destroy his enemies. However, the "Cleansing" protocol not only scrambled all the settings in the creatures' brains, but also burned out the communication channels so the enemy couldn't take control of them.

This modification and protocol had been devised long ago when the Lirdags encountered enemies capable of controlling their pets or creations. With the communication channels burned out, nothing could be changed, no matter the level of access. When the "Cleansing" protocol was activated, a planet was overrun by uncontrollable creatures. Then the Lirdags had to go in and destroy their creations to establish control over a now lifeless planet.

Finally, the map appeared before him, with an empty spot in the center, the nodes adjacent to the gray zone, the markers of all the deployed forces... And not a single Master's creature in the entire area.

"What the hell is going on over there?" The Regent muttered, automatically requesting a report on the activity of the bio-replicants and initiating a local scan. A few lines appeared, indicating the absence of the Chucklers in the specified area. This couldn't be so, but it was. A second later, responses from the system's equipment started coming in, and then the text turned bright yellow. All other data dimmed, leaving only one message:

Danger! Activation of an alien System detected.

Identification in progress...

The Regent couldn't believe his eyes. He had never heard of such a thing. The Lirdagi native system was trying to analyze a foreign one, going through all the known variants, of which there were many. Right now, it was comparing the features of the newly appeared system with those in its database. Suddenly, the message turned crimson. Filling the entire screen, it read:

System identified as that of a self-named race "Humans", bestiary code XSH124-5AK.

Attention! "A" class thread must be declared; infection source must be eliminated immediately!

The Regent's hand acted faster than his mind. He struck the "cancel" button — a physical button, not a virtual one, which required real physical pressure to activate. It also read the bioinformation of the one who was pressing it — no one but the Regent could do so.

Ignoring the system's annoying wail in his ears and the blinking red lights, the Regent stared at his hand in horror. He had just violated protocol.

An "A" class threat required a signal to be sent immediately to the planet's Central Sanctuary, where, according to rumors, one of the Masters lay in eternal sleep. If it had been a "C" or even a "B" class threat, the signal would have reached only the Sanctuary. However, in the case of an "A" class threat, it was also relayed through the planetary transmitter to the Central Nest. While "C" and "B" allowed the local Master to handle the situation, an "A" class threat had only one solution: the planet was to be destroyed.

The Regent listened to his feelings and was surprised to realize that he didn't want to die. He understood that it was necessary, but he still very much didn't want to die. He hadn't finished reading the books in his library; he enjoyed his periods of activity and wanted them to continue.

He raised his eyes to Maraktar: "Send everyone we have. Personally lead the assault. Destroy everything you see and the entire herd that witnessed this. No one must remain. Do you understand me?"

"I understand," nodded Maraktar Uru. "What should we do about the eyes in the Center, sire?"

The question was very unpleasant, but Kalamar Arku was glad his subordinate had asked it.

The eternal competition among the rulers required constant vigilance. Kalamar himself had surprised his sleeping colleagues more than once when the right moment presented itself.

No matter how much the rulers cared about the loyalty of the population in their main cities, there were always those ready to inform other Regents of any news. Especially if they were paid for the information.

A mass gathering of all troops in the Center would inevitably raise suspicions. While activity in territories far from the capital did not interest anyone, any stir in the Center would attract a lot of attention and would indicate that the ruler had problems. It would signify weakness and mark a good time for an attack. It would also mean that others would start looking for the source of Kalamar's problems.

The Regent quickly considered his options and the possible consequences. "Gather all the Araknat Eru. Only them. I'll announce the search for new servants and will activate the mechanism for initiating new nameless. I'll declare my intention to create a second hundred Araknat Eru."

"But sire," exclaimed Maraktar. Such a statement meant his master was preparing to expand his territory, which could only be done at the expense of a neighbor. There hadn't been a major war for a very long time. The Masters encouraged competition but punished wasteful resource use. If the war went poorly...

"That doesn't matter now," the Regent said.

"It's better if my neighbors are looking for informants and making sure their forces are in order, than paying much attention to what we are doing."

"As you command, my lord," Maraktar said and bowed his head.

"All gliders are at your disposal," the Regent continued. "Those within the palace rock. Send reliable warriors ahead to prepare the territory for your arrival. One of the herd leaders survived — Spatus. He has a good rating. Perhaps you can start solving the problem from his territory. You will personally lead the Ssarak-Maru. By the time you arrive, I should be aware of everything happening there. Begin!"

Maraktar bowed deeply and left the hall. The Regent stared at his alert system, which was currently in autonomous mode. He had ten days, after which its autonomy would be forcibly interrupted, and the signal sent to its destination. Within these ten days, the signal had to be neutralized.

The Regent could handle erasing the information about its existence, but he was unable to suppress the signal while one of the systems detected a foreign presence. So, in ten days, either the Regent would succeed and everything would return to normal, leaving only the problem of restoring the population of the herd, or... The Regent didn't even want to think about the alternative.

Chapter 22

Node 213
Edge of the Forest

I INSPECTED THE PANTS I was wearing and sighed heavily. The run to Wolf's node took about forty minutes, I didn't even have to use the energy matrices. Maintaining the necessary speed was almost effortless for me, but my only pair of pants had finally become completely useless. The boots were still holding up thanks to a piece of rope I had found somewhere. After multiple uses of Acceleration, I was surprised they hadn't fallen completely apart.

I dressed my fighters in the best gear taken in

battle but took almost nothing for myself. The clothes I was wearing I got back on the mountain from Ditras's guys. Conforming to any norms or status was always meaningless to me, but comfort was of serious importance. And now I felt it was time to update my wardrobe.

I purposefully headed towards the transport left by the nameless. The system showed the presence of guards nearby, which was very timely. My energy reserve had already dropped by a couple dozen RE and needed to be replenished.

A couple of raiders lazily sprawled on the ground a few yards from the gliders. It never occurred to them that someone might attack them. I didn't even have to use any energy matrices.

Now I was looking at the sturdy leather pants of one of the guards, wondering if I should change into them or wait until I got back to the base and choose something more decent from the trophy armor. It would not be a problem if I burnt out all the systems in it, because our reserves had energy now, and small losses weren't critical. At least the materials and quality of armor would be somewhat familiar to me.

Since my pants were already reduced to ragged shorts, I decided to change. I also took a good belt from one of the raiders and a travel bag. I had to carry all the items taken from the nameless in my hands, which was extremely inconvenient. Fortunately, I managed to attach the knives and sword to the general mount. I would need to figure out my own equipment and update it, but, as usual, it could wait.

"Detailed equipment analysis," I said, heading towards the gliders. The equipment looked strange, like it was another homemade machine. As it turned out, this only applied to the hull.

Identification according to the Confederacy catalog cannot be performed. The means of transportation have an internal identification marker Pain's Fang.

Load capacity: 200 standard units

Maximum speed: 60 miles/h

Maximum flight altitude: 50 meters

Range is not limited

No internal power source

Remote control capability: Available

Autopilot: Absent

Built-in weapon: Absent

Armor: Class 7 according to the standard classification

The innards were much more interesting than the rust-beaten scrap metal on the outside. Gliders never had serious armor, so this one having class seven didn't surprise me. If anything hit this contraption, it would fall. The speed was mediocre, too. Though for the locals, it was probably incredible. What I needed to deal with right away was the remote control capability, before these rusty birds flew back home.

"Block external signals," I ordered.

Block is impossible. Device functions as part of the alien system.

"Complete disconnection," I said after

considering the previous message.

Complete disconnection will lead to the transport becoming inoperable. Continue?

Yes/No

"Yes," I said confidently and stepped closer. I studied the structure of the machines for a few seconds before opening the discovered casing. Beneath it were internal mechanisms that looked much more familiar than I had expected. Another repurposing of Confederacy tech, which was all the better for me.

Equipment in this world had immense value. Judging by the external condition, even the nearest subjects of the Regent had issues getting their hands on the good stuff. This meant that after the death of the nameless, valuable equipment would be recalled. I didn't know why this hadn't been done already, but it no longer mattered.

Originally, I had planned to seize all three gliders for my own needs, but I had concluded that it made no sense. The gliders operated off the Lirdagi system, and without a proper autonomous power source, the transport would turn into a heap of scrap metal. Their consumption was quite high, and replacing the connection to the hostile system with ordinary batteries was not feasible.

"Well then," I grumbled. "Something useful gotta come from a dead lizard."

I connected directly to the nearest glider and activated the CES. I then set a number of tasks for the system and initiated a search. It was unlikely that the Lirdags had delved deeply enough into the captured units to clear out all the human engineers' traps.

It took me about five minutes to find the necessary nodes and activate the backup protocols. Having done this, I worked much faster with the second and third gliders.

"Activate device connections," I said, and green indicators went on on the gliders' control panels. A second later, a symbol of a flying apparatus with the number three appeared in the lower left corner of my vision, and I nodded in satisfaction. Now I could head back to the base.

I had just reached the edge of the forest when I heard a muted hum behind me. The owners of the gliders had finally taken noticed and flew them home. But I had no doubt that I would see them again soon.

The base was bustling with activity. Every one of my fighters was eagerly unloading the trophies. There was a huge pile of hem by the entrance shaft — so big, it was nearly impossible to get into the base. Ditras had ordered that everything even remotely related to the ancient era be brought back. Fortunately, I no longer had to handle the identification — it was now Herman's job.

The boy was clearly suffering from a lack of tasks. He even began stuttering again, like when we first met. So, he threw all his energy into examining and sorting the loot. I saw a decent pile of standard batteries, several sets of armor assembled from parts, and a whole heap of various weapons. At a first glance, we could already arm a respectable army. The only problem was there was no men to fight in it.

My combat group was down to just three people. Joker and his four refugees still weren't full-fledged fighters. We could muster a couple dozen strong men among the settlers, but calling them warriors would be premature. Ultimately, I was left with only one combat-ready unit — Fat Spat's squad.

We repelled the enemy attack, even though it had seemed impossible. But beyond this battle lay a stark reality of insufficient manpower. Alone, I could achieve a lot, and after deploying the system, I could do even more. But one person can't win a war. In the past, we had entire armies of Seniors and Juniors, to supplement the might of the Ideals. Now, the scale was significantly smaller, but the problem remained the same.

The nameless chief destroyed our main advantage. The forest was no longer an isolated zone where we could control enemy movements. I could still track them, but now it was merely reconnaissance. I couldn't influence the enemy or force it to change course. If the Regent's army descended on my base, we wouldn't hold out for long.

Personal energy: 179/200

"Herman!" I called out. "What's the status of the bio-replicator? How serious is the damage?"

"Achilles!" The boy yelled joyfully, and all work instantly stopped. Surprised, I realized that my arrival had gone unnoticed until that moment. "You're back!"

A dozen people, who I considered my unit, dropped everything and surrounded me. Each wanted to say something or make themselves known. I felt a nearly forgotten sense of peace and joy.

"We ventured beyond the forest, Achilles," Ditras said. "We gathered everything you left from the fight."

"Two hundred raiders!" Anar exclaimed. "Imagine that, Achilles! And you call that 'a couple of guys'?"

The men around laughed and patted each other on the back. I remembered many similar moments. People always rejoiced after liberating our planets from the lizards, or destroying another alien fleet, or breaking through enemy defenses. They felt alive, and that alone was true happiness. Many of them didn't think about what lay ahead. Just as my fighters weren't considering now that our victory was only the beginning of a great war that was yet to come.

Though this joy was different. In the past, none of the Juniors could have hoped to touch me, and few Seniors were afforded that honor. It wasn't about me, my snobbery, or an inflated ego. Before armies of millions, I appeared only as a huge holographic image, addressing everyone at once. To be patted on the back like a comrade and a good guy was something new. And I liked it!

"I've got gifts for you," I said with a wide smile. "Joker!"

"I'm here!" Joker yelled, puffing out his chest

proudly.

"For your bravery in battle and to help you develop your abilities," I said, taking the bag off my shoulder and untying the cord at the neck. "You get this. Use it well!"

"It's a bit short," Joker said, examining the gift with interest. "Hard to reach the enemy to knock him on the head."

"Fool!" Herman shouted, trying to snatch the rod. "That's sophisticated tech, not a club! Let me see it!"

"Private Herman!" I said sternly, and the boy instantly stood at attention. The sight was so comical that I couldn't help but smile. The rest of the fighters laughed. "For your heroism and achievements in training, you deserve a special reward."

With these words, I pulled the glass orb from the bag and handed it to the boy. Herman stared at it for a moment, then looked up at me with eyes full of wonder.

"Is this what I think it is?" He asked cautiously, hesitant to take the reward.

"Possibly," I smiled. "If you're thinking of a multi-channel accelerator and not a paperweight."

"I've read about these devices," he whispered, taking the artifact. To the others, his excitement was incomprehensible — it was just a glass ball, no big deal. "I thought they were long gone and never dreamed I'd have something like this. But... I'm not connected."

"We'll deal with that," I smiled, and the boy looked at me skeptically.

"You started the algorithm?" He asked cautiously, and I nodded.

"I express my gratitude to the rest of you for your heroism and bravery in battle," I said, looking at all my warriors. "Each of you may choose a reward from our trophies without restrictions. After the loot collection is finished, you can take a well-deserved rest."

"We don't need rest, Achilles!" One of the refugees cheerfully shouted. "We've got plenty of energy left! Just let the enemies try to come at us!"

The others immediately supported their comrade with cheerful shouts. I looked around and smiled, though there wasn't a hint of joy left inside me. I had managed to create a good starting point. We even withstood the first blow, but for our opponents, the previous battle was merely a reconnaissance. A plan for further actions was slowly forming inside my head. I needed a lot to implement it, but we could start right away.

"You need to rest!" I said categorically. "Because later, you won't have time for it. You will be defending the most important thing in this world — this underground shelter. The future of our planet depends on the preservation of this place. If the enemy destroys it, all our efforts will have been in vain. Ditras, you will lead the defense of our base. Joker, you'll manage the new squad of creatures if we can restore the equipment. If we can't, you'll have to find those lizards you were breeding on the farm."

My subordinates nodded seriously,

exchanging glances with one another. The importance of the mission was off the charts. Only Herman looked at me from under his brow and remained silent.

"Let's go check the bio-replicator," I said to the boy, nodding toward the hole in the ground.

The Chucklers' attack had indeed caused significant damage to the alien device. Usually, the monsters didn't attack other Lirdagi creatures, but the bio-replicator was connected to the shelter's system, and the Chucklers considered it an enemy. Fortunately, the hound producer was still alive and had even partially recovered. It was already capable of production.

"Am I staying here too?" Herman asked after I finished the inspection. The boy was looking down, turning my gift over in his hands.

"It's the duty of a true Operator," I said with a slight smile, patting the boy on the shoulder. "Who else will inform me of all the dangers? Who will ensure the system's main node defenses?"

"It's not forever, right?" Herman asked.

"Of course not!" I replied, though I wasn't completely sure of that.

"Alright," the boy sighed heavily and finally lifted his head. "Shall we try to create a hound?"

Personal energy: 175/200

"Yep," I said.

We had just enough energy and didn't add any extra enhancements or modifications. We needed material to fuel the bio-replicator, and if possible, to replenish my own reserves.

Personal energy: 200/200

Attention: Absorption of raze-energy is limited without before full deployment of the System

68,356% of the enemy's raze-energy absorbed

Just as I finished off the disoriented Hass-Arss, Joker walked in wearing a full set of the Alive armor and holding a plasma cutter.

"Mind if I help?" He asked.

"Not at all," I said. "Do you know what to do?"

"At our farm, we fed the lizards with whatever we could find," Joker smirked. "Even with other lizards. Where should I put the meat?"

"Herman will tell you," I said. "He's downstairs."

Joker left, and I headed toward the heaps of loot. Ideally, we needed to open the lower levels of the lab, but I didn't have time for that now. The current squad could be accommodated in the shelter as it was. I thought there should also be enough storage space for the trophies.

The loot couldn't be identified without Herman, so the men went about their own tasks. I initiated an analysis of the available equipment options and started to dig through it. The whole process took about ten minutes, and another five to synchronize the set I assembled to be suitable for my tasks.

Modular armor "Reserve"

Configuration: 11756

Armor Class: 4

Servos: None
Active Systems: None
Built-in Weapons: None
Condition: Lacks power elements
Status: Usable with power elements

This was the best option for me. It was a warrior's suit that consisted of a dozen-and-a half parts from seven different armor sets. The grayish brown color looked like skin from a distance. The armor didn't reduce mobility even in accelerated mode and had a good protection class. Its main advantages were the magnetic equipment fasteners, which couldn't fail under the influence of my energy matrices because they were too primitive — there were no circuits in them that could burn out.

I mounted the high frequency sword on my back, and the trophy knives fit perfectly into the chest sheaths. Then I strapped a handheld kinetic launcher to my thigh, got eight spare batteries, and a large emitter. In the loot, I found a flat backpack with a rigid frame. It was narrow, but spacious enough not to carry every little thing in my hands. I was ready.

There was no need to say goodbye to anyone, their tasks were defined. Herman was online. If anyone had questions, they could be handled remotely.

Fifteen minutes later, I was already climbing the slope of the mountain, where one of Spatus's men stood. As I approached, he quickly disappeared from sight, replaced by Spatus himself.

"Ready?" I asked as I got closer.

"For what?" Spatus asked cautiously.

"For a triumphant return home," I said with a wide smile.

Kill to Live

"For what?" Spatus asked cautiously.

"For a triumphant return home," I said with a wide smile.

Chapter 23

"I DON'T UNDERSTAND," Spatus said. "What return?"

"Home," I said. "You're a hero, Spatus. The sole survivor of a battle that became the demise of an entire army! A brilliant negotiator who managed to strike a deal with the Regent's cunning enemy and saved the lives of most of his fighters."

"That's nonsense," Spatus shook his head. "No one will believe that I escaped with my squad. There were five nameless that died there!"

My reasoning was quite simple. The technology on this planet was extremely primitive. There were no satellites, or they were inaccessible to the locals. I had scanned the sky at night and never saw anything. All these facts combined gave me some assurance that the enemy couldn't monitor the battle in real-time. More precisely, they couldn't see what was happening, but only had access to system logs and reports, which were a different matter altogether.

If one reconstructed the sequence of events, it would look like the nameless started the assault. Then the reconnaissance squad perished. Next, I killed Cyclops, the two Shadows, more raiders, and the Controller. The Operator was the last to die, but not before he deactivated the protective perimeter and sent the Chucklers into battle.

These are the facts the enemy would see and use to make decisions. The markers of Spatus's squad and Spatus himself would undoubtedly be visible to the Regent. The raider leader couldn't disappear even if he wanted to. But what was reflected in the system could be interpreted in different ways.

"The nameless chief ordered you to protect him," I said firmly. "And you followed the orders until his death. It's not your fault that he died too quickly, and the enemy from the forest used techniques unknown to you."

"That changes nothing, Achilles," Spatus said. "I survived and..."

"And managed to secure your position next to the target of the Great Hunt," I finished his sentence, and Spatus stared at me in fear. "Yes, I know about that order."

"I have no intention of carrying it out," Spatus

said.

"Oh, but you will!" I said with a predatory grin. "A general assembly has been announced on your territory, and you are obliged to lead it."

"No," Spatus shook his head. "How will I explain why I survived?"

"Tell the truth," I said. "It's not difficult."

"That I betrayed the masters and switched to your side? They'll kill me faster than the Regent's men arrive!"

"It depends on how you phrase it," I said. "You managed to negotiate with the enemy and secured a chance for yourself. To do that, you had to protect a village from a monster attack. Then you promised the enemy the moon and eternal loyalty, and you fled the forest at the first opportunity."

The Regent will see all the moves Spatus had made, and we needed to have a good explanation for them. This wouldn't help against the modificants, but I was used to handling problems on the go. My priority was a smooth transition into Spatus's lands. It was easy to assume that Spatus would be questioned by other raiders, maybe even without a direct order from the Regent.

I decided to change the battlefield for many reasons. The enemy wouldn't expect a counterattack on their own land. Spatus remained a loyal leader with a good reputation. Numerous raider groups were currently gathering at a specific section of the border, and their interest needed to be redirected. And these were just the reasons I considered most important.

"What if they want to verify my words?" Spatus asked.

"Who and how?"

Personal energy: 189/200

"Every leader I encounter will start asking questions!" Spatus said. "Everyone and their mother is over on my lands right now. I hope those idiots haven't started looting the nearby villages."

"And you can't come up with something to tell them?" I said.

"I can," Spatus replied grimly. "But what if they don't believe me?"

"Anyone who has doubts can go into the forest and see for themselves," I said.

"Even a complete idiot wouldn't do that, Achilles," Spatus said with an unexpected smile. "Raiders won't risk their hides without a clear order."

"Any more questions?" I asked.

"My people," Spatus said. "They'll be questioned, too. Not by the leaders, but many have friends in other nodes."

"You'll have to handle that yourself," I said. "You know your people better."

"Then it's best to do it right away," Spatus grumbled and headed down the slope of the crater, where his subordinates awaited his return. "You're coming with us, I assume?"

"Correct," I nodded. "Do we need to discuss this?"

"No, we don't," Spatus replied on the move. "I'll handle everything."

Personal energy: 188/200

Noticing their leader's approach, the fighters got up and formed a line — quite an unusual behavior for raiders. Discipline in Spatus's band was significantly better than in other raider groups.

"We have betrayed the Regent," Spatus said loudly. I expected to hear angry shouts or something similar, but the men remained silent. "Yes, all of us! We betrayed him because that bastard has been sucking us dry for who knows how many years. Borcha, tell us how they punish the Regent's traitors?"

A stern, fit man stepped forward and said clearly: "Every traitor must be killed. As brutally, painfully, and publicly as possible. If you catch a traitor, you can punish him right away. You only wait for the Regent's other decisions if there was a prior order to do so."

"Well said!" Spatus smirked. "Right now, there are leaders from a dozen neighboring nodes on our land. All of you are considered members of my squad and equally guilty of treason. There will be no mercy or leniency. If anyone finds out why we survived in that damned forest, we will all die in the main square of our own town. For everyone else, we just fled when this man," he pointed a finger at me, "killed all the nameless. Be grateful that I managed to negotiate with Achilles to protect that damned village. Only because of that were we able to escape the forest and return under the protection of the Regent."

Spatus gave everyone a stern look. The

warriors either nodded calmly or looked back in silence. It was an astonishing sight. Could it be that Spatus had managed to assemble a band of fighters so loyal to him personally that they didn't have any questions or doubts? Although, considering the order of things among the raiders, perhaps they knew what could happen to them.

"If any of you, in a drunken haze or in bed with a whore, blabs about what we saw, we're all dead," Spatus continued. "We, our loved ones, and the entire order we've worked so hard to establish."

"Be fair, Spatus," Borcha said calmly. "We've been under your command for years. We know the stakes."

"Good!" Spatus nodded and pointed to me again. "He's coming with us. If you have any questions, ask them now. We leave in five minutes."

"What should we call you?" Borcha asked. "The mission has your name, Achilles. Any coincidences would be suspicious."

"Call me Raven," I suggested after a moment's thought.

"Why are you coming with us, Achilles?" One of the guys asked. "If you killed even the nameless in the forest, what's the point of coming out?"

"They will come for you," I said. "And they won't care how many people die in the process."

"And what will you do when the Regent's army arrives?" Someone else asked.

"I'll kill them," I said. "Spatus said it right. Your only task is not to spill what happened in the forest. I'll handle the rest."

Just yesterday, any of these raiders would have laughed in my face after such a statement. No one in their right mind would say something like that. But each of them had seen the fight at the tunnel, and now they didn't doubt that I could actually kill anyone who came my way, even if it were an alien army.

"Do you still have a charge left in the accumulator?" I asked Spatus.

"Thirty units," he said.

"I'll need it," I said and extended my hand.

He hesitated for a moment but then pulled out the artifact and handed it to me.

Accumulator capacity: 32/100

Do you wish to use the energy accumulator to replenish your internal reserve?

Yes/No

Personal energy: 200/200

Accumulator capacity: 19/100

Good stuff. In my current situation, an extra hundred units of energy could significantly ease my life. Spatus looked gloomily at his precious artifact and then turned away, not expecting to get it back. He was wrong.

"I'll need it again when we reach the forest border," I said, handing the device back to its owner.

Spatus stared at me in surprise and barked: "Let's move out!"

The squad quickly reformed and headed toward the crater's summit. Interestingly, no one asked me what the ruins were or why the ground was still black with the blood of the hounds.

A group of fifty moved much slower than I did, so I constantly had to hold myself back to not surge ahead. I ran somewhere in the middle of the column, surrounded by Spatus's panting raiders. The squad didn't stop for a break once before reaching the forest border, which was a testament to these warriors' endurance.

After an hour of travel, the raiders started to cast surprised glances at me. Most of them were already wheezing from exhaustion and strain, while I wasn't even sweating. Our equipment was similar, so there were no allowances for a lack of extra weight. Yet no one dared to ask questions.

In general, Spatus's raiders were remarkably silent. The only thing I heard was Borcha's occasional commands when it was time to change scouts. Compared to the riff-raff that were the fighters of Baka or Wolf, I was now looking at what could almost be considered a proper combat unit.

Personal energy: 176/200

"Halt!" Borcha shouted, and the group began to slow down. There was a visible gap between the trees ahead. Beyond that lay the territory of Fat Spatus. Even from here, I heard the voices of many people.

I approached Spatus and silently extended my hand. The remaining energy in the accumulator wouldn't be enough to fully recharge my reserve, but it would buy me more time to assess the situation. Spatus didn't argue and handed over the artifact.

Book Two

Personal energy: 195/200
Accumulator capacity: 0/100

"Can you charge it fully?" I asked, returning the device.

"Only at home," Spatus said. "It'll take about an hour, but we still need to get there."

Home... Most node leaders had lairs or bases. I could hardly imagine Wolf talking about returning home. People were and still are very different.

"Keep a low profile," Spatus said quietly. "No matter what happens."

"I wasn't planning otherwise," I smiled and returned to my place in the formation.

The fighters had somewhat recovered, and we moved on. No one was running anymore; they just walked quickly, conserving energy. Outside the forest lay a vast raider camp. Off to the side, the bodies of the bandits I had killed were piled up. Two hundred corpses, which no one had bothered to bury or burn.

"Well, well! Look who's here!" Said someone in a cheerful voice. "Is that Fat Spat in the flesh?"

At the very edge of the raider encampment sat about twenty men. They were quite a distinctive bunch, much like their leader. Their muscular bodies were bare and covered in tattoos. All they had on were leather pants and heavy iron-studded boots. For weapons, they had massive hammers and two-handed swords.

"Yes, Vira, it's me" Spatus replied grimly. "Have the nameless arrived yet?"

"You'd know better," Vira chuckled. He

differed from his men only by the shield generator hanging on his chest. It was the same Droplet that Fiend had. "We're on your land, but from what I see, you're not keeping order very well."

Vira nodded toward the pile of corpses, a nasty smile on his face — the implication was more than clear. A truce was established between all the groups for the duration of the Great Hunt. This very fact allowed me to frame one of the leaders, but now Spatus was in a bad spot — he would need to justify and explain himself. But the fat man didn't even consider providing any explanations.

"You should take care of your own node," Spatus said. "You might lose your last workers with your games. I'm not lending you anything anymore — times have changed."

"Like I need it," Vira grimaced but quickly lost interest in the conversation — Spatus had obviously struck a nerve. "Why are you asking about the Regent's servants? I thought you were roaming the forest with them. Some even suggested going home."

"The nameless are dead," Spatus said grimly, heading around the main camp.

"What do you mean?" Vira asked, immediately tense. "That's a bad joke, Spatus."

"No jokes here," Spatus said. "That bastard hiding in the forest killed them all. Pirate, Raul, Baka, and five of the Regent's envoys too. Who knows what's going to happen now, but no one's going home until we root out this plague."

Vira stared after the departing Spatus for a few seconds, then caught up and walked beside him. The camp was already buzzing like a disturbed hive. The news of the node leader's arrival spread much faster than we moved. I could already see other faction leaders hurrying toward us — there were more than a dozen. If the nameless had waited a bit longer, they could have crushed us with their overwhelming numbers. Fortunately, the Regent's servants were too confident in their own strength.

A thunderous roar came from the center of the camp: "Spatus! "Stop right there, you cowardly bastard!"

Spatus slowed down and reluctantly looked toward the owner of that voice. He clearly knew the speaker. I looked in the same direction with interest. Until now, I thought that Spatus only answered to the Regent and his closest servants, and that none of the local leaders could speak to him as an equal. The stranger's voice carried an unmistakable threat. Then again, that was probably the only way this creature could speak.

I looked and saw a modificant approaching us. It was a massive mound of living flesh, twice the size of the Cyclops I had killed. A real flesh golem, over fifteen feet tall. How this creature had managed to reach the gathering point so quickly was beyond me.

The brute moved toward us, the ground shaking with each step. The closer he came, the more repulsed I felt. His enormous belly hung below his knees. No armor could fit this monster, not that he needed any — it would be a challenge to pierce such a layer of fat. And it wasn't just fat.

I watched the flabby body's movements closely. In some places, the muscles moved unnaturally, as if objects were hidden under the skin. Maybe protective implants, or maybe just chunks of metal — in this world, anything was possible.

Spatus watched the approaching giant from under his brow. The other gang leaders kept their distance. Even Vira, who had been walking beside Spatus, hurried to step back and join the others.

The commotion among the leaders quickly spread to their subordinates. Some raiders reached for their weapons. Others began to rise from their places and move in. Spatus's men clustered into a tight group, their hands resting on their weapons. If this was the usual way the local elite communicated, I was surprised they hadn't killed each other off yet.

Personal energy: 193/200

A name was glowing above the giant's head. It was a strange name for a person, but quite typical for a modificant. The creature was named K-7-3/1.

"Hello, Kasto," Spatus said calmly, tilting his head back to see the giant's face. "I'm glad you responded to the Regent's call and will fight alongside us in the upcoming battle. Our chances of victory are much greater with you."

"You can wipe my fat ass with your lies, Spatus," the modificant growled, leaning over Spatus and completely casting him in shadow. "Right now, I'm only interested in one thing: wy is your cowardly ass here, while the great servants of the Regent lie dead in that forest?"

Chapter 24

Bald Mountain
Node 213

KIRPAK BUMPED INTO HIS FRIEND who stopped all too suddenly right in front of him. "What the hell, Arbat!"

The two scouts knew their job well and were moving in a single line ahead of the main group and their boss, Turs — the leader of Node 199. For these young men, who weren't even thirty years old, this was the first Great Hunt of their lives.

Now, at the Regent's command, their reluctant and unhurried leader had gathered his fighters, and the group had set out slowly toward the gathering point. Strange rumors were circulating that something weird was happening around Node 213.

No exact information reached the ordinary raiders, but their boss, who certainly knew more, remained silent and angry. That made things even worse. Two murdered whores and one cook in two days — this was too much even for the impulsive Turs.

The two scouts were glad to be walking as far from their boss as possible.

"Do you hear that?" Arbat asked, looking toward the northeast.

"I don't hear a damn..." Kirpak began, but then he heard it too.

A strange buzzing sound was approaching from the northeast. The surrounding area was a steppe, covered with small shrubs. The peculiar lone mountain they were passing through was called "Bald" for a reason — it was nearly devoid of vegetation. This was a bad place. Nothing specific ever happened here, but it had a notorious reputation for being evil.

There was the recent earthquake, for example, which they had felt back at their Node 199, and after which things started going wrong.

"Look!" Arbat pointed into the air.

A low-flying dot was slowly increasing in size, becoming clear after a few moments.

"May the Masters keep us," Kirpak gasped.

"You said that right," Arbat said, ducking into the nearby shrubs just in case. "No one else would be out here."

A strange khaki, matte object flew right over their heads. It looked like either a massive log or a gigantic cigar. The object, with its strange buzzing, hovered over the mountain, a little higher up the slope, where fresh rock had piled up after the recent earthquake.

It looked alive, and when numerous bony legs emerged from its body, it became clear that it was. The semi-mechanical giant centipede landed on the pile of rocks and began scurrying around frantically, searching for something.

Two raiders nearly stopped breathing as to not attract the monster's attention. Having found something of interest, the creature froze and began to transform — a massive drill emerged from its head. It was similar to those Arbat had seen in the mines near the Center.

Next, an energy field flashed around the metal, the drill started spinning rapidly, and the monster slowly but surely began to burrow into the rock.

"Let's go," hissed Arbat, as the creature's head disappeared underground.

The two scouts had never run so fast in their lives.

Node 234

"I made a deal with our target, Kasto," Spatus replied clearly and loudly for everyone to hear. "That I'd run a couple of his errands, so he'd leave me alone, then I escaped from the forest."

The giant roared and struck his fist on the

ground. "What?!"

I stood a few feet behind them and could easily have stopped Kasto, but Spatus had asked me not to interfere. Besides, it would completely ruin my further plans.

The limb, resembling a fat log, struck the ground next to Spatus, who staggered and grimaced, clearly not from pain but from finding himself under the giant's armpit.

"You heard me," Spatus replied harshly. "You have no idea who we're dealing with, Kasto. This Achilles killed five leaders along with all their men. He killed all the nameless with his bare hands. Two of them right before my eyes. This animal possesses incredible abilities and completely despises weapons. He's like a wild beast, doesn't even know how to use a sword. And damn it, he killed five of the Regent's servants. Do you understand that?"

"That's nonsense!" Kasto growled back and reluctantly moved a few feet away. "That's impossible. You're a damned coward. You just ran away from the battlefield to save your skin."

"Is that an accusation?" Spatus asked. I noticed that all the leaders around were silent. They no longer tried to join the giant but were also in no hurry to side with Spatus.

"Yes!" The giant smirked arrogantly. "I, Kasto, master of Nodes 244 and 247, accuse Fat Spatus of cowardice and betrayal of the Regent. Of fleeing the battlefield and leaving our lord's servants to certain death."

"Challenge accepted!" Spatus said. "Who's

ready to confirm this man is challenging me?!"

"I am. I heard it," Vira said grimly.

Several more confirmations followed, and with each new voice, a sinister smile spread wider across Spatus's face.

"Now listen here, you fat piece of shit," Spatus growled. "All the nameless died within minutes. I arrived in the forest when three of them were already dead. The squad leader placed me last, to finish off the enemy if anyone was still breathing when we arrived. But this savage wasn't just breathing. He stormed into the tunnel we were in and killed nearly a hundred of Raul's and Pirate's fighters. Then the fourth nameless, who was controlling them, died of exhaustion. Achilles killed the group commander right in front of me while my men tried to escape from a cloud of poisonous gas. Every damn second of that fight is in the system. As soon as the Regent's servants arrive, I will appeal to them to resolve our dispute. Pray to the Masters that you only lose one node, you freak, because I will demand your life as payment for the insult."

Then Spatus simply turned and walked toward the road leading to his main settlement. The crowd of raiders was silent. Kasto's crimson face rapidly turned blue, as if he couldn't get enough air. When we had moved about thirty yards away, he finally got his voice back.

"Spatus!" He roared, devoid of his former rage. "Why the hell didn't you tell us this right away? Spatus!!! I overreacted!"

"I don't care," Spatus said, without even turning around. "Borcha, Raven, you're coming with me. Riko, you're in charge of the squad. Stand at the edge and wait for the Regent's servants to arrive. We must join everyone else in the Great Hunt."

The squad split into two parts. The three of us went on, while the others headed in a different direction.

"You knew he'd do this?" I asked once we were far enough away.

"Of course," Spatus smirked. "Kasto is a fanatic. He dreams of becoming one of the nameless and does everything he can to gain the Regent's favor. He just couldn't resist coming out of his hole. Loves to show off to the Masters."

"Not bad," I grunted. Spatus knew his neighbors' characters well. With one conflict, he conveyed the necessary information and his position to all the raiders. If anyone questioned him from now on, they would do so with much more caution.

I calculated the remaining time and shook my head. Nearly five hours had passed since the last nameless one was killed. In that time, more than five hundred raiders had gathered at the forest's edge. Ten groups were already there, but many were still on their way.

I didn't have the ability to track the flow of information in another network, which was the biggest disadvantage of my position. The arrival of new squads from the Center had to be anticipated every second. Just one small satellite could easily solve this problem, but where would I get it?

"How far is the Center from your main settlement, Spatus?" I asked.

"Around a hundred and eighty-six miles," he replied on the move. "About ten nodes of varying degrees of shabbiness. Why?"

"I'm trying to figure out when we should expect guests," I said.

"No one can say," Spatus replied. "The nameless never announce their arrival. Even if there's a system assignment to meet them, it never specifies an exact time."

"Distance will have to suffice for now," I said, and we continued walking in silence.

The main settlement of the territory was unusually close to the forest's edge. Just a few miles. Unlike most of his neighbors, Spatus didn't fear the foresters, and they didn't fear him.

The gliders I found flew back to the base two hours ago at a maximum speed of sixty miles per hour. The CES had issued its forecast. With a seventy percent probability, the Regent would use the entire fleet of high-speed gliders to deal with the emerging problem. The number of gliders and their characteristics remained unknown, but the speed of the group could not exceed that of the slowest one.

It was three hours to the Center, and three hours back to Spatus's settlement. A total of six hours, and two had already passed. I had at most four hours left to assess our positions and prepare. But there was still a probability of error in the calculations, so it would be better to wrap everything up in two hours.

"Where did you house the foresters?" I asked as the city walls appeared ahead.

"I still can't believe you used Valentina to bait me," Spatus shook his head, then pointed to the right. "Over there, I gave them a piece of land. Want to visit?"

"That would be good," I nodded. The detour was twenty minutes at a brisk pace, but I still didn't want to waste Spatus's time. I needed to talk to the dukuna, not Spatus. "But I can go their myself."

"Borcha, take him," Spatus agreed easily. "Then come back to me. I'll talk to my family and start preparing for the Great Hunt. I need to check the equipment, supplies, and the remaining fighters. You've battered my main squad pretty badly. It will be difficult to replace many of the guys. I'll also set the accumulator to charge."

"Thanks," I said, and we went our separate ways. Spatus felt completely at ease on his own territory and clearly not because he could kill anyone he met.

Personal energy: 186/200

"How about picking up speed?" I asked my silent companion, and he nodded in response.

I was critically short on people, which was one of the main reasons for visiting the foresters. I wanted to resolve this issue before the second phase began. The remaining energy needed to complete the system deployment could be harvested right at the forest's edge. I hadn't done so yet because of my own priorities.

Currently, the enemy had only received a signal about the appearance of an alien system. The Regent's troops would have to destroy the source of the signal and restore order in the region. Full deployment of the human system would mean more than just a signal. It would become a beacon demanding an immediate purge of the entire territory. And I had to be ready for that.

At the moment, there were a hundred people loyal to me in the forest. To complete the second phase, I needed one hundred and eighty. One hundred and eighty people who would without hesitation accept the offer to transition to the new system. If the delay in the second phase was significant, I'd face an unpleasant gap where I could only use internal matrices. The intermediates would automatically switch to an external reserve, which would be empty. Even after, such a small number of people would contribute mere scraps of energy.

There were also certain difficulties with the personal reserve. The status of the primary node would limit me for quite a while until the system fully stabilized and I established supporting nodes.

This wasn't too critical with a large number of easy targets, but any serious opponent could easily knock me off course, because I could only use a few matrices at a time. That's partly why I hadn't touched the raider's army yet. It was still too soon.

The foresters were settled in a small village. I

immediately saw several familiar faces. One man looked at Borcha and me for a couple of seconds before rushing off to the central house of the settlement and saving us time in finding the dukuna. When we got to the right house, the woman was already standing on the porch, anxiously peering at the stranger.

"Hello, Valentina," I bowed slightly. "I see you've settled in well at your new place."

"Hello, Achilles," the dukuna said. "Settled in, yes, but home is always better. People miss the forest."

"And you can return. It's much safer in the forest now."

"Spatus?" Valentina asked.

"I'll warn him myself," I replied. Valentina looked at Borcha, whom she'd seen before by Spatus's side. To her, this confirmed that Spatus was aware of what was going on.

"Will you come in?" The dukuna asked.

"Not right now," I shook my head, and she nodded. "Once I get everything in order, we'll sit down and chat about everything."

"How is Herman?" The woman asked.

"He's learning," I smiled. "He'll contact you when you cross the forest border. I'll tell him. There are no more tunnels or monsters, so you can take a direct route back."

"What do you mean, no more?"

"We killed them all," I said. "And the nameless destroyed the border. I couldn't stop them in time. How many people are in your tribe?"

"About a hundred, counting the children," the dukuna answered cautiously. "Why?"

"When you get home, you'll receive an offer," I said. "You need to accept it. It's very important. Adults first, and then children, if necessary. Herman will tell you when it's enough."

"Why?" Valentina asked. I had already brought them many upheavals. The woman saw what was happening in Spatus's node and didn't want more problems for her people, despite any prophecies.

"We repelled the first assault," I said. "Killed some nameless and many raiders. Now a new army is gathering, and I need your help again. None of the foresters will be harmed by this decision. The module you gave me became part of a larger mechanism. It needs human support. I can't do without it either. Will you help? Or should I look for volunteers among Spatus's people?"

"We'll help," Valentina answered after a moment of silence. "But this will be our last help to you, Achilles."

"So be it," I nodded. "Safe journey, Valentina. It's better for you to go through Naum's land. There are too many raiders at the border right now."

The dukuna silently nodded and went back into the house. She didn't even say goodbye. To her, my latest request was a heavy burden. It's hard to follow a person whose motives and actions you don't understand. But it had always been this way. For most people, the actions of the Ideals remained incomprehensible. They only saw the end result.

"Let's go to Spatus," I said to Borcha and we headed out.

It was less than a mile. There were fields beyond the last houses of the village, and the road was clearly visible. We also saw an endless line of people moving toward Fat Spatus's main settlement, among which, there was the giant Kasto. The entire mass of raiders waiting at the forest's edge had come into motion, and I didn't like the direction they were heading.

"What's happening?" I quietly asked Borcha, who had stopped beside me. The warrior was looking straight ahead and was clearly interacting with the Lirdagi system interface.

"The nameless," Borcha exhaled a second later. "They're almost here. The assignment now includes a time, and a summons for a general assembly in the main square of our city."

Chapter 25

THE CES WAS WRONG. Or rather, the enemy's decisions fell into the thirty percent that contradicted my plans. The requirement to gather all forces in one place could mean a change in the primary objective. If before it was to clear the forest and eliminate me, now there were some new developments.

"How much time until they arrive?" I asked, speeding up and turning off the path. A couple of people running through the fields would hardly attract any attention in the current situation.

"A little over an hour," Borcha replied.

"Herman, I need you," I immediately sent a message to the base. Until now, I had tried not to use the capabilities of my system. The status of the primary node prevented the enemy from detecting the location of the main base, and I didn't want to take any unnecessary risks. But time had come to stop being careful.

"I'm here," Herman said a couple of seconds later.

"Send someone to Vens," I said. "They need to be warned that soon, everyone will receive an offer to join the new system. Find the exact wording in the terminal. I need every person in the forest to accept this offer. Every single one!"

"Got it, I'm on it! Looking it up now!" The kid quickly replied. "What else?"

"Find all the foresters through the Brist and count them by heads. They need to receive the same offer. I've warned the dukuna," I continued. "Once we get the remaining energy to complete the first phase, the second phase will begin immediately. You'll have access to the Phalanx counter. We need to ensure the system is fully loaded. I need to know how many active connections we'll have within ten minutes."

"One hundred seventy-three," Herman responded almost instantly. "That's counting those currently at our base."

"Understood. Keep me updated," I wrote. "I'll place markers for the Brist on those who need to receive the same invitation."

There were just eight people left to find. I couldn't count myself, because the Ideals were initially created as consumers of raze-energy. But I didn't think there would be any issues. We could easily find eight people among Spatus's men. I just didn't like the fact that I couldn't solve this task on my own.

"Borcha," I said while running, "do you understand what's happening right now?"

"The whole world wants to kill you, Raven," he shrugged. "But I think you already know that. As for why... I do have questions about that."

"We are recreating the system that once destroyed the masters," I said, and Borcha let out a long whistle.

"And I thought this was just a local skirmish," Borcha said cheerfully. "So how do we do it?"

"For now, we just need enough people to start the system," I replied.

"Then I'm in!" Borcha declared. "What do I connect to?"

Talking to someone who had even a remote understanding of the principles of global systems was much easier. Even if his experience was limited to interacting with the Lirdagi algorithms.

"I need ten people who agree to connect to the new system," I said. "They'll receive a message with the offer."

"The one you mentioned to Vens?" Borcha asked.

"Yes."

"No problem. When we get to the city, I'll talk to the guys from my ten. We can also tell Spatus. I don't think he'll refuse after everything we've done."

The walls of Spatus's main settlement rose up

ahead. I hadn't bothered to find out what the locals called it, but a city this big definitely had a name. Tall walls surrounded a vast area of the city situated on a plain. One couldn't see what lay beyond the walls. Only the roofs of the tallest buildings peeked over the fortifications.

Our run allowed us to get slightly ahead of the raider forces, and we reached the massive gates a few minutes before the first of them.

"Close the gates!" Borcha ordered the nearest guard as soon as we passed inside.

"No need," I said. "The raiders have orders to come to the main square. Let them through."

The warrior looked at me for a second, then signaled the guards to leave the gates alone. Borcha didn't ask me any questions. Either he understood everything or feared someone might overhear our conversation. Not all of Spatus's subordinates were as loyal to their leader as his personal guard.

We raced through the town's streets toward the center. Somewhere there was Spatus's house. For now, the streets were still quiet. The residents were going about their business, completely unaware of what was happening.

It looked like the city had a population of several thousand people. The houses were clean and neat, and there were actual shops on the ground floor, which was a clear demonstration of the village's standard of living. I had seen what was going on in Wolf's camp and the outskirts of Baka's settlement, so there was something to compare to.

Spatus's home was a big, four-story house made of wood. There were numerous smaller houses within a fenced area, and guards guarding the premises. When they saw us, the guards moved to intercept us but immediately stepped aside when Borcha waved his arms at them.

"Spatus is upstairs," my companion said, catching his breath. "I'm going to get the guys."

"Bring them to me so I can see each one," I said, tagging Borcha with a marker for Herman. "Where should I go?"

"Pinta!" Borcha shouted, and one of the guards ran over to us. "Take Raven to the boss. Quickly!"

The guard dashed off without asking who I was — Borcha's authority was more than enough. If he said to take a stranger to the boss, the stranger was taken to the boss.

A huge porch, a series of rooms decorated with carvings, several corridors, a thick door. Pinta banged the doorframe with his sword hilt several times and stepped back.

"Who's there?!" I heard Spatus's angry voice.

"Raven is here, boss," the guard replied briefly. "Borcha told me to bring him to you."

The door swung open immediately, and Spatus appeared in the doorway. He hadn't even taken off the armor he wore while running through the forest. Behind the fat man were several pale women and a couple of young men. Frightened children's voices could be heard from somewhere in the back.

"You're dismissed," Spatus nodded to his subordinate and stepped aside. "Come in, Raven. I was just talking with my family."

Spatus had a sizable family — four wives, six sons, and two daughters. The women and children were visibly scared, the older boys wouldn't take their eyes off me.

"You already know?" Spatus asked quietly.

"Yes," I replied. "Borcha told me. We need to get the people out of the city."

"Are you kidding?" Spatus grumbled. "Who would let a herd flee without a good reason? We're being visited by the esteemed servants of the Regent, not enemies."

"Spatus," one of the women said cautiously, "maybe you should come with us? We could settle down somewhere. I have relatives in Node 400."

"Silence, woman!" Spatus barked. "I said, get moving and get out of the city!"

"Where will we go without you, husband?" Another one of his wives said, struggling to hold back tears.

"Raven, you tell them!" Spatus growled. "They're completely out of control!"

"You don't have to leave the city," I said calmly. "But you shouldn't stay in the center. If you stay near the city walls, that will be enough. Is there a suitable place where you can go?"

"Of course there is," The eldest son snorted. "Any resident would be happy to host the family of the Node's ruler. It's a cause for celebration for them."

Something clicked in my mind. Evacuating several thousand civilians in an hour was unrealistic — there'd be too many questions and too much noise. "Spatus, we need to announce a grand festival in honor of the arrival of the esteemed guests from the Center."

"Does anyone know what this man is talking about?" Spatus said, turning to his sons. "What festival, Raven? We're on the brink of war!"

"Just a regular festival," I responded calmly. "Every resident of your city must greet the esteemed guests. Let your guards go through the streets and announce your will. Everyone who goes to the city walls within an hour will be exempt from taxes for a whole month. You want to show respect to the Regent's servants and are ready to pay for it."

"Why?" Spatus asked grimly.

"So that no resident remains in the center," I replied. "Your fighters shouldn't be in the square and neither should you."

"But I have to be there to welcome my guests," Spatus said stubbornly. "If I don't show up, there will be many questions. Pierce, hide the mothers and the siblings. Graham, did you hear? The first shouters need to be walking the streets in five minutes."

Immediately, everyone started to run around. Only Spatus and I remained in place. Within minutes, we were alone in the room.

"What are you planning, Achilles?" Spatus asked grimly.

"The usual," I said.

"The usual, meaning kill everyone, including the nameless?"

"Something like that," I smiled. "What about the accumulator?"

"It needs about twenty more minutes to fully charge," Spatus replied. "Any specific orders?"

This was the first time Spatus openly acknowledged my authority over him. It had been clear from the start, but his verbal recognition was an important step. With just one phrase, Spatus set the necessary tone.

"Take the bare minimum of people with you," I began my instructions. "Just so the other leaders see you in the square. Stay away from the others. It doesn't matter what they think or say. As soon as the gliders appear in the sky, head to the city walls. Otherwise, I can't guarantee your safety."

"But you'll be alone!" Spatus protested. "There are six hundred thugs in that square. And we don't know how many nameless. And why do you think they'll arrive by glider?"

"Because it's the fastest way to get to the source of the problem," I replied calmly. "Don't worry about the rest. The only thing is, you'll have to part with the accumulator. Possibly forever."

"Who cares," Spatus said. "I'll buy a new one."

I nodded silently and headed for the exit. Spatus went to the next room for the artifact and caught up with me in the yard, where Borcha's ten men were already waiting.

"This is them?" I asked.

Outside Spatus's residence, the shouters were already doing their job, and the city was buzzing with excitement. People were cheerful and surprised, someone was loudly praising the generosity of their noble ruler.

"Yes," Borcha nodded, and I marked the ten men.

"I see eleven additional markers," Herman immediately reported. "George is with the settlers. The dukuna is still far away, but I've contacted her, too."

I calculated the remaining time and wrote to Herman: "You have ten minutes to get everything ready."

"Understood. Ready in ten minutes," Herman responded.

"Is there something I don't know?" Spatus asked.

"I asked Borcha for help," I said. "This group needs to be moved away from the center first."

"The western wall," Spatus ordered. "Make sure none of the residents fall down in their excitement."

A group of fighters in nearly identical armor came up to us. This was either the ruler's personal guard or a ceremonial squad. They formed up around Spatus and froze.

I remained outside the perimeter but that didn't bother me. The fat man gave me a slight nod and slowly headed toward the crowd of raiders. The main square of the town began just a few dozen feet from the residence of the node's master.

Personal energy: 163/200

I waited for a minute and then followed. The raiders immediately noticed the city's ruler and began to make way for him.

Spatus lazily nodded to familiar leaders, doing his best to appear gracious. Only when he saw the giant Kasto did Spatus act as if he were looking at an empty space.

I walked along the edge of the square, looking for a clear path between the jostling raiders. The crowd was diverse. Some, like Vira's guys, were flexing their muscles, showing off their strength. Others stood with hoods pulled low over their faces.

There were people in armor, ranging from simple leather to advanced tech gear. But all the raiders shared one thing in common: they were very nervous.

None of them understood why the main order had changed and why they were dragged into Spatus's city when they had been on the edge of the Great Hunt zone already. The information about the exact arrival time of the nameless added to the tension.

"Where do you think you're going, blackie?!" Someone growled rudely at me as I tried to squeeze past. "This is Node 170."

I lightly jabbed the loudmouth in the chest with my elbow, and he sank to the ground, gasping for air. His companion, presumably from the same node, quickly gave me a once-over and put on an apologetic look.

"Please forgive him, sir," he muttered. "Spek doesn't know what he's saying half the time."

I continued on my way and soon reached the center of the square. In that time, Spatus had crossed it entirely and was now climbing a small platform on the opposite side. It was probably from this spot that he usually announced his orders.

After a few minutes, a deathly silence fell over the square. Only cheerful voices of the city's residents could be heard in the distance.

Spatus's order had not gone unnoticed, and every one of his subjects hurried to fulfill their ruler's will.

I didn't have access to the Lirdagi interface and didn't know how much time was left before the nameless arrived. But from the tense expressions on the faces of the raiders, it was clear that we were in our final minutes of waiting.

Personal energy: 160/200

I clenched the accumulator in my hand and replenished my personal reserve up to two hundred. I would need what was left for other purposes.

"They're coming!" Someone nearby exhaled.

Twenty dots appeared in the sky, rapidly growing larger. Their speed was greater than that of the gliders I had seen before. They must have installed boosters, as I could clearly see markers of the systems I had recently modified. I decided to start with them.

An almost imperceptible pulse was sent toward the group of the nameless. It activated hidden traps, and I immediately saw the results of my command.

"What's happening?" Someone among the raiders shouted nervously, and commotion ensued.

Three gliders veered to the side and collided with their neighbors. The orderly formation of the Regent's fleet instantly fell apart. Black dots of the falling nameless and debris began to rain down. The raiders hadn't expected this, and panic erupted in the square

Out of the corner of my eye, I saw Spatus and his guards leaving the platform and quickly heading somewhere deeper into the city. It was time to begin.

"Ready in one minute," I typed, and gripped the emitter firmly with one hand. In my other hand was Spatus's raze-energy accumulator. The nameless were only five hundred yards away which would take just a few seconds to cover.

"Lights."

Personal energy: 60/200

Intermediate energy matrix Northern Lights activated

Attention! Energy levels below critical! If energy drops below zero, you will die.

Streams of rainbow-colored energy radiated from my body in all directions. They rapidly spread across the ground and began to rise into the sky, creating the very effect that gave this energy matrix its name.

It didn't kill anyone, but created an energy

sphere with a diameter of two hundred yards, within which all Lirdagi systems ceased to function for a long minute.

Moments later, the gliders flew into this sphere and started to fall uncontrollably.

"Destruction."

End of Book Two

Want to be the first to know about our latest LitRPG,
sci fi and fantasy titles from your favorite authors?

Subscribe to our **New Releases** newsletter:
http://eepurl.com/b7niIL

The Dark Healer
a historical progression fantasy series
by Alex Toxic & Nadya Lee

Ghost in the System
An apocalypse LitRPG series by Alexey Kovtunov

The Last Portal Jumper
a LitRPG series by Konstantin Zubov

Lord of the System
a LitRPG progression fantasy series by
Alex Toxic and Furious Miki

Kill to Live
a LitRPG progression fantasy adventure series
by George Bor and Yuri Vinokuroff

Kill or Die
a LitRPG series by Alex Toxic

The Strongest Student
a portal progression action fantasy series
by Andrei Tkachev

Living Ice
a portal progression alternative history series
by Dmitry Sheleg

Law of the Jungle
a Wuxia Progression Fantasy Adventure Series
By Vasily Mahanenko

Reality Benders
a LitRPG series by Michael Atamanov

The Dark Herbalist
a LitRPG series by Michael Atamanov

Perimeter Defense
a LitRPG series by Michael Atamanov

League of Losers
a LitRPG series by Michael Atamanov

Chaos' Game
a LitRPG series by Alexey Svadkovsky

The Way of the Shaman
a LitRPG series by Vasily Mahanenko

The Alchemist
a LitRPG series by Vasily Mahanenko

Dark Paladin
a LitRPG series by Vasily Mahanenko

Galactogon
a LitRPG series by Vasily Mahanenko

Invasion
a LitRPG series by Vasily Mahanenko

World of the Changed
a LitRPG series by Vasily Mahanenko

The Bear Clan
a LitRPG series by Vasily Mahanenko

Starting Point
a LitRPG series by Vasily Mahanenko

The Bard from Barliona
a LitRPG series
by Eugenia Dmitrieva and Vasily Mahanenko

Condemned
(Lord Valevsky: Last of The Line)
a Progression Fantasy series
by Vasily Mahanenko

Loner
a LitRPG series by Alex Kosh

A Buccaneer's Due
a LitRPG series by Igor Knox

A Student Wants to Live
a LitRPG series by Boris Romanovsky

The Goldenblood Heir
a LitRPG series by Boris Romanovsky

The One Who Changes the Future
a dystopian portal progression fantasy series
by Boris Romanovsky

Level Up
a LitRPG series by Dan Sugralinov

Level Up: The Knockout
a LitRPG series by Dan Sugralinov and Max Lagno

Adam Online
a LitRPG Series by Max Lagno

World 99
a LitRPG series by Dan Sugralinov

Disgardium
a LitRPG series by Dan Sugralinov

Nullform
a RealRPG Series by Dem Mikhailov

Clan Dominance: The Sleepless Ones
a LitRPG series by Dem Mikhailov

Heroes of the Final Frontier
a LitRPG series by Dem Mikhailov

The Crow Cycle
a LitRPG series by Dem Mikhailov

Interworld Network
a LitRPG series by Dmitry Bilik

Rogue Merchant
a LitRPG series by Roman Prokofiev

Project Stellar
a LitRPG series by Roman Prokofiev

In the System
a LitRPG series by Petr Zhgulyov

The Crow Cycle
a LitRPG series by Dem Mikhailov

Unfrozen
a LitRPG series by Anton Tekshin

The Neuro
a LitRPG series by Andrei Livadny

Phantom Server
a LitRPG series by Andrei Livadny

Respawn Trials
a LitRPG series by Andrei Livadny

The Expansion (The History of the Galaxy)
a Space Exploration Saga by A. Livadny

The Range
a LitRPG series by Yuri Ulengov

Point Apocalypse
a near-future action thriller by Alex Bobl

Moskau
a dystopian thriller by G. Zotov

El Diablo
a supernatural thriller by G.Zotov

The Fairy Code
a Romantic Fantasy series by Kaitlyn Weiss

***The Charmed* Fjords**
a Romantic Fantasy series by Marina Surzhevskaya

More books and series are coming out soon!

In order to have new books of the series translated faster, we need your help and support! Please consider leaving a review or spread the word by recommending *Kill to Live* to your friends and posting the link on social media. The more people buy the book, the sooner we'll be able to make new translations available.

Thank you!

Till next time!